The

I swung and dropp... ...trunk of Chang's ... ...came up, snapping off the safety. I put a three-round burst into the face of another of the cat-people and watched its nose and whiskers disappear in a fine spray of red and grey mist as the back of its head exploded, but the thing had too much forward momentum and kept coming until it hit me, knocking me to the ground. I shoved the cat-man off of me, rolled to the side, and came up drawing a bead on another one. My finger tightened on the trigger and the gun *burruped*, but I don't know if the rounds connected or not because at that exact moment, another one coming in from the side connected his forepaw-hand with the side of my head, and snapped the back of my skull up against the tree trunk. The last thing I saw before everything went black was about a billion exploding supernovas.

"The second book in this saga of future war among the stars has a nice, tight story and a good balance of action, hardware, and well-drawn characters both human and alien."

—Roland J. Green
Author of *Peace Company* and
These Green Foreign Hills

THE ALDEBARAN CAMPAIGN

KEVIN RANDLE
& ROBERT CORNETT

ACE BOOKS, NEW YORK

This book is an Ace
original edition, and
has never been previously
published.

THE ALDEBARAN CAMPAIGN

An Ace Book/published by arrangement with
the authors

PRINTING HISTORY
Ace edition/December 1988

ISBN: 0-441-23510-7

Ace Books are published by The Berkley Publishing Group,
200 Madison Avenue, New York, New York 10016.
The name "ACE" and the "A"
logo are trademarks belonging to
Charter Communications, Inc.

PRINTED IN THE UNITED STATES OF AMERICA

10 9 8 7 6 5 4 3 2 1

1

Headquarters, 504th Stellar Strike Command
5th Regional Combat Team,
SCAF 2nd IRF/A

10 September 2236

Stryker nodded an unfelt, cheerful acknowledgment to the guard's equally unfelt, cheerful "Good morning," and absently returned the man's salute.

"Please step up to the console and place both your hands palm downward on the screen for identification confirmation, Major. Then state your name, rank, and service number when the green light comes on."

It was a familiar drill which Stryker had performed an interminable number of times before. Occasionally the face of the young NCO seated behind the computer console or that of one of the guards positioned at intervals along the corridor with their automatic flechette carbines held at port arms would change, but the entry procedure into the 504th's Operational Intelligence Command Center had remained fixed and unchanging since the Second Fleet had departed Earth orbit, and that had been nearly three generations before Stryker was born.

For a fleeting moment, Stryker wondered what it must be like, to live out your entire life guarding an empty corridor against an alien intruder no one had ever seen nor was likely to, as the Security Tactical Command guards did with their little carbines that could shred a human with six hundred tiny krylon darts a second, but wouldn't breech the environmental integrity of the starship's outer hull. Did they ever ask themselves if a weapon that would shred a human being would also shred an alien suicide commando? Maybe it would just annoy him/her/it. Maybe it wouldn't even do that.

Strkyer complied with the NCO's instructions, and when the computer musically chimed its acceptance of proferred bonafides, signed and thumb printed the daily written log, returned the NCO's second salute in a haphazard fashion, and ambled off down the corridor, waiting patiently at the far end while the procedure was repeated by a second bored looking NCO at a second computer console. Finally, the impervium armored door to the inner corridor slowly swung open on its hissing hydraulics.

The scene inside was identical to the outer corridor, a long hall strewn at intervals with armed guards, with two notable exceptions. Regularly spaced along the corridor were a number of windowless doors of stressed impervium plate, and there was only one computer console with an NCO behind it, set out in the hallway, since there was only one way in or out. Except in the event of a shipboard fire, when a series of explosive bolts could be fired on coded order of the ship's captain to open a small escape hatch in the ceiling at the other end. Always presuming, of course, that in such an event the Captain had the presence of mind to enter the appropriate order in the ship's master computer, and that the necessary circuitry was still intact. And that he did it in the ninety seconds or so before the ship's automatic fire fighting apparatus evacuated all atmosphere in this section, effectively smothering any fire, and, of course, asphyxiating any personnel who remained behind. The system had never been tested, except for the computer which ran a self-diagnostic check on the circuitry every three minutes. Stryker fervently hoped it would never have to be.

Stryker stopped outside the door marked DIRECTOR, put a palm on the cathode ray screen set in the wall next to it, and when the green light came on, announced, "Major Stryker, SCAF 416229059, to see the Director." There was a delay of about a second and a half before the light turned blue and the door slid open.

Inside it might have been any office on any military installation anywhere in the Empire of Sol, instead of the most secure compartment aboard the flagship of a stellar battle fleet lying a few light weeks off the Alpha Tauri star system. The walls were covered in plastiform done in a fine, light shade of sandalwood, and lined with pictures of various high ranking military officers in their dress uniforms, most of whom were long since dead, and a few now little more than legends. On the far wall, looking curiously out of place amid all the army officers, was a painting of a fully rigged wooden sailing vessel of the type in general use for commerce nearly five hundred years ago. The painting itself was over half that old.

Beneath the painting was a battleship-grey, plastiform desk with an attached computer console, and behind the desk sat a very well endowed, and very, very young female second lieutenant, whose dark red hair hung down her back almost to her waist in flagrant violation of the Sol Combined Arms Force grooming regulations.

Stryker reflected that it was truly amazing at times what regulations you could violate when you worked for the Director of Operational Intelligence. Especially when you allowed the Director to violate you, occasionally. It occurred to Stryker that the Director's wife probably wouldn't have approved of her husband's regular screwing of an administrative assistant young enough to be his granddaughter, but then, the Director's wife was hardly in a position to do any complaining. She'd been dead for nearly half a century. The Director, unlike Stryker, and indeed unlike the majority of SCAF personnel in the 504th these days, had come from Earth and spent most of the last six decades in cryonic suspension.

Perhaps, Stryker thought wryly, it wouldn't have bothered the Director's wife so much if she'd known what a lousy lay his secretary was. Stryker could personally vouch for the fact that the girl was about as useful as a monkey wrench when it came to having fun in the sack and not nearly as enthusiastic. But then, perhaps that was what the old man enjoyed, the opportunity to play teacher with his cardinal haired fifteen-year-old administrative assistant cum mistress. Stryker couldn't imagine him ever winning the Fleet Education Award though. She'd had the questionable privilege of the Director's teaching that same night as well. The once had been quite enough, for both of them.

The administrative assistant gave Stryker a venomous smile, clearly intended to convey the message that Stryker was out of the running now because she was *so old* and presumably impotent, whereas the lieutenant was *so young and virile*, and said pointlessly, "How may I help you, Major?"

To her credit, Stryker suppressed the desire to reciprocate the smile and tell the lieutenant that a person of her obviously limited experience, and intelligence, could best help by stepping out a convenient airlock without an environment suit, gritted her teeth inwardly, and repeated that she was there to see the Director.

"Do you have an appointment?" The voice was positively syrupy.

· Jesus, Mary, and Joseph, deliver me from fifteen-year-olds intoxicated with the self-importance attendant on their sexual awakening, thought Stryker. "No," she said calmly, "but the Director is expecting me."

"Well, alright, then," said the lieutenant, forming her glossy, cherry red lips into a little pout that Stryker presumed was supposed to look thoughtful, "I'll see if the Director is in."

Stryker felt like shouting. "Where the hell else would he be? There's only one bloody way into the damned office." Instead, she amused herself with mental pictures of what the lieutenant would look like if she did go out through an airlock without an environment suit. It was a satisfying image.

The barely post-pubescent redhead finally ran out of ways to demonstrate her imagined superiority over Stryker and passed her through the double, sound and sensor probe resistant doors into the inner office.

Stryker always found seeing the Director to be something of a shock. Maybe it was just that meeting anyone who was over a century old was shocking, like meeting someone you had only read about in ancient history books and was now long dead would have been. Outwardly, of course, his physical appearance was that of a rather small, thin man in his late fifties, thanks to all the years he had spent in cryonic suspension, but he represented nevertheless, a physical link with a world and a culture that Stryker herself had never known. It wasn't, she decided, like meeting someone from the history books at all. It was like meeting an alien life form.

It wasn't just imagination on Stryker's part. She knew a bit about aliens. She'd met Taus before, the tall, dark inhabitants of Tau Ceti Four, who appeared as though they had all been stamped out by the same genetic machine, due to thousands of years of inbreeding. Like the fabled Amazons of old Earth lore, they were a race of fierce female warriors, who despite technologically inferior weaponry had held the stellar military might of Earth at bay for over a year. They were also a highly intelligent and imitative race, who with no previous knowledge of nuclear physics had, in that short year, succeeded in building a primitive fission bomb and mating it to a launch vehicle capable, at least in theory, of reaching the orbiting fleet of the invaders from Earth. The theory had never been tested, thanks to an intelligence coup that had enabled Earth to pull off an eleventh-hour victory. It was a victory that could have meant extinction for the Tau race, but like conquered Japan following the second world-wide war on Earth three centuries earlier, had resulted instead in a mutually beneficial cooperative arrangement with her conquerors. The newly formed Empire of Sol that had pushed outward from Earth needed troops for her stellar war with an enemy that as yet no one from Earth had met face-to-face, encountering him only in ship-to-ship combat that had left behind no biological clues. The Taus, their few breeding males destroyed in the combat with the Earth invaders, had required a new means of reproducing their species, and Earth medical technology had assisted with the introduction of parthenogenesis, and, once compatibility was established, with carefully controlled, experimental artificial insemination. Since Tau reproductive physiology followed a preferential natural selection for the female of the species in a ratio of about a thousand to one, it was a few generations too early to tell yet what effect such scientific interference would have on the long term Tau gene pool.

Yet because he *was* human, in the sense of Earth evolved man, the Director seemed somehow more alien than the very human appearing, but physically different, although not too different, native inhabitants of Tau Ceti Four. Everybody knew the Taus were aliens, but the Director was a native

Earthman, which made the difference in the way he thought and acted seem all the more alien to someone who had been born in space.

There was a little extra shock today. The Director already had a visitor. A short, stocky man with dark hair and black bushy eyebrows, and an incongruous red handlebar mustache. He had major's pips on his shoulderboards and Intell insignia on his collar, but unlike Stryker's blue Fleet uniform, his was tan and brown. STC. Surface Tactical Command. What the hell was Surface Intell doing here? Stryker glanced at the nametag, and then back at the face, and somewhere in her brain a tiny synapse made a connection. She'd heard the rumors of course. Everyone who worked in Intell had. But she'd never actually met one before. At least she didn't think she had. If she had, it had been a different model.

The stranger spoke, and his accent removed whatever doubts Stryker might have harbored.

"Good mornin' to ye, lass. Me name's Peterson, but y'can call me Pete. You'll be a bit surprised by m'being here, n'doubt, but that'll be clarified soon enough." He rose from his seat, and stuck out a hand.

Stryker reluctantly took hold of it, and received a firm, vigorous pumping. The hand felt warm enough, and a little of the doubt began to creep back in.

"Peterson series?" she asked hesitantly.

"Ah, ye'll have heard of me, then?"

"One of the worst kept secrets in Intelligence circles," replied Stryker more confidently. "What do I call you, man or machine?" It was an honest question. There was no slur intended.

"As I said, now, call me Pete. Major 'tis far too formal, Peterson does n' fit w' the accent, and a bio-medically engineered cybernetic w'full heuristic and mnemonic capability and cross-linked time-sharin' utilizing neuroskeletal and neuroeffector polysystems 'tis far more'a mouthful than I care t'hear repeated."

"All right then, Pete. Can I have my hand before you wear it out?"

"Sorry, lass," said Peterson absently, as though it were possible for that brain of his, a fusion of tiny supercomputer and organosynthetic material to have actually forgotten something. He immediately released her hand.

"If you don't mind, Major Stryker, we can get on with business," said the Director, clearing his throat. "I think we can dispense with the Morning Briefs until later. I've asked Peterson here so you can brief him on the rescue operation we've currently got underway.

"Rescue is a bit out of our line, usually, but there are some unusual circumstances involved in this case, and I think it's time you were briefed," the Director said to Peterson. "There may be a need for you to coordinate certain aspects of the operation from your end of things."

Peterson returned to his chair and Stryker, although she couldn't shake a feeling of unreality about the situation, began the briefing without preamble. For some reason or other, she'd always sort of assumed you just gave them their data on a diskette or bubble chip. It had never occurred to her that the artificial human-computers needed to be briefed just like anybody else.

"This," she said, touching a button that illuminated a life-size likeness on the floor-to-ceiling, wall-sized flat-screen, "is Brigadier General Britt Andersohn of the SCAF Imperial General Staff, a specialist in linguistics and digital logic, height just a shade over one-point-eight meters, weight of about seventy kilograms at the time of her last medical examination, hair blonde, eyes blue.

"Four months ago, the Brigadier, who is also a pilot, took it upon herself to borrow a two-man long range scoutship and go running off to the Alpha Tauri system, which as you probably know, 5th Regional Combat Team was scheduled to bypass. Fleet fighters were dispatched from the corvette *Achilles* on picket duty once the unauthorized nature of her flight was discovered, but were not able to intercept. Her flight was tracked by long range sensor scan, and found to terminate on the fifth planet of the system.

"The Imperial General Staff was understandably distressed by such behavior from one of their own, and a Search and Rescue team, along with a couple of MP's, was dispatched to bring the Brigadier back so the IGS could ask her why she'd gone and done such a fool thing."

"I presume they did n' find her," interrupted Peterson.

"That we don't know. We lost our comm-link with the S & R team about forty minutes after they made planetfall. It was never reestablished."

"Ock! An' th' o'course, took things ou' th' hands o' Search and Rescue, an' Criminal Investigation Division, an' made it th' special province o' Fleet Operational Intelligence, under FOI directive 2217/5.12."

"Precisely. Since the S&R team had been in communications contact from the planet's surface for nearly forty minutes, we knew nothing had gone wrong during atmospheric penetration and landing. Some sort of naturally occurring disaster was ruled out by analysis of meteorological telemetry from the S&R rescue ship. The ship's telemetric systems, by the way, continue to function."

"But n' th' comm-links?"

Stryker shook her head. "In addition to the three shipboard communications transceivers, each member of a five-person S&R team carries a personal neutrino transceiver. The probability of a simultaneous failure of all eight systems without outside intervention would be about the same as being struck twice by lightning in the same spot."

"N' precisely, bu' 'tis a fair enough gross estimate. An' since neutrinos have a penetration in lead roughly equivalent t' thirty-five hundred light years, I believe w' can safely rule o' th' hypothesis, th' yer Search and Rescue team encountered some form o' shielding phenomena, 'specially seein' as how yer still receivin' telemetric data. Yer next step, I suppose, wa' a Hard Landing Force?"

"Not immediately. We sent in an Imperial Marine Reconnaissance Unit by fast recon lander to conduct an armed reconnaissance of the S&R landing site. They put down five klicks away and approached the site by surface support vehicle. They made it a little over halfway there before they were forced to abandon their SSV due to terrain difficulties, and proceed on foot. For obvious reasons, the Recon Marines operated under a strict communications blackout until they reached the S&R landing site. The report from Gunnery Sergeant Sabena indicated that the site appeared intact but abandoned. It also indicated that he'd lost three of his eight marines to environmental hazards on the way in."

"Wha' sor' t' environmental hazards?"

"Sorry, uh, Pete. He didn't say. All I can tell you is the three marines weren't lost as a result of hostile action. We try to keep transmissions at a minimum, in case the enemy has monitoring equipment. Sabena and his unit were instructed to destroy any classified material or equipment, and prepare for extraction. When the fast recon lander came in for the pick up, they didn't find any marines waiting to be picked up. A normal pickup takes about ninety seconds turn-around time. The command pilot waited twenty minutes, then re-orbited and contacted OICC for further orders. We ran the mission ourselves, rather than direct it through RCT Fleet Ops. After that, we sent in the Hard Landing Force."

"How big?"

"Third Special Operations Platoon from the 7th Rangers."

"An' th' results?"

"We put them in right on top of the S&R landing site. They secured their perimeter and ascertained that there was no trace of either the Search and Rescue team and their two MP's, nor of the Marine Recon Unit. Then they set up their Mark Five Light Point Defense System, dug in deep, and settled down to wait out the night.

"It passed uneventfully, and the next morning Lieutenant Ammacker left his platoon sergeant in charge of the landing site and took half his troops out to conduct a patrol of the surrounding area. In five hours he managed to lose six of his people to the indigenous flora and fauna. Apparently there are some pretty virulent life forms down there. He found no indication of enemy activity, nor of any local indigenous inhabitation, and was instructed to return to the landing site in order to minimize any further casualties from environmental sources, and await new orders.

"He lost three more troopers on the way back, and when he got there, he found the site empty. The platoon sergeant and the rest of the troops had vanished without a trace."

"Is tha' when ye made th' decision t' call in STCI?" asked Peterson. He tactfully avoided mentioning the obvious, that it should have been done sooner.

There was a long, uncomfortable silence in the room.

"Ock, I see. There be more then, ye'v n' yet told t' me."

"I'm sorry, Peterson," said the Director, apparently finding nothing strange in apologizing to what was, in effect, an artificial human, if not exactly a machine. "You're right, of course. STCI should have been informed as soon as we put in the Marine Recon unit. But we didn't want to go stirring up a hornets' nest until we were sure we had one. It was my decision, and it's my responsibility."

"What, exactly, did ye do, now?" asked Peterson, just a hint of human exasperation creeping into his non-human voice.

"Tell him, Stryker."

"We sent in a company. Crack troops, all screened by the Battle Planning Computer, and hand picked. All combat experienced, all with special skills. We culled them from other units, pulled them out of cryonic suspension. Some were Rangers, some Special Ops, some Special Forces. Most of them we drew from the first and third Pathfinder Brigades."

"Good Lord! Wha' were ye thinkin' o'? A whole company o' Pathfinders? Have ye n' conception o' what a Pathfinder's job is? They be small unit specialists, like yer Marine Recce units. An' pullin' 'em all t'gether from various outfits like that. Pathfinders train as a squad, they live and work as a squad. Each one o' 'em knows precisely his 'r her job as members o' th' squad and does 't, know'n' th' each o' th' tothers can be relied upon t' do precisely 'is 'r 'er's. Pathfinder squads function on long developed trust, built o' longterm, mutually earned respect. Ye canno' throw a bunch o' total strangers t'gether in a Pathfinder team an' expect 'em t' function as an effective unit. And certainly no' in great whoppin' huge bunches. I canno' believe ye could do such a nightmare."

For someone who was supposed to be a coolly logical, reasoning machine, Peterson seemed capable of exhibiting a fair amount of very human emotion. Stryker wondered whether the human qualities were an outgrowth of Peterson's heuristic and mnemonic capacities, or had been programmed into him at creation.

"What else could we do?" said Stryker coldly. "We send in a Search and Research team, and they die. So we send in experts at reconnaissance in a hostile environment, and the marines died too. So we send in a bigger force, and it dies. At least, I think at this point we have to assume the Rangers are dead, except for those few with Ammacker who made it back. We've either got to raise the stakes, or fold our hand. And if we fold, we'll never find out what happened to Andersohn or any of the rest of them. I don't think the Imperial General Staff would want to bypass a planet that kills whoever we put on it without knowing why or how. As an intelligence officer, I'm damned sure I don't. And I'm beginning to wonder just exactly why a member of the Imperial General Staff would risk court-martial and disgrace to steal a scoutship and go there in the first place, unless she expected to find something there that she thought was worth risking both her life and her career for. Wouldn't you like to know what she was looking for?"

"Indeed I would, lass," said Peterson in a soothing tone. "I'm no' questionin' yer motives, only yer methods."

"Do you have something you'd like to suggest?"

"Aye. A different sort o' reconnaissance. Rather than a reconnaissance in force, a reconnaissance in stealth."

"I sort of thought that's what the Marine Recon unit was."

"Touché, lass, but maybe no' stealthy enough. Wha' I had in mind were jus' this. There be such a thing as economy o' force. Sometimes 'tis wiser t' do the job wi' one tha' wi' a hundred. Always assumin' o' course, ye can find the right person t' do th' job."

"You have someone in mind of course. Yourself, perhaps?"

"Heavens no," said Peterson. "This job requires a truly sneaky individual. Ye've go' t' understand me, lass. There be a difference between merely bein' able t' move wi' stealth, an' bein' truly sneaky. I' stealth 'twas all th' wa' required, yer Marine Recon chaps wou' o' done for 't nicely. Ye need a real Sneaky Pete ferr this 'un. An' whilst I can move wi' a reasonable amount o' quietude ferr a man o' three hundred kilos, 'tis my nature t' be logical n' devious."

"Well, the problem is a bit academic now, don't you think? The Pathfinder company should have made planetfall two weeks ago, so we ought to be getting our first surface transmissions from them sometime this morning."

"I were thinkin' abou' wha' yer next step'll be. Seems t' me ye'll be facin' the prospect o' sendin' an entire Para-Amphibious Infantry Maneuver Battalion down. Either that, 'r a single trooper. After this bunch all gets 'emselves killed."

Stryker glared, but said nothing.

"You think, then, that the company is bound to be wiped out too," said the Director calmly.

"Th' logic o' th' situation 'twould seem t' favor tha' hypothesis, Mr. Director. Ye've lost everybody ye've sent b'fore, in ever increasin' numbers. I' ye proceed in thi' fashion, I've little doubt ye'll soon be' facin' th' dark prospect o' loosin' a' entire division."

"Unfortunately, I'm inclined to agree. We reached the same conclusion a week ago, which is why the decision was made to bring you in. If for any reason, the current effort is not successful and we do lose the company, the IGS have directed us to attempt a limited reconnaissance before committing a major troop effort. No one wants to get bogged down in another sideshow war like Tau Ceti, but we can't leave a hostile planet behind us, either. Although long range energy scans have pretty well ruled out the possibility of it being the enemy's home planet, Alpha Tauri Five may be a base for the enemy. Or the inhabitants may be allied with the enemy. Or the natives may just resent our intruding on their sphere of influence. Or it may simply be a hellhole of a planet with a lot of deadly plant and animal life. Whatever it is, we've got to know.

"I asked you here this morning," the Director continued, "so that you could be briefed, and so that we could pick your series memory. We can feed a set of requirements into the SCAF Battle Planning Computer, and get a printout of individuals who might be technically qualified for the job, but it doesn't give us any firsthand observational data on how the trooper has actually performed in combat. It'll tell us how many awards and medals the trooper got, and a general description of what for, but it won't really tell us about the person. We need someone who has actually seen the candidate perform.

"The Peterson series had a representative with the Intell section of each of the major operational units during the Tau

Ceti Four Campaign, and especially during the final raid into the Tau North Polar Region, where the troops were facing an environment full of hostile flora and fauna. It would take us too long to hunt up the surviving unit commanders all the way down to squad level, defrost and debrief them. We want your suggestions, limited of course to those who are available to us from within the 504th. Can you help us?"

"I'll do me best, Mr. Director."

Peterson leaned back in his seat, appeared to relax, and sat unmoving for perhaps fifteen seconds, bringing all the power he could to concentrate on the problem. At last he spoke.

"Pardon th' delay, bu' I wanted t' make a thorough job of 't. There be six troopers w'in 5th RCT wha' could fill th' job. Three, however, be more'n five light weeks away, an' two o' those wou' require divertin' an assault transport significantly from 'ts current flight course. Th' one's tha' should b' available be First Lieutenant Anthony B. Fetterman, late o' th' Seventh Independent Ranger Company, his current duty station 'tis n' known t' me, but the Seventh Independent 'tis now a part o' th' Seventh Ranger Brigade aboard th' assault transport *Georgy Zhukov*; First Lieutenant Lara Masterson, formerly a Pathfinder, bu' now assigned to the 358th Training Company aboard th' *Jaroslaw Pelinski*; and Master Sergeant Duc Le Minh of the 5th Special Forces Group, detached, currently servin' as a' advisor t' th' Tau contingent aboard th' *Gronville Bromhead*."

There was a loud, audible groan from Stryker.

"I'm afraid the list is shorter than that. Masterson is in command of the mixed Pathfinder company we sent in. The Battle Planning Computer picked her because of her extensive Pathfinder experience during the Tau Ceti Four Campaign. We promoted her to Captain and gave her the company."

Peterson seemed to sigh. "A good lass. Very competent, bu' I fear sorely misused. Alone, 'r wi' a very small team, she might 'o had a chance. Ye best be checkin' on th' others."

The Director indicated his computer console with a wave of his hand and Stryker ran her long, slender fingers over the touch-pad. After a moment, she swore softly.

"Master Sergeant Duc is in sick bay. He suffered a malfunction in paradrop practice two days ago and broke his leg in three places."

"What about this Fetterman guy?" asked the Director.

"Just a second." Stryker's fingertips flew over the touch-pad again. "Must be some kind of screw up. Personnel records are showing he's assigned to Experimental Medical Cryonics Lab. What the hell would a Ranger be doing in Experimental Medical Cryonics?"

"Pull up his two-oh-one packet," said the Director. "Maybe that'll give us a clue."

Stryker manipulated the touch-pad a third time, then stepped back from the console as though she had been shocked.

"Good Lord," she said, "according to this, the man is clinically dead!"

2

Masterson, Lara
Captain, First Special Pathfinder Company
(Composite)
Hard Landing Contingency Force Charlie, SCAF

I sat there strapped into the harness of my main and reserve chutes and buckled into my ejection seat, staring at the lapsed-time readout on my helmet visor's Head Up Display, watching the seconds tick away and feeling the old pucker factor go to work like it had on my two previous combat insertion drops. There was nothing else to do. The smooth, gray-padded walls of the drop pod wrapped themselves around me like the egg crate cushions of an optics protective carrying case, and left me in total darkness, except for the faint L.E.D. readouts of the HUD. It wasn't a place for the claustrophobic.

I'd never made a combat drop in a pod before. In fact, I'd only been in one of the damned things half a dozen times, all during training in the simulator ship. This would be my first actual pod drop of any kind.

SCAF had come up with a lot of what the chairborne experts of Regional Training Command like to call "innovative tactical improvements" since I'd left Earth something over three quarters of a century ago. The pod was supposed to protect you from wind blast and shear effects, as well as wind friction burn, and lessen the likelihood of your blacking out when you pulled the five to seven negative gravities encountered during ejection from the new, high speed assault shuttles. On the other hand, it left you sightless, in a silent, dark cocoon, with much too much time to think about all the possi-

ble malfunctions that could happen and change the damned
pod into a funeral shroud before you ever got the chance to
punch out of it and use your chute. I guess how much of an
innovative tactical improvement it was all depended upon
your point of view. The experts claimed you couldn't survive
the drop without it, so I suppose maybe it was a good idea,
but we got along just fine without them back in the old days
on Tau Ceti Four. Of course, back in the old days, they didn't
punch you out of the shuttle at Mach Five.

Before you start wondering what an old octogenarian like
me is doing getting ready to have herself blown out of a high
speed assault shuttle over a presumed hostile planet, let me set
the record straight. Next month, *if* I'm still alive, I'll get the
chance to celebrate my twenty-first birthday.

I was drafted under the Universal Juvenile Conscription
Act back in 2150 when I was thirteen. My unit spent twenty-
five years and six months Earth time, or five years subjective,
traveling to Tau Ceti Four and then went straight into combat
for over a year. After the fighting on Tau Ceti Four, I got to
spend eighteen months as a first lieutenant in command of a
training company. The Table of Organization and Equipment
called for a captain, but SCAF likes to use experienced personnel whenever possible in training and instructor roles, and
SCAF was a little short of combat qualified officers after the
Tau Ceti Campaign. Most of them were dead.

After that, the cryonic life support technicians stuck me
and my staff and trainees into the cold tanks and chilled us off
for about six decades, sort of like a freeze-dried holocube
dinner. You don't age much in cryonic suspension, or at relativistic speeds. At least not physically.

That brings us up to a little over two weeks ago when
somebody turned on the defrost circuit on my hibernaculum
and thawed me out a couple of hundred years too early. Almost before I'd got the icicles cleared out of my brain cells, or
whatever they'd replaced the intracellular fluid with so the cell
membranes wouldn't rupture when they froze us, I was
briefed by some Fleet Intell major named Stryker, given a
copy of my written orders and told I had forty-eight hours to
organize, equip, and embark my new command on a Hard
Landing reconnaissance and rescue mission. There was no

time allocated for unit training and maneuvers unless I could come up with it, and if it made me feel any better about the whole mess, I'd been promoted to captain. I found five hours by ignoring a lot of mandatory regulations and compulsory safety directives, and it didn't.

The flight out to Alpha Tauri Five in the antigravity shuttle took fifteen days at near light speed. It was miserable. Like spending two weeks in the bedroom closet of your house with around a hundred and fifty of your closest friends. We only had the aisles to exercise in, and we had to sleep in the pods. The food was combat ration concentrates, and the lines for the two latrines always moved slower than your bowels.

To answer your next question, no, I don't know why SCAF insists on calling it Alpha Tauri Five instead of Aldebaran Five. I remember when I was a little girl and my father used to take me outside and show me the Iowa night sky, and point and say, "There's Orion, Lara, and there's Betelgeuse, and you see that bright one to the west and just a little bit north? That's Aldebaran. Both Betelgeuse and Aldebaran are Red Giants. Someday, maybe in your children's or grandchildren's lifetime, people will go there."

Dad was off by a couple of generations. I wonder what he would have said if he'd known his little girl would be one of the first people to set foot on a planet in the Aldebaran system. He's dead by now, I suppose. The last time I saw him was outside the Induction Center in Baltimore. He was crying. I didn't understand why. I do now. In effect, he was burying his barely teenage daughter.

As to your next question, the answer is also no, I don't have the foggiest idea how an antigravity drive system works. Not any more than your average paratrooper back in the second world wide war on Earth could have told you how his Douglas C-47 transport/cargo plane worked. I'm not a pilot, and I'm not a quantum mechanic. I'm a soldier. My job isn't fixing things, it's killing people. That's a bit of an oversimplification, I guess, but in the final analysis it's a fairly succinct job description.

There was a soft chiming sound from the bone induction speaker adhered to the tiny shaved spot above the mastoid sinus behind my right ear, and a tiny blue pinpoint of light flashed insistently on my HUD, telling me that the assault shuttle had entered the planetary atmosphere. Almost at the same instant, St. Croix's voice broke in on the command frequency of the shortcom.

"Captain Masterson? We've got the ten-minute warning."

"Thanks, Chief," I told her. "I've got it on my screen." I clicked up the company frequency with my dental switch, and keyed the throat microphone.

"Attention, Force Charlie. This is Charlie Six. Prepare for combat insertion drop. All troopers execute final systems and equipment check. Platoon leaders report when check complete." I scanned my own readouts and felt what gear I could move enough to reach while I waited. Ninety seconds later the reports came in.

"First Platoon, ready for drop."

"Second Platoon, ready for drop."

"Third Platoon, ready for drop."

"Fourth Platoon, ready for drop."

"Support Platoon, ready for drop."

Then St. Croix's voice cut in again. "Headquarters detachment ready for drop. All units ready for drop."

"Roger. Charlie Six ready for drop," I acknowledged. "All troopers ready for drop."

I clicked up the intrashuttle freq and advised the command pilot and dropmaster that Force Charlie was ready for the drop. When the blue light on my HUD changed to red and the receiver buzzed behind my ear. I keyed the company freq again.

"Force Charlie from the Six. Five minutes to drop. Stand by."

After that, there was nothing to do but sit in the darkness and wait, listening to the pounding of my heart and the growling of my bowels. My bladder felt like it was going to burst. I guess some things never change.

I could feel a slight buffeting, which I supposed signified that the pod ejection doors had slid open, spoiling the aerodynamics of the shuttle. I fingered the D-ring of the reserve chute across my belly with my left hand, and squeezed the safety lever, arming the pod's manual ejection trigger with my right, but I never got to use it. The automatic sequencer broke in for a five count. "*Beep, Beep, Beep, Beep, Beeeeep!*" Then the red light changed to green and I heard the recorded command, "*Eject! Eject! Eject!*" as the rockets roared to life and blasted me clear of the shuttle. A weight like a brontosaurus slid over me, then reversed itself and tried to shove its way up my ass as the gee forces snapped abruptly from negative to positive and back again, and my stomach turned flip-flops. There was a sickening lurch as the pod tumbled crazily, and I blacked out.

When I came to, I was still in the pod. Panicky, I checked the readouts, then forced myself to relax. According to the HUD, which was receiving its data via a fiber optic link with an automatic quick disconnect from the pod's systems, I'd only been out for about thirty seconds. The pod was still tumbling as the outer heat ablative layers were being burned away by the friction of the rarified air molecules at high altitude slamming into the pod about sixty-four hundred kilometers per hour. Finally, when the pod had slowed enough for the heat and shear factors to drop to a safe level, the stabilizer fins popped out and the pod quit tumbling and spinning just in time to save me from filling my face mask with my morning breakfeast. After that, the pod only dropped like a bomb.

It wasn't quite as haphazard as it seemed. The drop zone coordinates had been programmed into the pod prior to ejection, and the tiny gyro-inertial stabilization and guidance package in the pod had kept track of where we were supposed to land. A microprocessor fed the relevant data to the servos that actuated the stabilizers, and the fins adjusted their angle of attack to the atmosphere to glide the pod back toward the DZ. If you could call it a glide. Controlled fall is more like it.

At thirty-five hundred meters a little light came on and a buzzer sounded, reminding me to prepare for pod separation, which came off without a hitch at three thousand meters. The explosive bolts fired right on cue, and the pod split down the middle into two halves, as the ten kilogram thrust separation rockets pushed the two halves well out to the sides and the small thruster underneath the ejection seat kicked in, bouncing me two hundred meters back up into the air. It made you feel a little like a yo-yo, but it got you clear of the pod and above it, so you wouldn't have to worry about a lot of crippling or fatal debris landing on top of you when you got to the ground.

The visor on my helmet had automatically snapped down the polarizer and started darkening the tint of the photochromic lens as soon of the sunlight hit it, but it still wasn't quite fast enough to keep it from momentarily dazzling my eyes. I wondered if it were grammatically correct to call it sunlight when it came from Aldebaran. Probably not, but calling it starlight seemed too silly. To me, stars were still something you saw at night.

The thruster under the seat cut out, and at the apex of the flight back upward, the pneumatic rams in the back of the ejection seat discharged, pulling the seat fabric taut and tossing me unceremoniously another twenty-five meters up and to one side of the seat when the disconnect snapped on the lap belt. I wondered for a second what would have happened if the disconnect hadn't let go, or the one on the fiber optic link that had connected my helmet HUD to the pod, then tried not to think about it.

I stretched out in the prescribed reverse arch, sort of like being spread-eagled on your stomach over nothingness, to stabilize my descent. It helped to slow my fall and my angular momentum, and gave me a chance to have a look at the terrain below.

At 1x there were no discernible manmade patterns. Of course, you wouldn't expect there to be any *man*made patterns. What I mean is, there wasn't anything that looked like a cultivated field or an airstrip or a town or military base. Just a vast carpet of dense green jungle, broken at irregular intervals by high, rocky outcroppings and occasional scrub choked clearings that might be natural formations. I hiked the image multiplier up to 10x and scanned the area again. Just more of the same. I dropped back to 5x and checked the area more or less immediately below me, locating the Search and Rescue team's landing site with ease. We were almost right on target.

I dropped back to unity gain on the multiplier. Beneath me now, the remains of my pod and several others were beginning their electro-mechanical countermeasures programs. Some of the pods were designed to simply fragment. Others had extra thrusters built in designed to scoot the pods around all over the sky, a supposedly safe enough procedure, since their altitude was now five hundred meters below us. Still others were set up to throw out chaff to confuse enemy radar, always assuming, of course, that the enemy was using radar, instead of laser ranging equipment. A few of the pods ejected self-inflating dummy paratroopers that were weighted to fall at the same speed as a real SCAF trooper. Off to the right, I could see part of one pod crack open and rain out a shower of high intensity magnesium flares, designed to confuse infrared scanning systems and heat seeking surface-to-air missiles. In theory, the burning flares were supposed to fall faster than we were, and be self-extinguishing when they hit the ground. Not wanting to have one of those things on top of my canopy when I deployed the chute, I hoped the theory was a good one.

All the fancy tricks the pods were doing were designed to do one thing, keep a SCAF PAI trooper alive until he could reach the ground. When it came to movement to contact and engagement of the enemy, you were on your own. In the old days, we used to just dump an aerial bombardment or artillery prep all over the real estate, dust the DZ with a mixed bag of noxious chemicals, and jump fast from low altitude. That was then, this is now.

At twenty-five hundred meters, I saw the first laser pulse lance out briefly from the Light Point Defense System the ranger platoon that had preceded us had set up, then the rapid recovery gun went crazy as its defense computer began individually targeting the dummies, flares, chaff, and debris thrown out by the pods, vaporizing *something* every .08 seconds, selectively choosing those targets nearest the ground first. Nervously, I glanced down at the IFF neutrino transponder strapped to the Impervium II armored sleeve of my battle dress no-see-me's. The little lights all *said* it was switched on and working. I hoped they knew what they were talking about. Despite all the briefings, I was still less than totally enthusiastic about making a combat drop on top of one of our own point defense systems and trusting the transponder to identify us for it as friends, not foes, and therefore not to be targeted. The neutrinos, of course, moved at the speed of light, but then, so did the laser. What happens if you get a lazy neutrino?

I freefell to five hundred meters without getting fried by our own LPDS, and brought both my hands in to keep my body position stable, gripped the D-ring on the main, and yanked it away. There were both a barometric and a radar altimeter on the chute, either supposed to open the main container at four hundred meters whether I was conscious or not, but I didn't wait for it. By the time you're down to four hundred meters, you don't have a lot of time left to manually deploy your reserve if something goes wrong with the main. Call me paranoid if you must, but call me safe.

I heard the velcro rip apart as the cordura container flapped open and the spring loaded pilot chute popped out, dragging the suspension lines along with it. It must have worked, because the square canopy snapped open and yanked me to a momentary halt as if I had suddenly been slammed into a brick wall. The harness straps bit into my thighs, and I uselessly cursed the bruises I knew I was going to have tomorrow. Some things never change.

I glanced overhead to make sure I had a good deploy. The transparent polymer ram air canopy was nearly invisible, but with the polarizer on the helmet visor, I could see it well enough to tell it didn't have any holes, rips, or tears, and all the suspension lines leading down to the risers were intact. I had a good deploy and a good chute. I reached up and took hold of the steering toggles, and started my glide toward the S&R landing site below at my best maximum rate of safe descent. At one hundred meters I let go of the toggles long enough to reach down and pull the quick release covers that let the equipment bundles clipped onto the harness at my legs and the seat of my pants drop away and hang suspended on their deployment straps fifteen meters below me. Opening the covers exposed the manual release pull rings for the bundle straps, and also armed the bundle straps harness shoulder release button located on a little box near where the main chute D-ring had been. You were supposed to be able to reach down just before landing and punch off the bundles, then get your hand back on the right steering toggle in about a second and a half. The release pull rings were just backups.

I checked the wind direction indicator strapped next to the IFF transponder on my sleeve, and took another look at the

DZ. It wasn't an encouraging sight. The LPDS had stopped shooting, either because it had overheated or run out of targets. I could see it sitting serenely in the middle of the uneven clearing, about a hundred meters away from the S&R rescue ship, which looked about as lifeless as a brick. The whole area looked pretty lifeless.

There were bodies. Lots of them. They were littered all over the clearing. Some were missing parts of arms or legs or heads or chests. Some of them weren't much more than parts. A few seemed almost undamaged. I'd seen grisly scenes before, of course. You don't earn the Silver Crescent with Bar and "V" Device, the Tau Cross, and the Imperial Medal of Honor without seeing a lot of dead meat, but this scene ranked right down there with the worst of them.

It was a moment before the difference in uniforms sank in on me. I could see three different issues, tan and spinach for the rangers; gray, green, and black tiger stripes for the Recon Marines, and bright orange with a big blue six pointed star and gold caduceus on the back for the S&R team. It looked like the pickup pilot had lied about there not being anyone at the P.Z., and it also looked like we were a bit too late to be worrying about rescuing anybody. I wondered how whatever had killed them had managed to get past the LPDS. I'd already seen conclusive evidence that it had been armed and functioning.

At fifty meters I rechecked the wind speed and direction indicator which was registering negligible and variable. Since there was no wind to turn the canopy into in order to reduce my landing ground speed, I steered toward the LPDS. When the altimeter got down to 18 meters, I punched off the equipment bundles, made sure I had a relatively clear path ahead, and ran the canopy onto the ground. It was a much more dignified way of landing than the bone jarring crunch followed by a forward roll of the old Parachute Landing Falls we used to have to do back when we jumped round canopies.

As soon as I knew I was on the ground, I hit the quick release on my chest and ran out from under the canopy, dropping the chute harness, main container, and unused reserve behind me.

Unclipping the machine carbine from my combat harness, I dropped flat and scanned my surroundings. Nothing moved, and nobody fired at me, so I shoved myself up off the ground, whirled around, and ran over and grabbed my equipment bundles, dragging them into the imagined shelter of the LPDS. I scanned the readouts on its control panel, saw that they indicated the system was still armed and functioning, and put my back up against it for a bit of protection while I took another quick look around.

Troopers were dropping all over the DZ and as exposed as the location was, it seemed a better idea than trying to get all the way across the clearing to the edge of the DZ. SCAF considers it counter-productive for an officer to get a broken back, leg, or neck, by carelessly allowing one of her troopers to land on her head. I've always found myself in complete agreement with that policy.

Besides, I wanted to be in a position where I could best observe and control the movements of my troops, and short of standing on top of the S&R rescue ship and making myself an outstanding target for any enemy snipers, next to the LPDS was the best spot. Not to mention the little fact that any stray bullets, missiles, or assorted projectiles that came my direction would have to get through the LPDS before they got to me. For a moment there, I forgot that *something* very apparently *had* gotten through and killed all those people lying dead on the lawn around me.

It was time to go to work, and I keyed the company freq.

"Force Charlie from the Six. Platoon leaders report status."

"First Platoon down with thirty-three," the receiver crackled.

And almost instantly, "Second Platoon down with thirty-three," and "Third Platoon down with thirty-three."

There was a short delay, and then I heard Halvorsen say, "Support Platoon down with thirty-three." Finally, after much too long a silence, I heard Kittredge say "Fourth Platoon is down with thirty-two, Charlie Six. We lost Four-Six. Apparent pod malfunction. No one reports seeing him deploy his chute."

Damn! I thought. Not even on the ground yet, and I've lost one already. I sucked in a deep breath and keyed the mike. "All right, Four-Five. You're the Four-Six now. Move your people down the slope of the hill about two hundred meters and establish an outpost. Be careful out there. According to Intell, there are some fatal-type plants and animals out there."

"Roger. Go out two hundred and establish an outpost. Four-Six out."

I hoped I wasn't sending Kittredge out to get somebody else killed.

"Headquarters detachment down with eleven," said St. Croix. A moment later she loped up with the easy grace of a cat, her muscles rippling like waves beneath her camouflaged BDU's, and hunkered down beside me.

In the old days, they'd have called St. Croix a company first sergeant. Nowadays they're Field Warrant Officers, and the senior ones are called Chief. You get a two striper to run your fire and maneuver teams, a buck sergeant to run your squad, and a staff sergeant to run your platoon. Except that they don't call them staff sergeants anymore, just platoon leaders, whether they're actually running a platoon or not. The company commander is supposed to be either a first lieutenant or a captain, and if you're really, really lucky, you might get a second lieutenant for your XO. Except that most second lieutenants are green meat academy whiz kids, and having one of them hung around your neck is about as helpful as an anvil at a basketball game. I figured I was a lot better off with St. Croix. At least she had *some* combat experience, even if it was all gained in a series of counter-guerilla police actions back on Earth.

I don't mean that to sound deprecating. She distinguished herself well in a number of small, but very dirty wars in the jungles of Latin America, and she was a very demanding training officer. Plus, she had an innate ability to move through a forest of dry, dead leaves or a vine choked jungle with all the stealth and swiftness of a panther stalking its supper. The troops would do what she told them when she told them. And one thing more, she liked to do her killing up close and personal, an unarmed combat and knife expert. Me? I've always believed long distance is the next best thing to being there. Why get close enough to the other guy for him to be able to reach out and touch you, when you can reach out and touch him first?

St. Croix leaned over toward me, and I leaned toward her, so we could talk through the voice-mitters of our field protective masks without having to use the radio shortcom. As I did so, a big, fat drop of sweat hit me square in the eye and stung like hell. That was one thing that hadn't changed a bit since the Old Army. It wasn't as hot as it had been on Tau Ceti Four, but it was nearly as hot, and the humidity was unbelievable. I'd been down for maybe all of three minutes, and my uniform was already soaked through. The resistance against the filters in my mask was like trying to breathe with your head in a bucket of grain.

"I put First and Third Platoons on the perimeter with hand signals," said St. Croix, still almost having to shout to make herself heard through the mask. "I got everybody digging in. What's the status of this thing?" She jerked her head toward the LPDS.

"Still armed and operating. You saw it work on the way down?"

She nodded. "What's our next move?"

"We take any casualties besides Montoya?"

"Kershaw from Third sprained his ankle, I think. Sandburg's taking a look at it."

"What about Montoya? Did anybody see his pod go down?"

"Negative. At least not confirmed. One trooper *thinks* she may have seen a pod going down without opening. She's not sure."

"In that case," I told St. Croix, "I think our next move is to have a look inside that rescue ship. Then we'll hunt up Sandburg and see if the good doctor can tell us just what the fuck killed all these people."

"Yeah," said St. Croix. "It sure as the hell doesn't look much like a deserted pickup zone, does it?"

"No," I said. "It sure as *the hell* does not. Come on. Let's go have a look."

The lock of the ship was standing wide open. St. Croix and I got in and cycled the lock, then opened the inner hatch.

Okay, so I know it was a dumb move. We should have sent some poor dumb shag-assed private in first, in case the place was full of poison gas or a deadly virus of some kind, or worst of all, a vacuum where our masks wouldn't have done us any good at all. So sue me. Maybe we still had a few ice crystals in the brain from being people-pops in the cryo-tanks. Anyway, back in the Old Army, an officer used to *lead* her troops into combat, not *send* them.

As it turned out, there wasn't any poison gas or deadly viruses to contend with. What there was, was more bodies. Four of them to be exact, two of the S&R ship's five man crew, and two Fleet Military Policemen. I didn't know what the hell the MP's were doing there, nobody had briefed us about that, but I can sure tell you what they did there, at least one of them.

Sometime after the ship had landed and somebody had gone out through the airlock, presumably the S&R specialists, one whose body I had seen outside, one of the MP's had drawn his pistol and shot the other three men in the ship with him. He'd done it very methodically, and in an apparently unhurried manner. A single hypervelocity 3.5mm caseless round had entered the forehead of each man and fragmented causing severe tissue damage, and the hydrostatic shock had taken the back off of the victim's head in a very messy manner. Afterward, the MP who had done the shooting had used his belt to hang himself from one of the rungs on the ladder to the upper deck. He had apparently made no effort to save himself by putting his feet back on the ladder or taking hold of the rungs.

"Jesus," said St. Croix, "I didn't know you could kill yourself that way. Always figured the body's natural instinct for self-preservation would take over at the last instant and make you put your feet back on the ladder. He could have, you know?"

"Maybe he couldn't." I moved over and checked the corpse's wrists and ankles for signs of bruising or rope burns. There weren't any. "Oh, well, so much for that idea. I thought maybe he'd had help, and somebody wanted to make it look like suicide."

"Want me to cut him down?" St. Croix asked.

"Better wait until Sandburg has a look at him. Maybe she'll see something we don't. Let's check the rest of the ship."

We gave the little S&R vessel a reasonably thorough going over, although it was possible we might have missed something, since neither of us had ever been in a rescue ship before. It was a small craft, and there really weren't all that many places for an enemy spy to be hidden, at least not if he were human sized.

We checked everything except one compartment that had a sign on its small hatch reading WARNING: ACCESS TO ANTIGRAVITY DRIVE AND MANEUVERING THRUSTER FUELS COMPARTMENT. ENTRY RESTRICTED TO AUTHORIZED TECHNICIANS WEARING APPROPRIATE PROTECTIVE ATTIRE AND SELF-CONTAINED BREATHING APPARATUS. I figured if anybody was desperate enough to hide in there, all I was going to do was wish him luck. Besides, the hatch had been manually dogged down from the outside.

We went back out through the airlock. Everything was still quiet. Some of the troops were policing up the chutes out of the DZ. Nobody was throwing incoming fire at us, and Kittredge reported having established the OP without losing anybody else. It was a good omen, but I didn't like it. It was just too damned quiet.

I told Kittredge to have her troops blast anything that approached from the base of the hill, and then fall back inside the perimeter. Not exactly a friendly way to meet the natives perhaps, but from the look of all the bodies already strewn about the landscape, I didn't think we'd have to worry about offending the customary greeting sensibilities of any of the locals, nor accidentally wasting one of our own people. I had a strong hunch there weren't any SCAF personnel left around to worry about. Somebody or something had already wasted at least a full platoon of Rangers, a Marine Recon Team, and a half-dozen or so various other troops.

Hernandez, my exobiology toxicological pathology specialist came over and pronounced the area clear of all known disease causing organisms and toxins. The operant word however, was *known*, so I opted to have the troops keep their masks on a little longer, even though it was getting intolerably miserable in the damned things. I always figure being a little miserable, or even a lot, is preferable to being a little dead.

We found Sandburg still taping up Kershaw's ankle.

"How is it?" I asked.

"It's busted," said Sandburg.

"How bad?"

"No more foot patrols for Kershaw, here. At least not for a couple of months."

"Doctor, what I want to know is, am I going to have to call in an evac flight?"

Sandburg snorted. At least as much as you could snort with a field protective mask on. "For this? Nah. Not unless you want to move the company. Then we either need a medevac or somebody is going to have to carry him. It's painful and debilitating, not life threatening."

Kershaw frowned as if he didn't think we were taking his injuries seriously enough.

"What about all the rest of these people? Any of them still alive?"

"Are you kidding?" said Sandburg.

"No, damn it, I am not kidding. Are any of them still alive?"

"Of course not. We lost contact with these people five hours ago, remember?"

"Have you checked them?"

"I don't have to. They're all obviously dead. For Christ's sake, Captain, just look at them."

"Have you checked them, goddammit?"

"Oh, all right. No, I haven't checked them. I took care of Kershaw's ankle first."

"Then check them!" I snapped. "You just said Kershaw's ankle wasn't life threatening. It can wait."

Kershaw looked like I'd hurt his feelings.

Sandburg stared at me for a moment, then threw down her tape and got up slowly. "Yes, *sir*, Captain Masterson. I'll check the bodies for you, *sir*. It's always more important to treat the dead than the living."

I let it pass. It was just Sandburg's way of telling me she thought I was being a bit more macho than necessary. She was concerned with treating her patient. I was concerned with finding out what had killed everybody before we all became patients. It was a difference in philosophy, that's all. I knew when she'd had time to think about it, she'd understand my reasoning.

Sandburg stomped over to the nearest group of corpses and stabbed her finger at a body. "This man has suffered massive chest trauma. We can actually look into the thorax and see that both lungs have been shredded and part of the cardiac muscle itself is missing," she shouted through her mask in a lecture hall voice. "He is obviously and profoundly dead."

Her finger stabbed at another. "This man has sustained a severe blow to the chest in the area of the xyphoid process of the sternum, probably as a result of being struck with a solid, heavy object, such as a battle rifle, probably resulting in a puncture of the pericardium and the myocardium, leading to cardiac tamponade and rapid clinical and biological death."

She stabbed at another. "This woman has bulging eyes, a deep cyanosis of the chest and upper body, and distended neck veins, although they are not now as prominent as they would have been had we been here at the time of her demise. Her gross external appearance indicates sudden death from traumatic asphyxia, meaning someone or something squeezed all the air out of her lungs.

"This person we judge to have been a normally healthy female in her late teens, due to her general physical appearance, size, and the angle of her pelvis. The identification cannot be complete without further investigation, due to the fact that the patient has been decapitated and suffered disfiguring trauma to her upper chest, consistent with the characteristic signs of a hand grenade exploding while in contact with her upper body. We note also that one of the patient's hands is severed at the distal end of the radius and ulna, and we observe shattered fragments of bone extending from the right forearm that are again consistent with the actions of a low yield contact explosion upon human tissue."

Sandburg knelt next to another body and performed a triple airway maneuver, tilting back the head and forcing open the jaw with considerable effort. "Here we see a male patient with no obvious signs of injury. While further tests are indicated before we can accurately assess the cause of death, the severely clenched jaw suggests to us that the patient died under conditions of severe pain or stress or both, leading us to suspect acute myocardial infarction, in layman's terms, a heart attack. Need I continue, Captain?"

"You can skip the lecture, Doctor," I told her. "I just want to know if any of them are still alive enough to tell us what killed all the rest of them."

"Is that all you want, is it? Well, Captain Masterson, this is your lucky day, because I can answer both those questions for you.

"First, none of these poor bastards are alive. They're all dead, and you can take my professional word on that. I'll go ahead and check them all, just to keep you happy, but I can tell you right now, the only people alive on this DZ are the ones who dropped down with us.

"Second, since you asked, these people killed each other. Except for a few of them who evidently only killed themselves, like that girl there who held the grenade under her chin until it detonated. Just look at the body positions. Look at the weapons they've got in or near their hands. Look at the injuries of those people lying next to them. Compare the injuries to the type normally caused by the weapon held by the person next to them. You've seen combat wounds before. You don't have to be a doctor to see what I'm talking about."

"Sandburg, are you trying to tell me all these people went crazy and started shooting each other?"

"Shooting, stabbing, choking, you name it. That one there has a broken neck, and there are a couple I saw over by the perimeter when we were coming in that have been sliced neatly in half by the LPDS laser. I think if you check, you'll find they tried to run outside the perimeter safe zone without their IFF transponders. You may notice that the female of the two has had the buttons ripped off her blouse, and her trousers pulled partway down her thighs, while the fly of the man's BDU's is open. If you've got a morbid interest in such things, you might also note the priapism on the male, indicative of the neurological damage suffered when the laser cut a track through his spine.

"Did they all go crazy? I don't know, Captain. I don't know why they did what they did. But I do know what they did. These people killed each other, and then the ones that were left took their own lives. And *that* diagnosis, Captain, is credits in the paymaster's office.

"All right," I told her. "Finish what you've got to do, and then check the rest of them as you can get around to it. I want an identification and a probable cause of death on each one of them. We're going to have a hard time selling this one to Fleet Command. Document everything and take pictures. Afterward, there are a few more inside the ship you ought to have a look at."

"Yes, Captain. Pictures of everything. That ought to give the IGS something pleasant to look at over their breakfast tables."

I almost said something. Sandburg was going to have to do a rapid attitude adjustment, or one of these days she was going to find herself in a lot of trouble with some superior officer. I figured she was just still upset, though. No doctor likes to see a dead patient. Especially one that might have been salvageable if he'd gotten prompt medical attention, and most especially one that's suffered long and awful before expiring.

Sandburg had just seen more of them than the average SCAF MASH surgeon sees in a month, and these people had all died in a particularly grisly, senseless fashion. That was what really made it hard to take. The sheer incomprehensibility of it all. Why would fifty or sixty people just suddenly decide to start killing each other?

Besides, it's bad for morale for the CO to publicly ream out the company doctor's ass in front of the troops.

I turned to say something to St. Croix, but was interrupted by the crackling of the shortcom receiver. It was the third platoon leader on the company freq.

"Charlie Six from Three-Six. Can you come over to the northwest side of the perimeter for a moment? There's something here I think you ought to have a look at."

"What have you got, Three-Six?"

"I'd rather not say, Captain. I think you'd better have a look at this one for yourself."

"Is it important?"

"Yes, sir. I think it might be."

"All right, Three-Six. I'll be right over."

I looked at St. Croix, who shrugged, and we walked over to see what all the fuss was about.

As we neared the edge of the clearing, Tasco materialized from the tree line just outside the perimeter safe zone and motioned for us to follow. Mindful of Sandburg's description of the would-be rapist and his evidently intended victim, I made sure my IFF transponder was operating before stepping outside the LPDS's no-kill zone.

"This way, Captain, Chief St. Croix. It's over here."

"What's 'over here', Platoon Leader?" I asked.

"The body, sir. One of my fire and maneuver team leaders found it while he was looking for a place to take a leak."

"Couldn't he have done that inside the perimeter?"

"He's shy, sir. Besides, I think what he really needed to do was take a crap anyway. After he found the body, it scared the crap right out of him. He's over there changing his drawers now."

"Didn't the idiot hear the warning about avoiding contact with the local plants and animals until we can figure out which ones are dangerous?"

Tasco shrugged. I thought I could see the hint of a smile behind the field protective mask.

"All right. What makes this particular body so hairy-assed special?"

"It's one of them, sir."

"Platoon Leader, we got a whole drop zone full of dead *thems*. What are you talking about."

"Sorry, Captain. I don't mean one of us, I mean one of them. An alien, sir. Uh, that is, a native, I mean."

"What!"

"Yes, sir. Right over this way, sir. Be careful of that vine with the barbed thorns. They hurt like hell and they're a son-ofabitch to get out."

I said to hell with the thorns and pushed through the brush to where Tasco had pointed, almost tripping over the thing myself, then stared down at the form.

It was a little over a meter and a half long, or tall, if you stood it up on its hind legs. The back feet were long and skinny, and had claws. The legs were angled funny, as though there was an extra joint in them somewhere. The body was that of a well muscled human, as Sandburg would have said, but it was covered all over with coarse, tawny colored, short hair. The heavily muscled forearms ended in long slender hands with short, stubby fingers that had razor sharp, hooked claws about three centimeters long, and no opposable thumb, but the thing still looked pretty human overall. Except for the head and face. It had small, triangular shaped ears near the top of its head, a set of long, thin whiskers, eyes with pupils as big as a beer can, well, almost as big anyhow, and a mouthful of teeth that a sand shark would have been envious of. I'd have been willing to call it an animal, if it hadn't been for the bright green and gold colored loincloth about the waist. It was like something out of *The Island of Dr. Moreau.*

St. Croix muttered something, but I couldn't hear it through her mask.

"What did you say?"

"I said, is it still alive?"

"How the hell should I know. It doesn't appear to be. Get Sandburg over here on the double. Tell her to bring her medical bag. Then find Hernandez. Maybe she can tell us what the hell this thing is."

"You think maybe we've finally found the enemy?"

I knew what St. Croix was driving at. I'd seen several statues to one of the Tau gods on Tau Ceti Four that looked uncomfortably like what I was looking at now. Uncomfortably like, but not *exactly* like. It could just be coincidence.

I shrugged. "I don't know. Maybe. Or maybe it's one of the local natives." I wondered if I said that just because I associated the wearing of loincloths with primitives, an armchair anthropological theory that had already been pretty well disproven by the Taus.

I turned to Tasco. "Nobody touches this. You understand? Nobody even comes near it. Except for Hernandez and Sandburg. I'm holding you personally responsible for the safety and security of this thing until Fleet Ops tells us what to do with it."

Tasco nodded. "Yes, Captain. I understand. Protect the, uh, whatever it is."

"Captain, *do you think it's the enemy?*" St. Croix persisted.

"Whatever it is, Chief," I said, "I think I've got a very bad feeling about this."

3

Fetterman, Anthony B.
First Lieutenant, Seventh Rangers, SCAF

I was dead.

I knew that. There was simply no way I could still be alive.

Although I had only been dimly aware of the concussion when the anti-personnel mine exploded, within seconds I knew it had zapped me good.

Since it hadn't cut me off at the knees, I also knew it wasn't one of the radar-doppled claymores, and since it didn't kill me outright, it wasn't an ultrasonic mine. I couldn't remember stepping on anything or hitting any tripwires though, so it must have been a geophone triggered plastique and shrapnel model.

The pain was surprisingly little. I've read how, when the body undergoes a severe trauma, the shock to the system sometimes shuts down the pain sensing neurological response. I guess that must have been the case.

But I remembered Lara holding my hand, her soft touch on my cheek, the anguish in her voice, and I remember coughing up blood on the ground before everything faded to gray, and then finally black.

Later, I have a vague sense of being in a Close Support Craft cargo bay with a lot of bright lights and some plastic bags and tubing hanging over my head, and hearing somebody say, "We're losing him. I'm gonna shock him again. Clear!" After that, there is nothing, except for the memory that I wished someone would turn down those damned bright lights.

The lights still hurt my eyes, so I screwed them shut again, but somebody shook me and yelled at me to open them. I didn't want to, but whoever it was kept bothering me, and closing my eyes just made me feel sick, so I finally opened them again. There was just one bright light now, and it kept moving around in little circles, first in front of one eye, then the other. Finally it stopped and I closed my eyelids again.

When I reopened them, all I could see was a soft, diffuse, white light. I'd seen the scenario often enough in movies. Funny how they still call them movies, now that they're all in holovision. Nobody watches TV anymore. They all watch *The Cube*. But people still call the stories movies.

Anyway, I'd seen the scene half a hundred times, so I knew where I was supposed to be.

I have to admit, I was more than a little surprised. Given the kind of life I'd lived, I'd expected a lot of flames and a comical little guy in a red suit with a pitchfork. Well, to be honest, all I'd expected was that it would all end in some black hole in the ground, but *if* there was a life beyond the grave, I'd always figured I'd wind up in the other place.

What I couldn't understand though, was, if I *was* dead, why the hell did I have such a splitting headache, and why did I feel like I was freezing to death. How can you freeze to death, when you're already dead? And how was a guy supposed to get any sleep, when people kept shaking him every time he closed his eyes? And closing your eyes made you feel sick anyway.

"If this is heaven," I said, "it's a goddamned drag."

"'I' 'tisn't heaven my boyoh, an' yer n' dead. Although I'll a'mit fer a while ye were, an' possibly ye'll find i' t' be a preferable state, after y' hear wha's required o' ye."

There was something familiar about the voice, but I couldn't place it for a second. Then the owner loomed into view above me.

"Good Christ!" I exploded. "It's Saint Peterson. Are you dead too, Pete?"

"Th' lad's delirious," said Peterson to someone I couldn't see.

"I think maybe we'd better let him rest now," said the

disembodied voice. "He's been through a lot, and it'll be awhile before he's strong enough to talk to."

"Doctor," said Peterson, speaking to someone off to one side, "'Tis a matter o' gravest importance brings m' here t' talk wi' th' lad. We didn' have y' bring him back from th' grave jus' so's y' could practice yer medical skills."

"I'm sorry, Major," said the voice firmly, "but I'm afraid you'll have to consider that doctor's orders. It won't do you any good if you kill him again, will it? Come back in the morning when he's had some real rest."

"Doctor, th' man's been sleepin' fer over 'alf a century now. Jus' exactly 'ow much rest does 'e need?"

"Look, do you want to kill him? The man's system has been through two separate severe traumas, being severely wounded, *and cryonic suspension*. For your information, we lose about six percent of the people we bring out of cryonic suspension anyway, although I'm not supposed to say that. It's considered that it would be bad for the troops' morale, to say nothing of making it hard to get them to go into the damned cold storage tanks again.

"In his already weakened condition, I'm surprised he survived it. He shouldn't have survived the wounds to begin with. Let's not forget that they *were fatal wounds*. The man *was clinically dead* when he was brought in. He had no pulse or heartbeat, no electromechanical activity of the myocardium of any kind. And no respirations. The only reason he isn't *biologically dead*, was because the combat paramedics had managed to keep him artificially alive until he got here, and we got him frozen before the brain cells started to die. Another few minutes, and your boy here wouldn't have made it at all.

"You keep pushing him before his body's had a chance to readjust to what's been done to it, and he's liable to arrest again. Even the Almighty is a bit hard pressed to pull off the same miracle twice. Microsurgically repairing the man's lungs, heart, and brain, is a bit like patching a pair of pants. You can only sew up the holes so many times before you don't have a pair of pants anymore, just a bunch of sewed up holes."

"All right, Doctor. Bu' jus' a' soon as th' lad is able, I wan' t' talk wi' 'im. Clear?"

"Clear enough. I'll have someone let you know."

"An' one thing more. Ye best b' gettin' th' lad in shape. He's a' th' most two or three weeks t' b' ready fer a mission, an' there's a great deal dependin' on 'im bein' able t' do it."

"Now just a minute . . ."

"There'll b' n' argument, Doctor. Th' orders come from th' Imperial General Staff, no' me. I 'ave m' own orders, an' now y've yours. See to 't they're carried ou'."

"Goo' day, Doctor. I *will* b' hearin' from ye."

I think they argued some more after that, but none of what they were saying made any sense anyway, so I went back to sleep.

I dreamed of Lara, sometimes in her towel, and sometimes in her body armor, and sometimes in nothing but a smile. I liked that best. She had a great smile. Among other things.

At last I awoke, and for a moment, I imagined Lara was sitting beside me, holding my hand, but it wasn't her. I figured it must be an angel. She was certainly pretty enough to be. But it turned out she wasn't that either, and she wasn't holding my hand, she was holding my wrist and checking my pulse.

"Good," she said. "You're awake. How do you feel?"

I was going to tell her I felt like I'd been hit with a ton of shit, which would have been a fairly accurate description of how I did feel, but the question struck me as silly for some reason and instead I said, "With my hands?"

"What did you say?" she asked, bending over and putting her ear closer to my mouth.

"I said with my hands," I repeated. "You asked how I felt, and I said with my hands." I was a little surprised at how weak my own voice sounded. "Are you an angel?" I whispered.

"Whaaat?"

"I said, 'Are you an angel?' I'd like to know, please, if I'm dead."

She smiled prettily and said, "No. You're not dead. You're in a hospital. My name is Dinah, and I'm a nurse. Dr. Singh will want to talk with you. Will you be all right for a moment while I go and get him?"

I nodded and closed my eyes.

It couldn't have been long. A few minutes at most. The man who came in was a tall, thin man with a dark, pock-marked face and a great hook of a nose like a hawk's beak. He was dressed in a white jumpsuit with a white lab coat over it, and had an ultrasonic stethescope hung around his neck. When he spoke, I recognized the voice as belonging to the man who had argued with Major Peterson. I'd thought perhaps I'd only dreamed that.

"Ah, good morning. The nurse said you were awake. I am Dr. Singh. How are you feeling?"

"Like hell. How am I supposed to be feeling?"

He chuckled. "About like hell, I should think, considering what you have been through. Do you know where you are?"

"The nurse said this was a hospital. Beyond that, no."

"You're in the Experimental Medical Cryonics section of the hospital ship *Albert Schweitzer*, attached to the 504th Stellar Strike Command of the 5th Regional Combat Team."

"What the hell is that?"

"Part of the Second Sol Combined Arms Force, Imperial Retribution Fleet/Army."

"I didn't know there was one."

"I guess you'll have a lot of catching up to do. You haven't been with us for quite awhile."

"Coma?" I asked.

"Not quite. Please understand, Lieutenant Fetterman, this is rather difficult for me to adequately explain, and I'm not at all sure this is the proper time to do it."

"Explain away, Doctor. Suppose we start with how long I've been out."

He hesitated, then pulled up a chair and sat down, wiping imaginary dust from his hands on the legs of his jumpsuit before answering.

"All right. We'll start with that first. You've been, ah, well, that is . . . It's sixty years, Lieutenant. You've been out, so to speak, for sixty years."

"Sixty years! Is that some kind of a joke, Doctor?"

"Actually, it's sixty-one years and eight months."

I didn't say anything for maybe a whole minute, then my hand went up to my face, touched it, felt. "Am I . . ."

"You're still thirty years old, Lieutenant Fetterman. At least physically. Your body hasn't aged physically because you've been in cryonic suspension."

"Cryonic suspension? What in hell's that?"

"This is going to be tougher than I thought," said Singh. "Cryonic suspension is the process by which a human being or other living organism is held in a state of suspended animation by cooling the organism to a temperature near absolute zero. The process requires replacing the water in the body's tissues and cells with a complex fluorocarbon polymer in order to prevent rupturing of the cell membranes and resultant tissue necrosis. It was developed by Benge and Murphy in 2153, and perfected to a level considered safe for limited use on humans under special circumstances by Baer and Huff, working in conjunction with Rafferty and Bedford in 2162. The technique is now in fairly common usage for long distance space travel, where the time factor, even at relativistic speeds, is considered excessive from a practicality standpoint. While in such a state of suspended animation, the body's life processes temporarily cease, and no aging of the organism occurs."

"Doctor Singh, are you trying to tell me that I've been frozen like some kid's popsicle for the last sixty years?"

"Sixty-one years and eight months, plus five days."

"With all respect, Doctor, that sounds like a bunch of ba-hooey to me."

"I was afraid you'd feel that way. It makes the rest of what I have to tell you all that much harder. But I assure you, it's quite true. Tell me, what is the last thing you remember before waking up here?"

"An explosion. I was wounded by a mine."

"No, Lieutenant, I'm afraid not. You were not merely wounded by the mine, you were killed by it."

"Oh come on now, Doctor. I'm lying here in this bed talking to you. Do you expect me to believe I'm dead?"

"Not *are* dead, Lieutenant, but you *were* dead. Clinically at least."

"Now I'm supposed to believe that you can bring back the dead from beyond the grave?"

"Not from beyond the grave, Lieutenant. But yes, in some cases we can bring back the dead. If the person hasn't been dead too long, or too permanently."

"That doesn't make any sense."

"Is it any stranger than that we should be able to freeze people, to stop them from growing old, and then thaw them out again to fight another day? I said you were clinically dead, Lieutenant Fetterman. Your heart and lungs had stopped working. Once a person is clinically dead, it takes from four to six minutes for the brain cells to begin to die. Once the brain cells have died, the process is irreversible. At that point, biological death is said to have occurred.

"When the mine exploded, your wounds were sufficiently serious to be fatal. You did in fact die. But the combat paramedics were able to keep your blood oxygenated and circulating by artificial means until you could reach the major life support facilities of a hospital ship. The ship was in fact this one, a part of the SCAF Relief Fleet, dispatched from earth in 2163. We arrived too late to prevent the war on Tau Ceti Four, but were able to . . ."

"Prevent the war! Why would you want to . . ."

"I think we'd best leave discussion of that to another time, Lieutenant. For now, suffice it to say that the Relief Fleet's original purpose was to prevent the war, but that we arrived too late to stop it. The Relief Fleet was later redesignated as the Second Retribution Fleet, and the accompanying surface forces as the Second Retribution Army, with orders to seek and destroy the enemy."

"I thought we'd done that," I interrupted.

"Yes, you defeated the Taus, but I'm afraid the situation is considerably more complex than that. Major Peterson can explain all this to you later. Right now I'm more concerned with explaining to you what happened after you were killed."

"Ah! Doctor! This is all too much. You tell me I'm dead, but I'm not dead, that I was killed, but I wasn't really killed, and that you're part of a second fleet that came to stop us from fighting the war we were sent to fight, and on top of all that, you tell me you've had me frozen in a block of ice for the last sixty-one years. Just how much of all this crap do you really expect me to believe?"

"All of it, Lieutenant. Because whether you want to believe it or not, it's all true."

Something was bothering me with all this story, although I couldn't quite put my finger on it. Something just wasn't quite right. I was beginning to wonder if it weren't all just some kind of Tau trick to get information out of me, but neither the doctor nor the nurse had looked like any Tau I'd ever seen, and Peterson *had* been there. Then it finally hit me.

"Doctor Singh, you said I was clinically dead when the combat paramedics brought me in, but that I was frozen before the brain cells had a chance to die. Why was I left frozen for sixty years, Doctor? Why didn't you people fix me up then?"

Singh looked uncomfortable. "You must understand, Lieutenant Fetterman, that I was not involved with the original decision. I was not even born yet at the time. I was born in space, aboard the fleet."

"Didn't the technology exist at the time to fix whatever was wrong with me?"

"The basic technology existed, but was not sufficiently refined. While you could possibly have been resuscitated using advanced experimental techniques at the time, the repair work to your heart and lungs would not have been as successful nor as complete as we are able to accomplish now. Of particular difficulty was the removal of a tiny, but significantly positioned blood clot that had formed in your brain. Medical science's techniques of intravascular fiber optic laser surgery were rather primitive at the time. Also, the new pulmonary exchange polymers used to replace the alveoli that had been destroyed in the sections of your lungs injured by shrapnel from the mine, was as yet unproven except in laboratory animals. The medical staff felt that there would be little point in reviving a man whose weak heart, partial paralysis from a blood clot in the neuromotor control section of his brain, and severely reduced lung capacity would render him forever unfit for the only job he had been trained to perform."

"In other words, I was junk. Useless to them and an additional burden on SCAF's supply lines. They didn't need me any more. So why didn't they just let me die, Doctor? Surely that would have been cheaper than keeping me frozen all these years."

Singh said nothing. He just sat staring at his hands, trying to find the right words.

"You bastards used me as a guinea pig to try out your new techniques on, didn't you?"

"I, that is . . . While I am not trying to excuse the actions of my predecessors, Lieutenant Fetterman, you must realize that in a way, you were an ideal experimental subject. You were already essentially dead, so how could you be hurt any worse by the experiments? The field of cryonic surgery, that is, operating on a body while it is in a state of cryonic suspension, was advanced immeasurably by the techniques developed from experimental attempts on your, ah, body. Do not be too hard on us. Our work has enabled us to give you new life. In a way, you have saved yourself. The techniques you made possible, are what eventually gave us the necessary skills to return you to life."

"And what about all that experimenting that you and your predecessors did do, Doctor? Surely not every attempt was a success. What about all the times things went wrong?"

"Later techniques have allowed us to correct most of those mistakes. You will find, Lieutenant, that you will probably have some stiffness in your left leg, and you will have lost the use of the little finger on your left hand. You will also find a number of unfamiliar scars on your body, some from the fragments of the mine, others from more primitive surgical techniques. We may eventually be able to remove the scarring, or at least reduce it considerably, through cosmetic surgery. The stiffness in your leg and the paralysis of the finger will, I am afraid, remain permanent, at least for the foreseeable future. We simply have not yet learned how to regenerate, with any major degree of success, nerve tissue once it has died."

What the fuck do you say to a guy who has just told you something like that? You've gotten yourself killed fighting a war you weren't supposed to fight, only you weren't really killed, just sort of, and for the last sixty-odd years, a bunch of wacked-out latter day Dr. Frankensteins have been playing around in the insides of your frozen corpse, tinkering with it, and trying to find ways so they can bring other corpses back to

life. I was beginning to understand what had made Mary
Shelley's monster such a disagreeable fellow.

"All right, Doctor," I said. "Let's have the rest of it."

"I'm sorry. I don't know what you're talking about. That's
all there is to tell."

"Cut the bull. Why, after all this time, did you folks finally
decide to stop using me like a white rat and bring me back?"

"Th' di' it because I've need o' yer special talents, m'
boy," said Peterson coming in the door. "Thank ye, Doctor,
tha'll b' all."

Singh left, and Peterson took his seat.

"Now b'fore y' go gettin' all mad a' me, consider that I
didn' know wha' had happened t' ye, an' if I 'ad, I'd probably
'a' been overruled anyway. I am glad t' see y're back among
us, b' I fear ye'll no' be happy t' see me, after I tell ye wha'
I've come for."

"Tell me one thing first," I said. "Did we win?"

"The Taus y' mean? O' course. Ye were there yer self,
were ye no'? They b' our allies now, an' I think we'll b' a
needin' 'em, b'fore th' war is over."

"But I thought you said we'd won," I protested.

"Only th' campaign agains' th' Taus. As it turned ou', the
folks tha' destroyed th' *Star Explorer* an' started th' war,
didn' even come from th' Tau Ceti system. Th' *Star Explorer*
merely tangled wi' one o' their scoutships. W' drew all th'
right conclusions from all th' wrong data, an' conquered th'
wrong race o' people."

He let that sink in for a minute.

"I think I'm going to be sick," I said.

"Shall I get th' Doctor back?"

"I just don't believe it," I said, waving him back to his
chair. "How could such a cock-up have happened?"

"There were many contributin' factors, laddie. Th' hows
and whys d'n' matter much now. What's done's done. There's
no undoin' it. Now, we're faced wi' an entirely different
problem."

"Is he awake? Can I come in?" called a voice from the
door.

She was a real knockout, one fine looking woman, with
shoulder length brown hair and gray-green eyes, wearing a

blue jumpsuit with major's pips on her shoulderboards. She looked to be about my age, maybe a little older. Uh, that is, in her mid-thirties, not her nineties. Peterson introduced her as Major Stryker from Fleet Intell, and together they told me what they knew about the Aldebaran situation. It wasn't much.

When they got to the part about Lara leading the Hard Landing Force, my heart leapt for joy. I'd never expected to hear of her again. After spending sixty-one years in the freezer, I'd figured she was dead for sure by now. They said she was a captain now, though, which made me wonder about other things. How old was she now? Was she older than me? Would she still remember me, and if so, would she even care? Sixty-one years is a long time to stay in love with someone. I wasn't even sure if we had been in love, but it had been something like it, something more than just lust and loneliness.

I was also worried about Lara's safety. From the sound of things, Aldebaran Five, or Alpha Tauri Five as Major Stryker seemed to prefer calling it, was a wonderful planet. Set foot on it, and it killed you. And Pathfinders aren't set-piece battle experts either. They're recon and guide specialists. The damned fools shouldn't have sent a whole company of them. If you need more than a squad of Pathfinders, you need something other than Pathfinders. I told them as much.

"Which," said Stryker, "is exactly why we've come to you."

"Maybe you'd better come again," I said.

" 'Tis like this, lad," Peterson explained. "As yet, we've n' determined a definite need t' send y' down there. Based on Masterson's report abou' findin' the cat-person, we've detached a special task group t' close on Alpha Tauri Five fer further investigation, an' sent her a message t' protect th' thing a' all costs. If everythin' goes well, she'll do exactly that, an' when we get there we'll send down a PAI maneuver battalion t' secure th' area, and a team o' exobiologists t' study the critter an' bring it back t' the Fleet for detailed analysis.

"But as ye know fro' what we've told ye, th' previous track record o' th' units we've sent 've n' been all tha' impressive.

If anythin' should g' wrong, we've decided to send down a single expert t' perform a reconnaissance, rather than droppin' a whole great whoppin' huge bunch o' troops down there an' maybe losin' all o' them too."

"A one-man recon? Who's going to be dumb enough to ... Oh, no. No-oh. Peterson, you can't be serious. I've just come out of the freezer. I'm not even working right. Ask Singh, he'll tell you. I'm going to have a stiff leg for the rest of my days, and one of my fingers doesn't work."

"S' long's it's n' yer trigger finger, I d' n' see that as a serious problem."

"But why me? I'm a Ranger, not a Pathfinder or a Recon Marine."

"Rangers perform reconnaissance patrols, d' they no'?"

"Well, sure," I said. "Sometimes, but it's not our primary..."

"An' y're trained in th' use o' unconventional weaponry an' silent killin' techniques, are ye no'?"

"Special Forces have more training in those areas than Rangers. Besides..."

"An' yer 201 File shows ye've go' plenty o' experience under fire."

"So have a lot of other..."

"No' all tha' many, lad. No' anymore, an' those tha' 'ave, 'ave been dispersed throughou' both the fleets. In truth, we've a shortage o' combat experienced personnel, especially surface officers. Besides, statistical analysis by th' Battle Planning Computer indicates ye've survived enough combats t' kill a dozen men. Ye're a natural born survivor, y' are, an' tha's precisely wha' we need most a' present."

"Yah, well, one of those combats got me killed, remember? Which sort of shoots your theory all to heck."

"Tush, lad. A minor mistake. Happens t' all o' us, sooner 'r later. The Battle Planning Computer did n' find it statistically important, s' why should we concern ourselves wi' it? Besides, as I need hardly point ou', ye're n' dead now, are ye? S' strictly speakin' y' were n' actually killed, even though y' were. Now tha's wha' I call a man wha' can really beat th' odds agains' survival."

"You people are nuts," I told him.

"Laddie, I canno' b' nuts. 'Tis n' logical t' be deranged when there's n' call for it, an' it runs contrary-wise t' me programmin' t' be illogical 'cept when th' logic o' th' situation dictates a' illogical response."

"I give up. It's like trying to reason with an alien life form. We're just not broadcasting on the same wavelength."

"Besides, lad, you'll wan' t' see y'r girl again, an' if she does ge' 'erself in trouble, y'd want t' be in a position t' 'elp 'er now, wouldn't ye?"

He had me on that one, the bastard. For a machine, he could be awfully humanly sneaky at times. I guess it must have been that tiny biogenetically synthesized heuristic center of his.

"Maybe we picked the wrong man," interrupted Stryker. "Maybe he isn't what we need after all. Maybe we should let the medical research people have him back."

"Lady," I said, "if that's supposed to be a threat, I suggest you reconsider it before I decide to get up out of this sick bed and tear your goddamned head off. Respectfully, of course, sir."

"At ease, laddie," said Peterson, laying a hand on my shoulder. "Major Stryker 'ere's n' aware of y're sensitive nature. There's a good fellow. We d'n' wan' t' be upsettin' the major unduly now, f'r she's a truly nasty bitch an' jus' might do as she says."

"So might I," I replied, glaring at Stryker who had turned beet red at Peterson's slur, letting me know that perhaps she wasn't quite as tough as she pretended to be. But then, neither am I, and I'd sure as hell meant what I said.

"So, I take 't y'll accept th' mission, if an' when we need ye?" said Peterson.

"What other choice have I got?"

"There's always a choice, laddie, provided y're willin' t' pay the consequences o' tha' choice."

For a minute there, I thought Peterson was trying to threaten me too, but I finally decided he wouldn't do that. He knew me well enough to know that it wouldn't be logical, so I decided he was just making a philosophical observation.

"All right," I said. "Let's say just for the sake of argument that I do accept. What, exactly, is my mission? If all you wanted was a reconnaissance, you could send down a bunch of drones to holomap the area without risking anybody. Why don't you guys stop shitting me, and tell me what I'm really supposed to do down there?"

"Once the mission is under way, your actual progress and immediate goals will have to be dictated by what happens down there. Basically, you'll have three priorities, and the order of those priorities may change as the mission situation changes," said Stryker.

"First, if for any reason contact is lost with the landing force or pickup of the alien cat-person is delayed, you'll have to locate and secure it until it can be retrieved. Second, if possible, you'll have to determine for us what went wrong and caused us to lose contact with the landing force, *if* we do lose contact. If we don't, we probably won't be sending you in at all. Third, we want you to try and locate Brigadier General Andersohn and return her to the fleet."

"Is that all?"

"For the moment, yes."

"Have either of you geniuses considered what happens if I find General Andersohn and she doesn't want to come back with me? Suppose she just tells me to go to blazes. Generals do sometimes have a tendency to tell first lieutenants to do that."

"We ha' considered tha' possibility," said Peterson, "so f'r purposes o' th' mission, ye'll be appointed th' rank o' simulated major general."

"Simulated major general?"

"Aye."

"Wonderful. Just frigging marvelous. And suppose as a simulated major general I give Andersohn an order to return with me, and as a real brigadier general, she still tells me to go stuff myself. What then?"

"Then," said Stryker. "You will place the brigadier under arrest and return her to the fleet using whatever force may be necessary to accomplish the task. The orders come direct from the Imperial General Staff."

"Terrific," I said. "Just what I always wanted to do. Arrest a general. When does this boondoggle start?"

"It may n' start a' all," said Peterson. "Keep in mind tha'

th' distance between us an' Alpha Tauri Five's still almost two light weeks. Even wi' neutrino communications, it still takes messages two weeks t' reach us fro' Masterson's group, an' another two weeks f'r them t' receive our reply. It may well be awhile befor' we're sure o' what th' situation truly is. B' be ready when w' need ye. If y'ave t' go, the notice'll be mighty short."

"Fine," I said. "Now if you people will excuse me, I'd like to get some rest. If you'll pardon the expression, I'm simply dead."

4

Masterson, Lara
Captain, First Special Pathfinder (Composite)
Hard Landing Contingency Force Charlie, SCAF

"Is it dead, Sandburg? I've got to know."

"Yes. No. Hell, I don't know. Maybe."

"Could you try and be a little more specific than that, Doctor?"

"I can't find any pulse, or heartbeat. I don't hear any bowel sounds upon auscultation, and the capillary response appears nonexistent. The beast, or whatever it is, has a laser track through the spine. On Earth, or even on Tau Ceti Four, I'd say it was dead without hesitation. But . . ."

"But what?"

"But in the area of the thorax, I can hear what sounds like lung sounds. And the pupils still react to light. And the foot exhibits a positive Babinski response."

"What's a Babinski response?"

"It's a test for lesions of the pyramidal tract. If it's positive in an adult human, it indicates injury to one of the three descending tracts of the spinal cord arising as fibers from the giant pyramidal cells of Betz present in the motor area of the cerebral cortex of the brain. That would be consistent with the obvious laser injury. The only problem is, an injury like this should have severed all the tracts. There shouldn't be any response at all. And there shouldn't be any pupillary reaction or respirations occurring, but there are. And anyway, a positive Babinski is normally occurring in an infant under six months of age."

"So what are you telling me, Doctor? Is it alive or isn't it?"

"I'm telling you I don't know. I can't tell. Maybe this thing has a naturally occurring Babinski like an infant. Maybe it doesn"t have a circulatory system like we do. In that case it might not have a pulse or heartbeat, at least not like we have or where we have. We're dealing with a life form here that we've no previous information on. I don't know what makes it tick, and I can't tell without an autopsy. I might not even be able to tell then. I'm a general practitioner and trauma surgeon, not an expert in extraterrestrial life forms."

I turned to Hernandez. "You're the exobiologist. What do you think?"

Hernandez shrugged. "I'm not an exobiologist, Captain. I'm an exobiology toxicological pathology specialist. That means I'm trained to operate certain equipment which is supposed to detect any micro-organisms that might be hostile to humans. It also detects known molecular toxins. It doesn't identify new life forms the size of that thing, and it doesn't teach me how to identify them either."

"You're a great lot of help."

"Sorry, Captain, but I can't do what I can't do."

"Sandburg, is there anything we can do for this thing? What I mean is, is there any treatment you can give it to keep it alive, assuming it is alive. The fleet exobiologists and Intell people are damned sure going to want it alive if it's not dead already. You can't interrogate a corpse."

"Captain Masterson, I don't know what to do. If we move it improperly and it does have a spinal injury but isn't dead yet, we might sever the spine, which might kill it. We can assume it breathes pretty much the same kind of air we do, because that's what this planet has, but I can't be one hundred percent sure that it's an oxygen breather. Maybe oxygen is just an annoying trace element to it, and if I put it on high concentration oxygen we'll kill it. If we follow normal procedures and make a few assumptions, the thing ought to be dead right now. Frankly, I don't know what's keeping it alive, or even if it is. It has some of the *normal* signs of life, but not all of them. You tell me what to do."

Sandburg was leaving me to dig my own grave. If I guessed wrong, it would be my responsibility and my court-martial. As the commander on the spot, it would have been anyway.

"All right then. Give it some oxygen and figure out your best guess on how to move it without damaging it any more than it already is. We can't leave it out here. One way or the other, I want it inside the perimeter safe zone of the LPDS within forty minutes."

St. Croix and I walked back to the ship and sat down in the shadow of the hull.

"So what do we do now, Captain?" St. Croix asked.

"Now we wait, Chief," I told her. "We wait for an answer from the fleet. What else is there to do?"

That had been two weeks ago. A lot had happened in that time.

We'd lived in our field protective masks for three days, subsisting on liquid concentrates, until the damned masks got so intolerable that the troops started ripping them off. In order to prevent a complete breakdown in discipline, I had to go ahead and give permission to unmask. So far, nobody had died from it.

Sandburg had used up most of her supply of medical oxygen, uselessly treating the alien that refused to do anything but lie there and apparently keep breathing. The oxygen didn't do any harm or good as far as she could tell. When we stopped giving the thing oxygen, it didn't seem to make any difference either.

We rigged a parachute canopy over the cat-person to keep the sunlight off it, outside the rescue ship, and mounted an around-the-clock guard on it in case it suddenly decided to come back to life and start killing SCAF soldiers.

After five days it started to stink and Sandburg pronounced it dead, even though it was apparently still breathing. We waited another three days until the smell got really bad, then we put the alien in a storage compartment of the rescue ship and reduced the air-conditioning to cool just that one compartment at maximum output. It made a fairly decent walk-in freezer.

We ran a couple of short range patrols outside the perimeter without losing anybody, but there were some fairly close calls.

One of the troops got too close to what he thought was a bunch of hanging vines, and wound up screaming in pain after being stung by something that turned out to be a sort of arboreal Portuguese man-of-war. His arm swelled up like a personal flotation device, and Sandburg figured she was going to have to amputate it to save the guy, but about the time she got her surgical tools set up, the guy stopped screaming and the swelling started to subside. By nightfall the trooper was back to normal.

Another trooper brushed up against some colorful looking wildflowers that resembled orchids and got covered with a sticky, nectar-like substance. Five minutes later she got violently sick, fainted, and went into muscle spasms reminiscent of a grand mal seizure. When she finally stopped convulsing she vomited. One of her squadmates was brave enough, or foolish enough, depending upon your point of view, to turn her on her side so she wouldn't aspirate her own emesis. It took her about three days to fully recover.

The only other close encounters were with the animal life, although I guess you'd have to say one of them was insect life. At least maybe it was insect life. One of the guys tripped over a large, jade-green thing that looked like a beetle about the size of an armadillo, and scraped his nose on a rock. The beetle, which had a set of pincers big enough to take a man's wrist off with, looked the trooper over, but evidently decided he wouldn't make a good meal and scuttled off into the brush. The other problem was with the birds.

I suppose we'll have to wait for some ornithologist to come along and classify them before we know whether or not we can really call them birds, but they looked like birds and had wings and feathers, and that's good enough for me. They were about the size of sparrows, but had sharp, ice pick like beaks about five centimeters long. They were apparently highly territorial, and whenever anyone came near one of their big, cone shaped, communal nests which hung from its apex in the trees, they would swarm out like a bunch of angry hornets and throw themselves at the interloper in a series of kamikaze wave attacks, skewering themselves into their victim. We were saved any fatalities by our body armor, which they blunted their beaks on, but a few of the troops did pick up some nasty punctures of the hand or cheek. One day a bunch of the damned things got after a patrol and just kept following them, a few of the birds peeling off periodically to hurl themselves at the troops, until finally our people had to retire to the safety of the perimeter. Several of the birds got fried by the LPDS, exploding in little puffs of smoldering feathers when they tried to fly inside the zone protected by the LPDS. The rest of them seemed to get the message that it was dangerous to fly into the clearing, and they buzzed around just outside the activation range of the LPDS for a couple of hours, squawking and stirring up quite a fuss, but they didn't try to follow their former comrades. Most of the troops found it mildly amusing, except for the ones that had gotten stuck before they got back inside the safe zone.

It was a welcome bit of levity among the grim business of burying all the bodies.

I wasn't too sure that Fleet Ops would be real pleased with us doing that, because I knew they'd love to study the casualties and theorize over the cause of death, but we had to do something to prevent the spread of disease and get the stench down to a tolerable level. It didn't take corpses all that long to start turning pretty ripe in the sun. We finally compromised by selecting one rescue man and one MP, and one each from the Recon and Ranger personnel to accompany the alien in our makeshift morgue. Sandburg took a lot of blood and tissue samples from various locations in several of the other corpses, and we refrigerated most of them as well. A few we stored at ambient temperature in vacuum containers, since we weren't sure if refrigeration might not kill some microbe used to living at near forty degrees centigrade. It was all just guesswork. We really had no idea what we were doing.

Other than that, there wasn't a lot to do but sit around and wait for word from the fleet. A couple of the troops had brought along some cards, and there were some marathon bridge and pinochle games, and Halvorsen and Sandburg improvised a chess set by drawing on the back of a spinal immobilizer with a marking pen and using various sized pill bottles with different tops from Sandburg's portable pharmacy. I tried to follow their game for awhile, but the distinctions between pieces were too subtle, and I kept getting confused.

After a few days, St. Croix set up a schedule of calisthenics and immediate reaction drills for those platoons not on perimeter defense duty, more to give the troops something to occupy their time with than anything else, and we dug a lot of bunkers and filled a lot of rubberized nylon sandbags. Pretty much the same sort of stuff soldiers do anywhere when they're not fighting and there're no bars around.

There was a fair amount of recreational sex, but that was nothing new, what with SCAF being an equal opportunity employer. As long as the troops weren't fucking around on duty, I really didn't care what they did on their own time, so long as they were reasonably discreet about it, and I probably couldn't have prevented it if I had.

There was only one rule which I rigidly enforced. Everybody had to have their weapon within reach, and had to wear their IFF transponder at all times, whether they were wearing anything else or not. The transponders weren't really necessary once you were within the safe zone of the LPDS, since it was programmed to target only whatever tried to cross the perimeter, not what was within it, but I remembered what had happened to the male and female we'd found near the perimeter when we first landed, and the transponders stayed on, period.

Things fell into a state of lethargic monotony; not good, because it tended to dull a soldier's alertness and reactions, and I reduced the duration but increased the frequency of patrols outside the perimeter. It did, perhaps, unnecessarily jeopardize the safety of the troops a few at a time, but the risk factor helped to keep them thinking and lessened somewhat the mind dulling effect of sheer boredom.

We finally got a reply from the fleet, ordering us to make all possible effort to preserve the body of the alien and a representative sample of the SCAF casualties. I was pleased we'd guessed right about that. The message further advised that a special task force was being dispatched with a para-amphibious infantry brigade to relieve us, and that it would bring in a team of exobiologists and pathologists to study the alien and the dead troopers and return them to the fleet. It was

taking a little time to get everything organized, and Fleet
Operations advised us to expect the relief force about ten days
after we got the message.

There was an almost continual stream of messages from the
fleet after that, most of them updates about the progress of the
relief force, and a lot of questions about things we didn't have
the answers to, like the mobility and settlement patterns of the
indigenous population, and sources of potable water for the
relief force. The only indigenous population we'd seen was
the one alien, and we were drinking canned water we'd
brought with us and recycling it through the rescue ship's puri-
fication systems. There were some small streams nearby that
had been located by our patrols, but I wasn't going to risk the
lives of any of my troops testing the stuff. Hernandez had a lot
of testing equipment she used to check it out and it seemed
okay for the most part, but there were a few trace elements the
spectrograph couldn't identify, so we stuck to recycling.

It rained almost every night, and the troops got soaked and
never really managed to dry out because of the high humidity
during the day. At least the rain cooled you off some, but by
ten the next morning, the whole damned planet was a steam
bath. Finally about fifteen hundred, it would simply get hot
and stay that way until after dark, so that you almost, but not
quite got dried out. Then about midnight it would rain and
soak everything again. Hernandez said the rainwater showed
the same unidentified trace elements as the streams, so we
didn't try to drink any of that either, but we did use it for
washing. You couldn't get out of the stuff anyway, and since it
hadn't killed us so far, I figured we might as well use it for
something.

In a way, I suppose we were fortunate. If the planet hadn't
had an Earth-type atmosphere, we'd have had to go in wearing
environment suits and set up our own biosphere shelter so we
could occasionally stand-down without the suits. Living in an
environment suit is a bitch. They're tolerable for about
twenty-four hours, but after that, everything smells and tastes
like recycled SCAF trooper, which is pretty much what it is.

About the third day after we got the initial reply from Fleet
Ops, I got a really strange message asking me about some
brigadier general who was evidently supposed to have been

with the Rangers or Recon Marines. I couldn't figure out what such a high ranking officer would have been doing with them in the first place, and we hadn't found any bodies wearing general's stars when we landed. I messaged back that we had seen no sign of a general officer and requested further information.

The attack came on the evening of our eighteenth day on the planet.

I think the time was around 0200. I'd been sleeping sort of out in the open, beneath the bow of the rescue ship at night because it was cooler than in my bunker or inside the ship, now that we'd rearranged its air-conditioning. The overhang of the bow also gave you a little protection from the rain, which arrived reliably as clockwork at midnight and lasted for about an hour. It seemed kind of unfair to me that the LPDS let the rain come through, but zapped anything else that tried to penetrate its detection cone.

After the rain that evening, I lay awake listening to the sounds of the jungle animals we so rarely saw. It seemed as if most of the animal life on the planet must have been nocturnal.

It began at first as a general uneasiness, difficult to describe. Just a sort of feeling that all was not right. Soldiers get it all the time, and usually nothing nasty happens. It's those other times, the ones when you get it just before the war turns to shit on you, that makes the short hairs on the back of your neck, and other places, stand up when it happens.

I tried to shake it off and go back to sleep, but I just couldn't do it. I had this weird feeling that someone or something was out there, just beyond the perimeter, watching me. That was the way it felt. Not watching all of us, just me in particular. Like it was trying to read my mind.

One of the patrols on outpost duty had reported seeing something that looked like a panther a couple of nights before, and for some reason I thought of that. Have you ever tried to stare down a cat? Try it sometime. I'll bet you can't do it. Have you ever been sitting alone in a room with one, just you and the cat, and suddenly you can feel, I mean really *feel* that somebody's watching you, and you look around and the cat is staring at you and you try to stare it down first, but the cat always wins. I remember doing that with our family pet, Carlyle, when I was a little girl. Well, that's what it felt like.

I couldn't shake it, and I couldn't go back to sleep feeling like somebody was out there getting ready to cut my throat. The fact that nothing could come in through the perimeter while the LPDS was operating was small consolation. Something had killed all those troopers that had been there before us.

I got up and picked up my carbine, a bullpup affair about sixty centimeters long, and checked the hundred-round magazine. It was full. I'd been sleeping in my armor, which is about twice as uncomfortable as it sounds, but a lot safer, so all I had to do was put on my helmet and pick up my web gear, a big kevlar and krylon harness that holds all of a trooper's munitions pouches and assorted other combat gear. I slipped into it, and trotted over to the command bunker to see St. Croix who rotated watch with me. I found her outside the bunker, pacing up and down like a caged animal.

"You feel it too?" she asked.

I nodded, and felt my short hairs stand up even more. When two old combat hands get that same feeling at the same time, it's not just a feeling anymore. "Like someone watching me," I said.

"Yeah. Not just watching us, but watching me. Guess they can't be watching both of us individually though, can they?" said St. Croix, her smile flashing briefly in the darkness. "What the hell do you suppose it is?"

"I don't know, Chief. Maybe one of those things looking for its lost mate." I jerked my head toward the ship, and St. Croix understood I meant the alien.

"Suppose I'd better wake up the troops, Captain?"

"I reckon you'd better, Chief. If you can find any of them that's still asleep. I've got a hunch nobody's having very pleasant dreams this evening."

"We're going to look awful foolish if we're wrong."

"Better than being awful dead if we're right and we don't do anything about it."

"Right you are, sir. I'll notify the platoon leaders personally."

"Who's on outpost tonight? Kaiserhaus?"

"No, sir. Kittredge's platoon again."

"All right. See to the others."

St. Croix moved off with that easy, muscular grace of hers, vanishing into the blackness, first a cat in the night, and then the darkness. For some reason, I couldn't get cats off my mind tonight. I clicked up the command freq on the helmet transceiver and keyed the mike for Kittredge's platoon.

"Four-Six from Charlie-Six."

"Four-Six."

"I want you to pull out of your position and fall back inside the perimeter as quietly and quickly as possible. Do it now."

"Roger."

Then I keyed the company frequency. "Force Charlie, this is the Six. All troopers hold your fire. Fourth Platoon is coming in. I repeat, do not fire. We have friendlies coming in through the perimeter."

The tension was becoming unbearable. I felt as though some giant cat had its paws on either side of my head and was squeezing in slow, slow, slowly. My temples started throbbing. Then suddenly, on the perimeter, I heard the low, bull-fiddle moan of a carbine firing on open cyclic, and all hell broke loose.

Within seconds the air was filled with the shattering blast of grenades, the moan and growl of carbines and battle rifles, and the sharp staccato trilling of squad automatic weapons, a charming anachronism, now that all the weapons were capable of automatic fire.

I cut in the passive night optics on the helmet visor and scanned the perimeter. The scene was total chaos. Troopers were running all over the place instead of staying in their fighting holes, and were shooting at anything that moved, including each other. The air was filled with the screams of terrified and wounded men and women. It shouldn't have been. These people were professionals, some of the very best SCAF had to offer. Nearly all of them had been in at least one combat before. They weren't the kind of people to make mistakes and panic under fire, but that was exactly what they were doing. In fact, as far as I could tell, we hadn't even taken any incoming fire yet. And when I realized that, I felt my own panic beginning to rise.

"These people went crazy and killed each other, except for the ones that only killed themselves," Sandburg had said about the dead troopers we'd found when we first entered the drop zone. And now, to my growing horror, the same thing was beginning to happen all over again.

I keyed the company frequency and talked rapidly, trying to regain control of the situation, but nobody seemed to be paying any attention to me. The combat had gone hand-to-hand all over the clearing, Pathfinders trying to kill each other with their knives or helmets or bare hands.

Off a little way to one side, I saw a group of troopers running through the perimeter and into the clearing, firing madly at our own people. Then, incredibly, I saw them change form, their features melding into alien shapes, into the shape of *the alien*. I raised my carbine to fire, and then saw that *all* of the Pathfinders were changing shape into aliens. I hated them. They were evil, and they were destroying my command, and I wanted to kill them all, and I flicked off the safety, ready to shoot, but the blast from a concussion grenade exploding nearby knocked me to the ground.

I shook my head to clear it, and struggled to get back up on my feet, stunned. The helmet PNV display wasn't working any longer, and I flipped the visor up out of the way so I could see. A Pathfinder came charging at me from out of the darkness, screaming and trying to bayonet me with the blade on the end of his battle rifle. I sidestepped the thrust, feinted to the left, and banged him on the right jaw with my carbine as he rushed past. He dropped like he'd been hit over the head with an anvil. I didn't know if I'd killed him or not, and right at that moment, I didn't much care. He'd been trying to kill me.

I spun back toward the north slope of the perimeter, trying to reorient myself and get a feel for what was happening. As I watched, Pathfinders started slipping back into alien cat-people again. I didn't understand exactly what was happening, but a part of me realized that something was persuading the troops that everyone around them was the enemy. In some fashion, our minds were being manipulated.

St. Croix loomed up out of the darkness with such catlike suddenness that I wheeled on her and almost shot her head off, but I recognized her just in time, although she was beginning to look a little like our guest in the improvised cooler in the ship.

"Captain Masterson!" she screamed at me. "They're all changing, and they're killing each other. They won't listen to reason. I tried to talk with them, but they just kept killing each other. If we don't get out of here, they'll kill us too."

Hearing St. Croix speak helped to stabilize the image of her in my mind, but she started rapidly slipping into a cat-person again.

"Run!" I yelled. "Get away! Up the hill to the south. Whatever it is, we can't fight this thing. Keep away from everybody, including me. Get into the jungle and hide. If we make it, we'll rendezvous at that high rocky outcropping to the east we saw coming in, day after tomorrow at oh-nine-hundred." Then I turned and ran away from St. Croix as hard and as fast as I could.

5

Fetterman, Anthony B.
Major General (Simulated)
Seventh Rangers (Detached)
Fleet/STC Joint Operational Intelligence Task Force,
SCAF

"Get ready," said Stryker, bursting into the room. "You're
going in." She seemed to be carrying a bush in her hands.

I pushed aside the graphics flatscreen linked to the ship's
library computer that I'd been using to catch up on the last
sixty-one years, and sat up in my hospital bed. "When?"

"Now. Here, put this on." She tossed me the bush, which
turned out to be a camouflaged jumpsuit with a lot of little
plastiform leaves fastened all over it. "We're not one hundred
percent sure of the match, but based on reports from Masterson's Hard Landing Force, it ought to be fairly close. I
brought your socks and boots too, size nine narrows, hope
that's right."

I nodded, throwing back the sheet and thermal cover and
swinging my legs over the side of the bed. "What happened?"

"Communications monitored a transmission from Force
Charlie about twenty minutes ago. It would have been sent
early yesterday morning their time. It indicated they were
under attack, but didn't say by what. After that, things got
really garbled. Everybody down there was trying to talk at
once. Whenever anyone keyed a mike, you could hear firing
and explosions in the background, people screaming all over
the place, then, after about twelve minutes, silence. There's
still an open mike down there. We know that because the

carrier beam is still open, but nobody's talking anymore. It's been silent since. Will you please hurry up?"

Stryker stood watching with a detached, almost clinical interest while I peeled my way out of the hospital gown and struggled into the no-see-me's. It dawned on me that she hadn't brought any underwear, and I wondered if she'd just forgot it, or if she knew that combat troops didn't wear underwear in a hot environment because all it did was make you hotter and chafe hell out of you. It didn't occur to me until later that maybe she'd just wanted to see me naked, but I dismissed that notion as the wishful thinking of a male ego. She was far too cold a lady for that.

"Where's Peterson?" I asked, pulling on the socks and jamming my feet into the boots.

"In the morgue, drawing some special equipment. We'll meet him on the flight deck. Come on. Most of your equipment is already there. We had it transferred aboard along with your transportation."

"What about a mission briefing?" I protested.

"There isn't time. Besides, you already know as much about the current situation as we do."

"I was thinking in terms of a planetary environment pre-insertion briefing," I said, following her as she charged back out into the hallway.

"It's all on this, what there is of it. You can play it back enroute." She handed across a microdiskette as we trotted down the corridor, drawing a startled look from the nurse behind the station desk.

"Say, don't I have to sign out of here, or something?"

"Forget it. We'll take care of it."

We made our way out of that particular section of the hospital ship, and jogged along a main traffic corridor until I started to wonder whether or not all that exercise was good for a man who'd been through everything I'd been through in the last sixty-one years. Just when I was about to suggest that a more reasonable rate of progress might be in order, Stryker found an elevator she liked, and we took it to the flight deck.

Peterson was waiting, standing next to a big pile of clothing and equipment, when we got off.

"Och! There y' be, laddie. I wa' afraid y' were goin' t' be

late. Good. I see th' cammies fit, 'r maybe I should say I d'n' see 'em. Well, anyway, off wi' that lot, an' slip into this one, will ye?"

I was getting kind of tired of being asked to change my clothes in front of other people. There were several maintenance crews and flight crews on the flight deck, tinkering around with Mobile Intensive Care Shuttles and loading some smaller ships, Close Support Craft medevacs, into a big transport shuttle. Besides that, it was cold on the flight deck. Peterson and Stryker were waiting, however, and neither of them was showing any marked signs of patience, so I shrugged out of the bush suit and tried to put on the other thing. It was some kind of environment suit, similar to the one I'd been trained on, but not identical. I had to have help getting all the appropriate recycling connections hooked up in the lower section. That seemed to perturb Stryker at first, then to amuse her. I couldn't see anything funny about it at all.

Peterson stuck the camouflage suit in a polypropelene bag and tossed that inside a big induraplast drop container, along with several other bags. "We've jus' time enough t' go over a wee bit o' equipment wi' ye before departure. I'm confident ye're resourceful enough t' figure ou' most o' th' items, bu' there be a few ye'll be needin' t' know about, s' pay attention."

"I'm all ears," I said.

"Not from what I've seen," said Stryker.

We both ignored her, and Peterson went on.

"In selectin' yer equipment, we've 'ad t' take into consideration tha' th' enemy has apparently been able t' detect an' annihilate th' previous forces we've sent in, s' we assume they've a sophisticated intruder detection capability. As such, we've tried t' optimize both electronic and mechanical countermeasures in yer gear."

"Meaning what?" I asked.

"Meaning we had to decide whether to arm you to the teeth, or send you in naked," said Stryker. "Arming you to the max seemed a little bit pointless, considering that an entire heavily armed company couldn't defeat the enemy when they encountered him."

"Given the alternative, I hope a compromise was arrived at," I said.

"Quite," said Peterson. "F'r one thing, we've reduced all possible use o' metals, t' shield ye from any radars or magnetometers th' enemy may be employin'. You'll find y'r grenades 'ave thermoplastic resin cases wi' hardened ceramic pellets imbedded in a plastique matrix f'r fragmentation effect; even th' detonator cap's plastic. A' th' last moment, we also included a couple o' ultrasonic ones. There was some debate abou' that, since we couldn' eliminate all th' metal 'n those, bu' they do be a mite quieter than th' explodin' kind. Besides, there be minimal metal an' electronics 'n y'r chronometer an' communications transceiver. Ye'll 'ave t' decide f'r y'rself whether 'r no t' risk 'em, 'r bury 'em once y've landed. There be also a small amount o' electronics 'n th' IFF transponder y'll need t' get through th' Light Point Defense System at th' rescue ship, if it's still 'n operation. There be nothin' we can do abou' that."

"Terrific," I said, not finding anything terrific about it at all. "From what you tell me, that planet is mostly jungle down there. Has anybody thought about what I'm supposed to do if I need to cut a path or defend myself from some wild animal?"

"Indeed we 'ave, laddie. I think you'll find this t' be satisfactory."

"What is it?"

"It's a knife, laddie. Surely y've seen 'em before."

"Never like this one."

It had about a thirty centimeter blade, cut roughly on the Bowie pattern, with a drop point and a false edge sharpened about a third of the way along the spine until it terminated in a bunch of sawteeth. It had an oversized finger guard, and the handle was wrapped in black nylon and Kevlar II cord. The thing had a dull black finish overall. It looked like it would be just the thing for hunting Cape buffalo.

"It'll weigh a ton, and produce a radar return that'll stick out like tits on a Tau King," I told him.

"Faith, lad! Have y' n' trust 'n me own good judgment? 'Tis made o' glass composite resins and hardened ceramics. It'll be producin' no returns, holds a good edge, sharpens easily wi' th' ceramic stone on th' back o' th' sheath, an' 's strong enough so's y' can drive it through a two centimeter teak board."

I hefted it. It was too light to deliver a good slashing blow, and the blade design was all wrong for thrusting.

"Couldn't I just have a standard issue combat knife?" I asked hopefully. "Or don't they make those anymore?"

"They do, but y' can't. Impervium, like all metals, 's too easily detected by radar an' magnetometers, an' anythin' tha' size 's sure t' be detectable."

"In that case," I said without much feeling, "I heartily accept. Now then, what about a gun?"

"Th' higher ups were no' 'n favor o' givin' y' one. Said there'd be too much metal in 't. Besides, they said, a man what 'as a gun's likely t' get 'imself 'n a fire fight, whilst a man what's got no gun's likely t' avoid trouble."

"He's also likely to get himself killed. I won't go without a weapon, and I don't count that so-called knife of yours, so you'd better find me a good assault rifle or SMG or I'll just take this damned environment suit off and we can forget the whole damned thing right now."

"At ease, laddie. I said th' higher ups were no' 'n favor. I did no' say I agreed wi' 'em. After all, I found ye th' grenades did I no'? An' I also found ye this."

At least it resembled a gun. A toy gun to be sure, but a gun nevertheless. Well, sort of. It had a pair of vertical pistol grips attached to something that might have been a receiver, what I took to be a magazine well, and a folding zytel plastic stock. There was a simple, ring protected post front sight, and a little rotating drum rear with apertures marked 1, 2, and 3 which I assumed stood for one hundred, two hundred, and three hundred meters respectively. I thought that was a rather optimistic estimate of effective range on a weapon with such a small sight radius. What the dingus didn't seem to have was any ejection port, barrel, muzzle, safety, or trigger. Just a few minor little details like that.

"Oh, no," I groaned. "A plastic gun. It doesn't even have a trigger."

"'Course it's got a trigger, lad. Only ye can no' see 't. When y' squeeze th' front grip, which inactivates th' automatic safety, th' trigger pops out o' th' rear grip, an' the muzzle cover opens. Otherwise it all stays sealed up t' keep ou' th' elements."

"Cute. What's it shoot, rubber bullets?"

"Plastic. Krylon t' be exact. An' I'll thank ye t' maintain a more serious attitude when I'm briefin' ye. There be fifty little needle-like darts packed into a sabot wha' discards once out o' th' weapon. A dollop o' fuel on th' rear o' th' sabot drives it ou' th' barrel, which is internal t' th' receiver, an' ignited by a piezo-electric crystal 'n th' weapon. It'll cycle twelve sabots 'n a second from a thirty-six sabot magazine, an' at a muzzle escape velocity of twenty-one hundred meters per second, it'll shred a textured Impervium 'n Kevlar II combat vest an' who-ever's behind it at a range o' from three t' three hundred meters. It weighs jus' three kilograms wi' a fully loaded magazine, has seven movin' parts, includin' th' trigger, front and rear sights, an' muzzle cover, an' I could stand here an' beat it on th' deck all day long, an' it'd still be in operatin' condition."

I stared at the little weapon with a newfound respect. "Sorry. What's it called?"

"Officially, it's an Automatic Flechette Carbine, Mark I," said Stryker. "Unofficially, the SETAC guards who use them call it a meatgrinder."

"SETAC guards, huh?" I said, wondering what in hell a SETAC was. "Sound like real sweethearts."

"They're not paid to be."

Peterson packed away the knife and AFC, and shouldered the enduraplast container like it weighed five kilos instead of the fifty-five it must have really weighed. "This way t' y'r ship, me boyoh. Y'r carriage awaits."

We stopped in front of a tiny little vessel. It was maybe half again the size of a Close Support Craft, bulkier and less streamlined.

"Where's the rest of it?" I asked.

"What do you mean, the rest of it?" replied Stryker. "This is all there is."

"This is a near light speed, antigrav space ship? I thought it was just the crew compartment."

"It's a one-man reconnaissance ship," Stryker explained patiently, talking as one might to a very small child. "It only holds a one-man crew, fuel and engine, and it's only for short trips, so it doesn't need to be big."

"One man? Well, boys and girls, I've got some very bad news for you. I'm not a spaceship pilot. Not even a Close Support Craft pilot. And I'm certainly not checked out on antigrav drive systems. I don't even understand why the things work, let alone how, so I guess that finishes the mission right here and now."

"Guess again," said Stryker. "The entire flight has been programmed into the onboard computers. You don't have to fly the bird, it'll take care of itself."

"The landing sequence too?"

"There is no landing sequence."

"Then how am I supposed to . . ."

"You're not. You bail out at ten thousand meters, wearing the environment suit, and freefall to opening altitude. The ship will slow up enough for you to make a safe exit, but once it does, you've only got five seconds to get clear. After that, it'll go through a series of pre-programmed flight maneuvers designed to make it appear as though it's in mechanical difficulty before it finally crashes about a hundred kilometers away.

"They're bound to pick the ship up on their sensor scans when you enter the planetary atmosphere. We figure that's how they spotted the other units, although we haven't been able to detect what frequency they're scanning on. In fact, we haven't been able to pick up any EM radiation at all. They must be using some form of scanning unknown to us, or have a well developed shielding system. At any rate, we're going to sacrifice the ship and pilot to throw them off you. Hopefully they'll be so busy tracking the ship that they won't notice you leaving it. If they do pick up what little metals are in your equipment, we hope they'll think it was a piece that fell off the ship when things went haywire. By the time they get around to searching the jungle for it, you should be long gone."

"What do you mean, you're going to sacrifice the ship *and* pilot? I thought you said the computers were flying this thing?"

"'Tis no' really much o' a sacrifice, me boyoh," said Peterson. "Th' lad's already dead."

"Will somebody tell me what the fuck you people are talking about?" I demanded.

"The enemy is sure to detect your ship," said Stryker. "And they're just as sure, given all the other teams we've sent in, to expect us to send another reconnaissance mission of some kind to find out what happened to the others. If we just flew you over in a shuttle and dropped you out, even if they didn't pick up your separation from the ship, I think we can assume that they will assume we tried to insert someone. What we're doing instead is trying to mislead them. By giving them what's obviously a reconnaissance ship, we've pulled the classified gear, but left enough cameras and sensors to make it look convincing. We're hoping they'll believe that we opted for a high altitude reconnaissance instead of another ground team. But they've got to have a body to make it believable. They're going to have to find the pilot's corpse in the cockpit, or they'll put out a ground search to find him.

"Well, we got lucky. There was an accident in propulsion engineering the other day, and one of the technicians died. He wasn't resuscitable. Some heavy equipment fell on him and crushed him beyond biomedical repair. It was a real break for us. The injuries aren't unlike those that could be expected to be encountered following a crash in one of these things. Since the body was available, we stuffed what was left of it in an environment suit and put it in the cockpit. We've rigged a number of self-destruct charges on part of the equipment, so it'll look like they were intended to destroy classified gear in case the ship went down in enemy territory. They'll go off just before this thing hits, starting a couple of pretty big fires. By the time the impact scatters the ship all over the landscape, there won't be enough left of the 'pilot' for anybody to tell exactly how or when he died, but there will be enough left for them to find at least parts of a body. At a minimum it'll confuse them for a little while, and that might be just long enough to give you the time you need."

It was a rather cold-blooded plan, but I could almost believe it might work. Then I had a couple of thoughts that convinced me it was impossible.

"What about the computer? Suppose there's enough left of

it for them to figure out that it flew the ship instead of the pilot?"

"There won't be. Even if there were, the system has been programmed to erase itself, once it's activated the destruct charges and locked the ship into its final dive."

"You've thought of just about everything, haven't you?"

"We've tried to."

"Well, have you thought about this? What are they going to think when they find the wreckage and notice that the rear ejection seat is missing or am I just supposed to stand up in it and jump over the side?"

"Tell him. Peterson," said Stryker.

"Neither, me boyoh. We thought o' tha' too. Tha's why we chose a ship wi' only a single capacity. There be no second seat 'n this model."

"'So what the hell am I supposed to do, hang on to the tail fin?"

"'Course not, me boy. Ye couldn' survive tha' way. Why d' ye think we gave ye an environment suit wi' recyclin' connectors? Y'll 'ave t' ride 'n th' defensive weapons bay."

I stared at him aghast, unwilling to believe what I'd just been told. "You can't be serious," I finally choked out.

"'Tis th' only way, Leftenant. We've removed enough o' th' missiles t' make room f'r y'rself an' y'r equipment container, an' scorched th' pylons t' make it look as though some o' th' weapons had been fired, s' there's a reason f'r th' pylons t' be empty, should enough o' 'em survive th' crash t' be recognizable. It'll be a mite tight, but there'll be room enough."

"Here," said Stryker, unzipping a pocket on my environment suit and stuffing something inside. "Your stars, Major General. You may need them if you run into Andersohn. If you're in danger of being captured, I'd recommend throwing them away. If they figure out you're supposed to be a general officer, I imagine they could be pretty rough on you."

From the sound of things, I imagined I wouldn't live long enough for things to get rough. Based on the reports from Masterson's group, it didn't sound like the enemy made a habit of holding on to prisoners long enough to interrogate them.

"What?" I said angrily. "No cyanide capsule?"

"Do you want one?" asked Stryker, apparently in complete earnest.

"No thanks," I told her. "It was just sort of a joke. I think there're enough ways to get myself killed already in this mission."

"Follow me, laddie, and I'll show ye t' y'r seat," said Peterson, ducking underneath the ship and disappearing behind the half-open maw of the weapons bay.

I threw a last, forlorn look at Stryker, hoping she would now tell me it was all just some nightmarish joke and we could all go drink a beer now, but she didn't even wish me good luck. I swallowed hard and followed after Peterson.

The weapons bay *was* small. It was meant to be. After all, the ship was a recon vessel, not a fighter. It carried the minimum ordnance necessary to throw off or deal with pursuers, break contact, and get away with the intelligence it had gathered. With the equipment container in place, there was just room enough for me to lie supine alongside it, beneath an empty missile pylon. There wouldn't be room enough for me to turn over, or even scratch my nose. Not that it mattered much. In the suit I wouldn't be able to scratch my nose anyway. For the next day and a half, I'd have nothing to do but lie there in the darkness, incapable of moving, and hope nothing went wrong.

Peterson got me into the main and reserve chutes, and got me situated in the bay. The chutes weren't all that much different from the kind I'd used before, and I'd had some experience with running-on a ram air canopy a long time ago when I used to do sport parachuting, so at least I didn't have to worry too much about getting psyched out by ground-rush effect and tensing up and breaking a leg on landing. It was a minor comfort.

As Peterson was getting ready to leave, I suddenly reached out and grabbed his arm. "Hey!" I said. "Stryker said I only have about five seconds to get out of this thing when the time comes. How will I know, and how do I open the damned bay doors?"

"No t' worry, laddie. It's all been programmed into th' onboard computers. Th' five-seconds delay's jus' t' give ye a bit o' time t' untangle y'r self, in case ye get hung up on somethin'. At th' right time, y'll feel th' ship slow, then th' doors'll open, an' y'll jus' fall right out."

"Yeah, just like a dead weight. Suppose the doors don't open when they're supposed to?"

"In tha' case, laddie, we'll all o' gone t' a lot o' trouble f'r nothin'. D'n' worry, boyoh, it'll be all right. We've done our part, now y' do y'rs. Good luck t' ye."

He shook my hand and slapped me on the shoulder before he left. A moment later the earphones crackled in the helmet and Peterson told me to watch my arms and legs, and that I wouldn't hear from any of them again until it was over. Then the open bay door hissed shut on its hydraulics, and I lay there in the darkness and the silence.

For awhile, I pondered why a machine would shake your hand and slap you on the arm and wish you good luck, when a human did none of those things. I suppose maybe Peterson had been programmed to show compassion, at least when it didn't interfere with the mission, while Stryker, being human, had the capacity to be an asshole all the time if she felt like it. But that wasn't a totally satisfactory explanation. It didn't allow for Peterson's biogenetically engineered heuristic center, which gave him the capacity to learn from his experiences. Maybe being compassionate wasn't something that you either had to be born with or have programmed into you. Maybe it was something that you learned, and either decided to be, or not to be. It sort of made me wonder which of them was really the more human.

At last I felt a gentle throbbing, indicating the recon ship was powering up, and then a little bumping motion as it rode its maneuvering thrusters across the flight deck and out the launching lock to where the antigravs could take over. A few minutes later, the thrusters cut off, and I assumed the ship was coasting out a ways. Finally the throbbing built up to a low pitched hum, more felt than heard, and I assumed that the little scout was accelerating away from the hospital ship under antigravity power, despite the lack of any sense of motion. I was weightless in the weapons bay, and would have floated around like a soap bubble, if there had been any room to float.

After that, there was nothing to do but lie there in the darkness and silence, trapped in the weapons bay of a recon ship taking me to a hostile planet, with the computers running the flight, and a dead man at the controls.

6

She that runs swifter than the shadows of the night, but chooses the path of aloneness to preserve the land and the waters, the grasslands and the forest, the fish and the animals, in the ancient ways of our forebearers.

The night was warm.

The heavens had rained in the time of middle darkness, and the smell of the liquid that gives life was thick among the leaves that give life and spring from the soil that gave life to them and to our forebearers and continues to give life to us now.

The nighttime air was heavy with the sound and the smell of a myriad number of creatures that the Great Spirits had created in the ancient past, long before they battled in the sky among themselves, slaying each other with fang and claw, until only two were left, and they, in trying to slay each other, lost their balance and fell from the star they were fighting upon, and in so doing, tumbled to the land and lost all of their magical powers but one, and became like the animals they had created, in their folly to destroy one another.

It is said that the Great Spirits, although they were great, and did many great things, were very vain, and became bitter at what had happened to them and that they learned nothing from their misfortune, but that each blamed the other for his fate, until they grew to hate the very sight of each other and became the most bitter of enemies. This was easy to do, because they did not look very much alike, and it is easier to hate someone who is different from you, but they also looked enough alike that they hated the other for trying to look the same as they did.

And so it was, that they parted company, each going to live on opposite sides of the world because they could not stand the sight of each other and wished to be as far apart as possible.

And in their leaving, each swore eternal hatred for the other, and vowed to kill the other whenever they should find him or find her.

In time they each littered, and told the story of the other's treachery to their offspring, and taught them to hate those who were like them, but also unlike them. But with the passage of the generations, the progeny of the Great Spirit that had settled in the forests and the grasslands, learned to accept what fate had given them, and came to appreciate the beauty around them, and became as one with their world and the creatures that took life from it and returned life to it.

And so it remained, until one day, when the children of the Great Spirit that had settled in the forests and the grasslands were out hunting for food, and encountered the children of the Great Spirit that had settled in the mountains and the valleys of the land where it is always cold.

And those that had lived in the forests and the grasslands said to the others, "You are strangers. You are like us, and yet you are not like us. You are strangers. Tell us, strangers, why have you come here, to the land of the forests and grasslands?"

And the strangers answered them saying, "We have come from the mountains and the valleys to hunt and kill food, for the game is all gone now from our lands, and we must feed our families."

And those who lived in the forests and grasslands, and who had become as one with their world and the creatures that took life from it and returned life to it, forgetting the lessons of their ancient forebearers said, "Then come and hunt with us. For here there is plenty, because we understand the land and its creatures and are one with them. If your families are hungry, you must feed them, and here there is plenty, so we will share our wealth with you. Come now and hunt with us."

But the strangers who came from the mountains and the valleys in the land where it is always cold did not agree to this. For they had lived too long in the land where it is always cold, and the everlasting cold there had frozen their hearts.

And the strangers said to the dwellers of the forests and the grasslands. "No. We will not hunt with you. For in our hunting grounds, we are not one with the land the lower creatures, we are masters of the land and we hunt wherever it pleases us, and we are masters of the lower creatures, and we hunt and kill them as it pleases us, and we shall do the same here, in this new land."

And the dwellers of the forest and grasslands said, "We are very sorry, but we cannot allow you to do that. For the land here is sacred land, and the land gives life to all creatures and to us, and we return life to the land. If you wish, we will share our riches with you, but you must become as one with the land. Here there is no master, either of the land, or of those who take life from it, and return life to it."

And the strangers said, "We are the descendants of the Great Spirit Yil, and are called the Yilii, which means masters of the land and all that walk upon it, and of the sky and all that fly in it, and of the water and all that swim in it, and we take whatever we want. And we shall do the same here."

And those who lived in the forests and grasslands replied, "We are the descendants of the Great Spirit Chat, and are called the Chat, which is also our name for the world, and which means those who are one with the world and draw their life from it, and return their life to it, and who have no masters, because they are one with the world. And we co-exist with the world, and protect it for our future generations, so that there will always be a world to give life, and to receive it. And while we will share our world with you, we will not let you master it, for to become a master of a thing, is to take away its freedom, and once you take away a thing's freedom, you destroy it, and make it into something else. This you have done in the land you came from, and this you would do here. We have no wish to fight with you, but we cannot permit you to do here what you have done in your own land."

And this angered the strangers who called themselves the Yilii, and they fell upon the Chat and tore at them with their fangs, and slashed at them with their claws, and killed a great many of them, and scattered their survivors.

And the Chat abandoned their beloved grasslands, and went deep into the forests where they could hide their young and where the young would be safe from the Yilii. And there the Chat held council and roasted meat in the Sacred Fire, and thought much about what had happened, and about what kind of creatures the Yilii were.

And when the Chat had thought about it long enough, they vowed to rediscover the lessons and the ways of their ancestors.

And then there was war.

Even the old ones cannot count the passings of the three moons since the time the war began. There are those who say it was a hundred generations ago, and those who say it was a hundred times a hundred. For as long as the oldest Chat can remember, and longer still, the Yilii have hunted us, and we in turn, have hunted them. Not as we once hunted only for food, but to protect the land that they would master, and to return to the land that life that they have taken from it, but would not return.

The Chat were born as hunters, the Yilii as killers. In this we are alike and different from our enemies, and also in appearance. The Yilii hunt to kill. The Chat kill to have hunted. The Yilii find pleasure in causing death. The Chat finds neither joy nor guilt.

The smells of the warm night air told me that the Yilii had hunted much in this area within the last two days. Their musty odor, like long dead grasses, left to dry in the sun and then rained upon, was not strong in my nostrils, but was everywhere about me. Either there had been many of them, or they had crossed the area repeatedly.

There was also something else. An odor such as I had never smelled before. Faintly reminiscent of the Yilii, but more fecund, and, in a way, more revolting. It had a sickly, sweet odor about it, and the scent of dried blood. The smell of death.

It would have been safer to leave the area, but I did not think the Yilii were still about. Their scent was not that strong. I was driven onward by that insatiable curiosity that afflicts all my race, and decided to follow the new smell to its source.

After a time, I came to a clearing with many strange objects in it, but I did not enter the clearing to investigate them, for they gave off strange smells, like the smell of the air after a rainstorm, only stronger, and they seemed alive, although they did not move, for they gave off a low humming sound, like that of bees in their hive.

On the soil of the clearing, surrounding the strange objects that hummed like bees, were the lifeless bodies of a great many creatures. They looked something like the Yilii, and for a moment I thought that perhaps the Yilii had struggled here among themselves and killed each other, but this was not so. I looked at them more closely, and saw that they resembled the Yilii only a little. They looked more like the Yilii than like the Chat, but the Yilii had evidently hunted them, as they did all creatures, and had mastered them. There were a great many of the strange creatures. I thought perhaps I was witness to the Yilii's mastery of an entire tribe.

The Yilii had hunted well indeed.

7

Masterson, Lara
Captain, Hard Landing Force Charlie, SCAF

I ran blindly through the rain forest, crashing through brush and tripping over vines, feeling thorns tear at my face and hands until I ran headlong into a tree trunk and fell down. I lay there for a moment, the wind knocked out of me, then forced myself up off the ground and ran again, my breath coming in ragged gasps, my lungs burning, my legs aching. I hadn't run so hard since basic training. Finally I tripped again, and this time couldn't get up.

I lay there, smelling the wet earth in my nostrils, fighting for breath, while the adrenalin level in my bloodstream slowly returned to something like normal, and along with it, the process of reasoned, rational thought.

It wasn't perhaps my best performance as a soldier. In fact, I figured my court-martial, when it came, would itemize some of its specifications under the charge of "Cowardice in the face of the enemy." Perhaps I had been guilty of cowardice in the eyes of the Uniform Code of Conduct, but I don't think I've ever been guilty of gross stupidity, and only a fool would have stood there and let herself be killed by something she was smart enough to realize she couldn't fight. If that's cowardice, call me guilty, but don't call me stupid.

I didn't know exactly what had happened, except that my troops had suddenly started killing each other. There were a

lot of possible explanations for it, but none of them very satisfactory. An illusion, some form of mass induced hysteria,
even thought control if I wanted to get really weird theorizing.
About the best I could come up with was that the enemy had
hit us with some kind of mind-altering drug gas. But if that
were true, why hadn't everybody started acting weird in different ways, instead of just killing each other? Or maybe they
had. Maybe the gas did affect everyone differently, and I'd
just hallucinated that my troops were killing each other. Hell,
maybe nobody had killed anybody at all.

But that didn't really wash either. Not with all the bodies
we'd found littering up the landscape when we landed. Those
people had definitely been dead, and we'd buried them. Sandburg had been quite positive they'd all killed each other. Unless the dead in the clearing had all been an hallucination too.
Maybe the clearing had been empty all the time, like the
pickup pilot who had gone in to retrieve the Marine Recon
Unit had insisted, and we'd dug a bunch of holes and only
thought we'd put bodies in them, and then filled the empty
holes back up again.

And then I had an even worse thought. Suppose the bodies
had been real, but they hadn't been dead, and we'd buried a
lot of SCAF troopers alive.

That kind of thinking could definitely drive you crazy, and
the situation was crazy enough without me making it any
worse by thinking up weird theories that were, in any event,
unprovable. I rejected that train of thought, and stuck with the
notion of some kind of hallucinogenic weapon. It made the
best sense and didn't require self-examination.

I took stock of my situation and tried to decide what my
next move should be.

I'd lost my helmet somewhere, probably when I ran into
the tree, and with it, the neutrino transceiver that would have
allowed me to send a warning message to the fleet. I was still
wearing the throat mike, but the fiberoptic transmission line
had pulled out of its connector jack. I felt behind my ear, but
the flat little trapezoid of the bone induction speaker was
gone. Evidently the sticky goo that was supposed to hold it in
place had separated when I ran into the tree and it had stayed
behind with the helmet.

I still had my battle carbine, whatever good that might do me, and my combat harness with most of my spare ammunition and grenades, and two canteens full of water. When that ran out, I'd have to use my pocket purifier and take my chances with the local supply. At least I wouldn't have to worry about a shortage. It rained every night.

Food was going to be something of a problem. There were three days worth of concentrates in the little pouch on the belt. With careful rationing, I might be able to stretch that to six or eight, but after that I was going to have to find something to eat, and I had no idea what might be safe, and what might prove fatal. I might not have to worry about that. I was going to have to start drinking the local water a long time before the food ran out, and if it wasn't safe after running it through the purifier, eating was never going to become a major concern.

There was still plenty of food and water back at the rescue ship of course, but I didn't think trying to get to it would be such a hot idea, at least not right away. The enemy obviously had kept the landing site under observation for some time, and there was no way of knowing how long they would continue to do so. It seemed probable that they might even reason that any survivors of the raid would attempt to return to the site to use the communications equipment in the ship, or to scrounge supplies. If nothing else, it was a good bet that a survivor would want to return to reconnoiter the damage, and it was also a good bet that the enemy would think of that. The safest policy would be to stay well away from the area for several days.

I didn't know if the LPDS would keep the enemy from entering the perimeter to search the camp and ship or not. Anything larger than a few microns except in air and water shouldn't be able to slip through into the safe zone without setting off the defense system, but then a lot of things that had happened shouldn't have been able to happen.

I felt something warm and sticky on my hands, felt around, and determined they were bleeding. That reminded me to check my face. Ny nose hurt, but didn't seem to be broken. It

felt like it was bleeding too, and since an uncontrolled nosebleed can lead to mild shock or even become life threatening
if it goes on long enough, I let the scratches on my hands go
and concentrated on the nosebleed first.

I remembered from my combat first aid classes that you
could usually control a nosebleed by putting pressure on the
upper lip beneath the nostrils, or by pinching the nostrils together and holding them for awhile, but I couldn't remember
which was supposed to be best or done first, so I did both,
lying there in the mud and holding my nose while I listened
for the sound of any pursuing enemy.

The night was warm and humid and surprisingly quiet,
considering all that had happened. I didn't know how far I had
run or in what direction, but figured I was still close enough to
the camp to hear the sounds if the one-sided battle were still
continuing. Since I didn't hear anything, I assumed the enemy
had successfully neutralized all resistance. I didn't think
they'd overrun the camp, because I figured the LPDS would
prevent that, but I wasn't sure.

After awhile, I used a capful of water from one of the
canteens to wet my handkerchief and wipe off my face and
hands. I felt somewhat better after that, and the bleeding
seemed to have stopped, so I dug out the little first aid kit
from its pouch on the leg of my Battle Dress Utilities and felt
around inside it until I found the tube of antibiotic ointment. I
smeared some of that on my face and rubbed a bit of it into my
hands and hoped it would be sufficient to keep the scratches
from getting infected. Wounds infect easily in a jungle environment and the resulting sepsis can be fatal in a matter of
hours.

After that, I felt around on the other leg and found the tiny
survival kit. A somewhat optimistic name for it, I've always
felt. It was a standard issue item consisting of a little metal
container that could be used as a cup or tiny cooking pot, and
contained a magnesium fire starter, a cable saw, a twelve centimeter metal saw blade with the spine of it sharpened to make
a crude knife edge, a couple of pieces of snare wire, some
iodine pills, and a handful of fishhooks and sinkers with about
ten meters of Kevlar line. The whole thing was wrapped in a

thermal foil blanket and a polyfilm sheet that could be used as a ground cloth, poncho, or tube tent, and packed in a plastic bag that doubled as a water carrier and solar still. According to the survival manuals, a well trained, inventive, and resourceful SCAF soldier could stay alive indefinitely using only the items it contained, always assuming of course that he was stranded in an environment with a breathable atmosphere and some kind of life form small enough for him to catch and eat, and which wasn't poisonous to the human digestive system. The only really decent piece of equipment in it was a miniscule compass with luminous needle and markings, and of course that would only do you any good on a planet that had a magnetic field, which fortunately, this one did.

There were several directional and navigational aids built into the SCAF battle helmet, but I'd lost the use of those when I'd lost the helmet, so the compass was all I had to work with, and I needed to get it out so I could use it. The damned polyfilm wrap defeated me in the dark, however, and I finally had to dig out my little hand generated flashlight and have a look at the closures in order to avoid tearing the blasted stuff. I hadn't wanted to use the light, because I figured the enemy was still in the area, but it was either that or go without the compass, and without the compass I had no idea where I was going and might as well stay put. The light did have a red filter on it, thank God, and by cupping my hand around it and pumping the lever with my thumb, I was able to use it and still restrict the illumination to a faint, narrow cone of red light. It was enough for me to get the packet unsealed.

It never ceases to amaze me how stuff that's packed at the factory absolutely refuses to fit back in the box once you open it, and the survival kit was no exception. Once I had the compass, I stuffed the rest of the junk back into the kit as best I could and crammed it back in the pouch. Then I just lay still for a long time, listening to the night and trying to detect the sounds of any enemy troops. Once I heard something rustle past, but it just kept on going. I lay still for about an hour after that, then took a rough compass bearing and headed off toward what I hoped would be the rendezvous with St. Croix, if she had gotten out alive.

I spent two hours moving about five hundred yards before I finally gave it up. With the passive and active night vision equipment of the battle helmet, traveling through the jungle at night wouldn't have presented many more special problems than movement in daylight; without it, it was a nightmare. True, I had charged pell-mell into the bush to escape the insane carnage back at the ship, but that had been the unthinking flight of panic, I'd been lucky I hadn't broken my neck tripping over things, or worse, run into some local lethal head of lettuce. We already knew there were plenty of things in the Aldebaran jungle that could kill you without the addition of panic, and even the greenest of rookie SCAF recruits is taught while still in basic training that the single biggest killer in a survival situation, including combat survival, is panic. I'd survived the attack on our base back at the rescue ship by plain dumb luck.

Well, okay, maybe that is being a little hard on myself. Having the presence of mind to realize I was in over my head and get the hell out might have had something to do with it, but mostly it had been luck. I didn't bank on that kind of luck. Soldiers who do, don't live long.

It was practically impossible to follow a compass heading in the rain forest at night. There were no visible landmarks to shoot a bearing on and then walk to. In fact, you could hardly see your hand in front of your face, unless you held it up to the sky where a little bit of light from the twin moons could filter down through the triple tiered canopy of leaves overhead. And trying to hold the compass where you could see it and just follow the needle didn't work at all.

For one thing, the degree markings were only luminous-coated on the eight main points. Using the flashlight didn't help all that much, because the small compass was only divided into five-degree increments, so at best, all you could get was the general direction, and using the flashlight increased the likelihood of being spotted by the enemy. Further, unless you did use the flashlight, you had to feel your way in front of you with your hands in order to keep from walking into trees and bushes and vines, and sort of shuffle forward with your feet to keep from stepping in a hole or tripping over some thing. I'd left my gloves behind in camp, and grabbing a big handful of briers wasn't much more attractive than the possibility of stepping on the Aldebaran equivalent of a bushmaster or bear. It gave me a real appreciation for how truly helpless the modern soldier is without the aid of all his electronic battlefield gadgetry.

I finally got to where I really couldn't tell if I was walking around in circles or not, so when I bumped up against a tree that had a branch low enough that I could jump up and grab it, I hauled myself up, used my combat harness and the sling from my carbine to belt myself to the trunk so I wouldn't fall out, and settled in to wait out the rest of the night.

I woke just before dawn to the sound of something that must have been as big as an elephant crashing through the jungle beneath my perch, and a short time later the stillness that followed was broken by a cacophony of chirps, whistles, screams, howls, and snarls as the nocturnal creatures blundered off to bed and turned the forest over to the daytime critters. It was like something out of an old movie-gram, the kind they run late-night on the cube, "Frank Buck's Bring 'em Back Alive." I guess jungles must sound pretty much the same the galaxy over, even if they're not.

When it finally got light enough for me to see, I found I was sharing my branch with a brilliant purplish-red snake about three meters long with a row of yellow trapezoid patterns running down its back and either side. It had woken up too, and seemed fairly annoyed at finding a perfect stranger sharing its sleeping quarters. I didn't know if it was poisonous or not, but I figured anything that brightly colored couldn't have many natural enemies. I spent about an hour working my hand down by millimeters until I could open the flap on my Personal Defense Weapon's holster and ease the pistol out, while the snake watched me with ill concealed hostility. It probably took me about another hour to work the flat little semi-automatic back up to where I could use it, and just as I was about to blast the bugger, the snake dropped off the branch and slithered away in the undergrowth.

That was just too much. I started shaking like the proverbial leaf. I snapped the safety back on the PDW and reholstered it, needing only three passes at the holster to get the job done, then leaned back against the tree trunk and tried to get my trembling hands back under control. I didn't quite get the job done before my tortured bladder forced me down off the limb, and I had to drop my BDU and take a squat. I kept a nervous eye out for the snake, but it didn't reappear. After that, I covered my modesty back up, longed for a Tau cigarette to soothe my jangled nerves, took a small sip from one of my canteens, and gathered up my gear.

It was a little easier to make progress during the day, but not much. I wrapped my handkerchief around my left hand to make a sort of rudimentary fingerless glove, which offered more imaginary than real protection for my hand, and used that whenever I had to push aside a branch or vine. I'd take a compass bearing on a tree or bush some fifteen or twenty meters away, farther when the vegetation allowed it, which wasn't often, and walk to that, then shoot another heading and repeat the process. The only way I could tell how far I'd come was by counting paces, which wasn't all that accurate in the uneven, plant choked terrain, but I figured I was making about a kilometer an hour. At that rate, I figured I'd miss my rendezvous with St. Croix by about a day and a half. The only consoling factor was that she probably wasn't making much faster progress than I was.

Around mid-afternoon my growling stomach finally persuaded me to stop and nibble a little bit of a concentrate bar and take a sip of water. While I was doing that, I heard a rustling in the bushes and eased the carbine into position. The rustling stopped for quite a long while, then finally started again, moving slowly toward me. It stopped every little bit, waited a few moments, then came on a short distance before stopping again.

It didn't take a genius to figure out that whatever it was, it was looking for something, and I figured I was the only something around interesting enough for anything or anybody to be looking for. As it got real close, I eased the safety off the carbine and sighted at the bushes where I expected it to come out. Only the remote possibility that it might be St. Croix kept me from riddling it with a burst of hypervelocity 3mm frangible bullets when it finally pushed into view. It was a good thing it did.

It was so unexpected and startled me so much, that I nearly did blast it, but I got my finger off the trigger just in time. It was a SCAF Imperial Marine, wearing one of those tiger-striped recon uniforms.

"Just don't make any sudden moves, Marine, and neither of us will get hurt," I told him.

For a second, I thought the poor bastard was going to die of a heart attack, then he spotted me and a look of relief spread over his grimy face. I lowered the carbine, and he lowered the little SMG they issue to recon types.

The marine reached up and pulled the boonie hat off his head, letting a cascade of jet black hair fall to his shoulders and mopped at his face with the hat. He was so filthy, and there was so much camouflage makeup smeared on his face that even with the hair, I didn't realize he was a she until she spoke.

"Damned glad to see you, whoever you are. I'm Chang, Mai Lin, Lance Corporal. I think that's what you army types call a Fire and Maneuver Team Leader."

I nodded. "We used to call them that too. Times and titles change, but not the job."

The smile grew a little wider. "Back in the Old Corps, eh? You don't hardly look old enough. What's your unit?"

"It *was* Hard Landing Force Charlie. Name's Lara Masterson, Captain of Pathfinders."

The marine stiffened just slightly, but knew enough not to salute in the field. That just identifies the officers for the enemy snipers. If any are around.

"Sorry, sir. I didn't see your rank."

"I'm not wearing any. No point in advertising for the enemy."

"Yes, sir. Recon has the same policy in the field, sir."

"Let's not get too hung up on this 'sir' stuff, Chang. It's liable to get kind of monotonous after awhile. You and I might turn out to be the only humans left alive on this planet."

"I was afraid you were going to tell me that. I heard the firing last night. Your bunch getting clobbered?"

"Clobbering themselves is more like it. I don't know what

happened. Everybody just suddenly went wacko and started shooting at each other."

"Well, I'll be a Tau Sand Spider. Same thing happened with my unit, near as I can figure. I was on listening post duty with Marines Sanchez and O'Toole outside the perimeter when I had to go take a leak. I crawled off a little ways, and when I got back they were gone.

"Next thing I know, there's a bunch of firing from the direction of the ship, so I start working my way back there to see what in hell's going on. When I get there, everybody's lying around dead, and there's this bunch of big catlike guys hanging around.

"At first I figured they zapped my team, but they haven't got any weapons. I'm lining them up in my sights, trying to decide whether or not to smoke 'em when another bunch of cat-guys shows up. Then they get real excited and go charging off into the jungle straight toward me, so I figure I'd better get the hell out of there. I've been hiding out in the jungle ever since.

"The cat-guys are still around though. I've seen them twice. I figured they were looking for me, to finish the job, but they don't seem all that sharp. They've got good eyesight and seem to hear pretty well, but I don't think they can smell much, and I got a hunch they're colorblind. They seem to rely more on movement for seeing things. One of them walked right past me, almost close enough to touch. I'm pretty sure one of our people would have spotted me at that range, my cover wasn't all that good, but I suppose it could have just been careless."

"Well," I said, "that's something. At least it does tell us who we're up against, and we do know they're not perfect. I suppose it's useless to ask if you've got a neutrino transceiver or even a radio on you?"

"Afraid so, Captain. Marines get mostly hand-me-downs, whatever the other services don't want or won't use. No disrespect intended, sir. We did have two neutrino transceivers. One of them was a mobile unit mounted in our SSV. We disabled that when we had to abandon the vehicle. The other was with Gunnery Sergeant Sabena back at the ship. I tried once to sneak back and get ahold of it, but the cat-guys were still there."

I nodded. "That would be the one the Rangers reported finding."

"What Rangers?"

"When your team didn't make pickup, Fleet Ops sent in a Special Operations Ranger platoon."

"What happened to them?"

"The same thing that happened to your people and mine, I guess. What about a helmet radio? Don't you people normally get issued battle helmets with radios?"

"Sure, all the time. Only we were operating under a strict communications blackout, except for vital messages to the fleet, and nobody knew if the enemy had monitors or not, so we were ordered to leave them behind rather than risk somebody getting stupid and forgetting or accidentally triggering his mike."

"Terrific. A typical bureaucratic solution to a non-problem, practically guaranteed to create another problem, which it did. When radios are outlawed, only outlaws will have radios."

"How's that, Captain?"

"Nothing. It just reminded me of gun control, that's all."

"Gun control? What's that?"

"Being able to hit your target," I grumbled, then seeing the still blank look on Chang's face, "a political football of a couple hundred years ago. Some politicians and a lot of other people got the bright idea that you could get rid of crime by taking guns away from everybody, instead of getting rid of the causes of crime and punishing the criminals. Eventually, even the cops were disarmed, based on the theory that they didn't need weapons since the criminal element didn't have them. Then they started disarming the military. The result was THE EXCHANGE and about three hundred and fifty million dead Americans and Russians, and another five hundred million Chinese."

"Stop crime by disarming the public?" said Chang. "That's crazy. Uh, Captain Masterson, what's a football?"

"Never mind," I said. "How have you managed to stay alive this long without food or water?"

"No mystery there. Plenty of water, Captain, it rains every

night. I've been eating mostly snakes. They're about the only thing around here that moves slow enough to catch. The big bright green ones that resemble a tree boa are the best. I'd give the burgundy colored ones with the yellow spots a pass if I were you though. I tried one of those, and the flesh burned my lips."

"Thanks for the advice. Do you know the water around here contains trace elements we haven't been able to identify?"

Chang shrugged. "All I know is, I haven't died from it yet. I'd sure as hell have died without it."

"Well, I don't suppose it compares with snake, but how about a bite of concentrate to chew on?" I offered generously. I broke off about a third of the bar I'd been nibbling on, and not really feeling all that generous, passed it over to Chang. I rewrapped the rest of the bar and tucked it back into my pouch.

Chang bit off a mouthful, tipped back her head, and closed her eyes like she was savoring a drink of good brandy, or the afterglow of a good orgasm. I thought she was going to hold it in her mouth until it melted, but she finally chewed the dry, crunchy, protein and vitamin concentrate and swallowed.

"Purely delightful," she said. "If I try real hard, I can imagine it's *moo goo gai pan*."

"That's trying pretty hard," I said.

"Captain, you try eating snake for as long as I have, you'll be amazed what you can make that stuff taste like. If you don't mind, I think I'll save the rest of it until later. I feel like *mu shu pork* for supper," she said, zipping the rest of the piece of bar into a pocket of her uniform. "What's the game plan now? Are we going to try to sneak back to the ship and get a call through to the fleet?"

I shook my head. "Negative, at least not right away. I think we can safely assume our friends with the pointed ears and whiskers are still hanging around watching the ship. Besides, my warrant officer is wandering around out here somewhere, if she managed to get away. I want to find her first. St. Croix was wearing a battle helmet the last time I saw her, and Pathfinder helmets have both radio and neutrino comm circuits built into them. She may have been able to get a message out to Fleet Ops already. Do you know the big rocky outcropping to the east of here?"

Chang nodded.

"I'm supposed to meet St. Croix there tomorrow morning. If she made it out, and managed to get a message to the fleet, she might even have a reply by then. They were supposed to be putting together a task force to relieve us, a whole PAI brigade, so they shouldn't be too many days away by now. If we can just hang on a little longer, I think we can expect some help."

Chang felt differently. "Do you really think they'll drop in that big of an outfit, after what happened to your command? It wouldn't look too good on some brigadier general's record to lose a couple of regiments."

"None of what's happened down here is going to look too good to the Imperial General Staff. They'll hardly just go off and leave us with so many unanswered questions. It's just not sound tactically to leave behind you a planet that's proven itself hostile to the Empire of Sol. If anything, I think we can expect them to send in half a dozen divisions instead of just a brigade."

"Well then," said Chang, "in that case, I guess we better hurry if we're going to keep that rendezvous with your warrant officer. I'm probably a little more familiar with what all can kill you around here, so I'll take the point, if that's okay with you, Captain. Don't stop to sniff any flowers, some of them are nasty. And if you see anything that looks like a giant Venus flytrap, stay the hell away from it. That's exactly what it is, and it can move. Not very fast, but it *can* move."

"A plant that walks? You can't be serious."

"I wish I wasn't. One of the damned things ate my machine gunner. He was a damned good marine, and real talented with that machine gun. Sort of an Aldebaran mantrap, I guess. They've got a big sticky tongue about five meters long that's attached at the front like a frog's, and they can pop it out just about as fast. And to make matters worse, they hunt in packs, anywhere from four or five of them up to fifteen or twenty. They don't fight over the kill, though, or share it. Whichever one gets the prey, gets the meal. They seek food like other plants seek water or the sunlight.

"Just follow along back far enough to cover my butt in case we run into those cat-guys, but don't lose sight of me. If I move too fast, let me know and I'll slow down the pace, but we've got a lot of ground to cover between here and that escarpment, and you can't move all that fast in this stuff anyway."

"Lead on, Macduff," I told her.

"Macduff? It's Chang. Mai Lin Chang."

"Never mind," I said. "It's just an expression. Comes from a play written by a guy named Shakespeare."

"Shakespeare, huh? Never heard of him. Has he written anything good?"

"Not lately. The guy's been dead for about six hundred and twenty years. Some of his stuff was pretty good though, lots of intrigue, violence, even a little romance. Sex if you read between the lines."

"If you don't mind my saying so, Captain, I've got all the intrigue and violence I need in my life."

"I can't argue that one with you, Chang. Anyway, like I said, it's just an expression."

"Yes, sir. Just never heard anybody use it before."

"Well, it's kind of an old-timer's expression."

"Back in the Old Corps again, eh, Captain?"

"Sort of. I learned it from a Ranger Lieutenant I knew once. Good soldier, came up through the ranks. He used to quote a lot from Shakespeare, and I kind of got interested and read some of his plays and sonnets."

"Whatever happened to him?"

"Shakespeare? I don't know. Died of old age I guess."

"Nah, I meant the Ranger Lieutenant. Don't often meet a first rate soldier with an interest in ancient literature."

I wasn't real sure if that was just an observation, a left-handed compliment, or an insult. "He's dead too. He was killed on Tau Ceti Four."

"Mmmm. Some pretty rough fighting there, from what I understand. Captain, if you don't mind me saying so, seems like you know an awful lot of dead people. What say we get the hell out of here while we're still breathing?"

I suppressed the desire to get theatrical again, and simply gestured with my hand. Chang moved off, and I followed along, trying to keep her in sight, but leave enough space between us so that one grenade wouldn't get us both. So far I'd seen nothing to suggest that the enemy had any grenades, but it was SOP.

It wouldn't be fair to say we hiked the rest of the day. Hiking implies a more or less steady progression, usually along roads or well marked trails, sometimes carried out for recreational purposes. Pathfinders don't, as a general rule, hike, nor do Recon Marines. We worked our way slowly through the bush, sidestepping vines and rotting, fallen branches, spending twice as much time frozen motionless, listening, looking, smelling, as we did moving. Ordinarily we'd have spent three or four times as much time listening and observing as we did moving, but as Chang had pointed out, we had a lot of ground to cover if we were going to make the rendezvous with St. Croix on time.

I'd like to give the impression that we cut through the jungle with the speed of the wind and the silence of a pair of shadows, that's the popular storybook conception most people have of professional soldiers experienced in jungle fighting. It's also a myth. You can't move swiftly through the jungle without sounding like a herd of elephants, and that's exactly the last thing you want to do, especially if the enemy is about someplace, looking for you. You softfoot it along at a snail's pace, trying not to disturb any of the local fauna whose alarmed flight might tip off the enemy, and straining to hear any disturbance that might signal the enemy's presence to you. You don't move with absolute stealth either. With luck, you move with sufficient stealth. Absolute stealth is as impossible as speed. There are too many vines to entangle you and trip you up, too many rotted, fallen tree trunks to crunch and crumble underfoot, too many branches to whip back sighing and slap you in the face, too many thickets that are too big to detour around that you've got to chop and hack and fight your way through. Good jungle fighters don't learn to master the jungle. They learn to co-exist with it.

To make matters worse, the ground was uneven, not just hilly, but running all up and down like a roller coaster. In a lot of places you had to hack out a clear path in front of you while you held on with your other hand to bushes and exposed roots,

easing your way slowly down a ravine bank, then use vines
for handholds as you chopped and pulled your way back up
the next slope.

About dusk Chang's tiger-striped uniform got too hard to
see in the lengthening shadows and I had to whistle to her to
slow down the pace. Instead, she doubled back to meet me.

"Might as well pack it in for the night, Captain. We're
going to have to rest sometime anyway, and besides, it's too
dangerous to move after dark. I've got a set of passive night
goggles, but you'd have to stumble along behind me with your
hand on my shoulder like a blind man. In this terrain you'd
fall and break something for sure. The batteries are getting
pretty weak in them anyway. It might be smarter to save them
until we really need them. Besides, they're not all that hot for
use in this heavy cover. Not much starlight gets through the
overhead canopy and anything in shadows remains shadowed.
A person really needs active infrared down here. Unfortunately, all we've got is one set of passive goggles with weak
batteries."

I nodded. "I presume we sleep in the trees. I did last
night."

"It's safer than the ground. Too much animal traffic around
here at night. A lot of the wildlife seems to be nocturnal. So
do the cat-people. I don't think we want to be wandering
around in the dark with those guys on the prowl. I guess I
don't need to ask if you can climb. I'd recommend staying off
the lower branches, the snakes seem to like those, and although I haven't actually seen one, I'd judge from some of the
tracks I've come across and the cries I've sometimes heard at
night, that there's a couple of varieties of feral cat around,
besides our markedly unfriendly cat-people."

I nodded and we found ourselves a couple of trees about
twenty yards apart, just at the limit of each other's range of
vision in the dense foliage, with a couple of likely looking
perches, climbed up with some difficulty, and settled down to
supper. I sat there with my feet dangling down either side of a
big branch and my back resting up against the trunk, belted in
by my harness and carbine sling, and chewed slowly on a
lump of one of the ration bars, listening to the jungle taking on
the sounds of night, and hoping to hear something. I'm not

really sure what. The thrusters of a shuttle bringing the relief force or a reconnaissance shuttle we might somehow signal, I suppose. Maybe it was the forlorn hope of hearing another of my troops crunching through the brush. After all, if Chang and I had survived, perhaps someone else might have too.

Chang moved slightly on her branch, the movement making her camouflaged suit momentarily visible against the background pattern of leaves, branches and shadows, and held up a hand, forming her thumb and forefinger into a circle, asking if everything was okay at my end.

I gave her a thumbs-up reply and she flashed a tight smile back at me, before becoming motionless again and changing into just another part of her tree. I was impressed. Pathfinders are quite a bit beyond your average SCAF PAI trooper when it comes to camouflage and concealment, but Chang was really good, almost a magician. I crunched down on the ration bar and wondered whether or not she'd had her *mu shu pork*. To me it still tasted like cornflakes, oats, wheat germ, and textured, vitamin enriched soyabean meal rolled in ersatz chocolate to make it all at least partially palatable.

I swigged down a couple of mouthfuls of water to get the taste out of my mouth, and resisted the temptation to guzzle the whole canteen. The water only whetted my thirst, but the reminder of how truly thirsty I was did make me forget about the awful taste of the food concentrate bar.

After that, there was nothing to do but get as comfortable as possible and wait for the darkness to engulf the jungle, then try to get some sleep. It should have been easy enough to do after the day I'd put in, but it wasn't. There was a big knot on my limb in just the right place that I couldn't get into a comfortable enough position to sleep without pushing up against it in just the right way that I then definitely couldn't get to sleep. On top of that, I was high enough up to catch the breeze I'd missed sleeping on the lower branches of the tree I'd spent last night in, and as the slight air movement began to evaporate the sweat from my skin, I started chilling.

I tried just buttoning up my BDU's and toughing it out, but I finally got to shivering so much that I was shaking the leaves on the smaller branches, so I dug around in the pouch down on my thigh until I found the thermal foil blanket. It made

godawful loud crinkling noises while I got it unwrapped and
figured out which side had the camouflaged finish so I could
put that to the outside. It was a bit tricky without using a
flashlight, but this high up off the ground there was a little
light filtering down through the overhead branches and I could
tell that one side was a little lighter than the other so I figured
the dark side was the camouflaged one. I had to unbuckle the
combat harness to wrap the thermal blanket around me, then
rebuckle the harness around that. After that I sat there shaking
and rattling like a sheet of aluminum foil until my reflected
body heat finally warmed things up.

There was a small gap in the overhead cover, and through
it, I could see three or four stars. I wondered what constellation they were part of, then almost chuckled. It wouldn't be
any constellation I was familiar with. Constellations were just
names we gave to groups of stars as they appeared from Earth.
Other stars would be visible from Aldebaran Five, and even if
they were the same stars we could see from Earth, we'd see
them from a different angle here, so the constellations
wouldn't look the same.

Sitting there thinking about those stars and wondering
which ones they were, combined with the rain forest surroundings reminded me of a childhood memory I'd almost
forgotten. My father had taken us all on a camping trip into
northern Wisconsin, to the boundary waters area, and late one
afternoon I'd wandered away from our camp and gotten lost.
It got dark and I was cold and hungry and scared, but I kept
myself from crying by looking at all the stars and trying to
remember the names of the constellations and of the individual
stars that my dad had taught me. It never occurred to me that
someone might never find me. I guess because Daddy was so
special to me, and I just knew he wouldn't let anything really
bad happen to me. I suppose all little girls think of their fathers as being just a little bit godlike. He used to call me his
"Little Princess" and I called him my "Knight in Shining
Armor". I didn't worry about what might happen to me that
night because I just knew Daddy would come and find me,
and take me back safe to camp. And that's just what he did.

It was only later, when I was thirteen, that I learned that
parents aren't really godlike, and that fathers can't always

keep bad things from happening to their children. Daddy tried hard to keep me from being conscripted into SCAF, but he just couldn't do it. He was a fairly well known writer and had a lot of friends, but none of them were members of the Congress or Senate. The last time I saw my father alive, he was standing on the front steps of the Baltimore Induction Center waving good-bye as they herded me and several hundred other teenagers inside. There were tears in his eyes and I felt a terrible dread, although I was still too young to fully understand why at the time. It was a few days later before I realized my "Knight in Shining Armor" wouldn't be coming to rescue his "Little Princess" anymore, and I'd have to slay my own dragons and lions from then on out.

I've gotten pretty good at taking care of myself since then, and at slaying my own dragons and lions, and human beings. But I guess there must be a tiny part of every woman that stays a little girl, no matter how old she gets, and still wishes for that knight in shining armor to come take her home safely when she's in trouble. I sure wished for my dad right then.

And then, thinking about it, I wished for someone else. A kind of small, wiry young Ranger lieutenant. He'd been a sergeant when I first met him. My training platoon sergeant back in basic in fact. I hadn't liked him then. I'd maybe even hated him just a little bit. He was cool, aloof, efficient, and more than just a little bit deadly. Everything my dad wasn't. He told the platoon once that he'd killed more people than we had friends, and we believed him. I found out later it was no boast. I think we were all a little afraid of him. We used to bitch and moan a lot about the way he treated us and all the extra duty and extra training and extra calisthenics he put us through.

Later, after I'd been in combat, I understood why. He wasn't hard on us because he hated us like we all thought. He was hard on us because he loved us. Every one of us in his training platoon. He loved us and cared about us. And he knew the hell we'd someday have to go through, so he was hard on us to toughen us up, so we'd have some chance of surviving that incomprehensible nightmare soldiers call combat. The little hell he put us through prepared us for the big hell we went through later. As I look back on it now, I realize he wasn't just teaching us to be killers or to take the objective or complete the mission. He was teaching us to complete life, to take impossible odds and make them work for us, rather than against us, to be survivors. He always insisted that combat was a survivable experience. "The only way to get killed in combat," he used to say, "is to make a mistake." For him, the acid test of warfare was survival, and death was not a passing grade. He judged himself more harshly than he judged us, and measured his success by the number of his trainees who survived their first encounter with combat.

When I figured that out about him, I cared for him too, and loved him just a little, like I had my father when I realized he'd been stern with me on some matter or other for my own good. Later still, when I crossed paths with that Ranger again, we met not as training platoon sergeant and recruit, but as equals who shared the common bond of combat. We talked then, in a way we could never have talked before, and got drunk together. And I realized something else about him then. He was like a hard-boiled egg, a real tough exterior presented to the outer world, a kind of self-protective armor, but with an interior that was soft, compassionate, capable of love as well as hate, of life as well as death. In that moment, I loved him in a way like I had never loved my father. He wasn't a knight in shining armor, but he was a much more useful fellow to have around. I missed him.

They're both dead now, I suppose. both my knights. Daddy's probably succumbed to old age or a broken heart at losing his little girl. And the young Ranger, who was not so very much older than me, is gone too, killed by a mistake I suppose he would say. I held him in my arms and watched him die on Tau Ceti Four. But when he faced death, he faced the reaper squarely and fought long and hard before he died. He didn't surrender to death. He was overwhelmed by it. For his kind, there's no other way to die. Death took him by surprise, or it never would have gotten him.

I sat there on that tree limb, staring up at those stars and thinking of the father I'd been taken from and the ranger that had been taken from me, and wishing one or both of them were there to take me home safely. I had the strangest feeling that one or the other of them would do just exactly that. I can't explain it. I knew they were both dead, but I still felt like when things got really grim, one of them would come to my rescue.

Neither of them did, of course. Instead, an hour before dawn, the enemy came.

8

Fetterman, Anthony B.
Major General (Simulated)
Seventh Rangers (Detached)
FLEET/STC Joint Operational Intelligence Task Force,
SCAF

I'd been wrong about having nothing to do but lie in the darkness for a day and a half. The ship's onboard computer kept feeding me what little background information we had on the planet from the previous missions into its biosphere, and then quizzing me on it over the little fiber optic data link plugged into my helmet. Peterson had taken Stryker's data diskette from my pocket before tucking me into the defensive weapons bay of the miniscule recon ship and fed it into the onboard main, which promptly developed the annoying habit of playing twenty questions with me every time I tried to get some sleep. By the time the computer once again interrupted my efforts to catch some shut-eye in order to tell me we were about to enter the planetary atmosphere, I was beginning to think of a day and a half in soundless, sightless, solitary confinement as a pleasant way to spend a vacation.

There was no sensation of motion when the antigrav propulsion system was operating, but for some reason or other it was apparently against standard operating procedures to use antigravity in close proximity to large masses of metal, like the hospital ship, or within a planetary atmosphere. Don't ask me why. Like I said, I don't even know why the thing works, let alone how. Maybe the attractional field of any massive object interferes with the operation of the system when you enter its gravitational envelope. I know even less about gravitons than I do mesons, and about those I know quark.

At any rate, in the close proximity of any massive object, the antigravity drive was shut down and ion or chemothrusters were employed. I'd found that much out from what little reading I'd had time to do while I was in my hospital room. So when the computer chimed its little annunciator bell and politely requested that I prepare for atmospheric entry, I knew what to expect.

Or so I thought.

No amount of reading or imagination could have prepared me for what it was like when we hit Alpha Tauri Five's atmosphere and nearly bounced back off. It was like slamming into a brick wall on your back. I bounced my helmet against the overhead missile pylon and bounced my head off the inside of the helmet. Fortunately, neither of them cracked.

The computer, in a voice so pleasant it made me want to pull out its logic and memory circuits with my bare hands, apologized for the "inconvenience," and informed me that the turbulence was due to our entering the outer layers of the planetary atmosphere at a shallower angle than normal landing procedures, due to the rapid braking maneuvers we had experienced while we were in the antigravity propulsion mode, and which, unlike the encounter with the planet's atmosphere, had gone totally unnoticed. I was assured that our angle of atmospheric entry had been properly readjusted to compensate for the difficulty, and that there was nothing to concern myself with.

I almost choked on that one. Here I was, locked into the weapons bay of a ship being flown by computer, with a dead man who wasn't even a dead pilot, mind you, seated at the controls, and me getting ready to do a high altitude, low opening paradrop into some of the densest jungle of a hostile planet, which had presumably already claimed the lives of a hundred and seventy or so SCAF soldiers, all by my lonesome, and the damned computer was assuring me that there was nothing to concern myself with.

We hit the atmosphere again, apparently at the right angle this time, as the effect was more like riding a washboard on your back over a rocky road full of potholes, instead of being thrown into a wall.

After a minute or so, I noticed that I was starting to feel a bit warm, and checked the environmental homeostasis readouts on the suit's head up display. The cooling mechanism was functioning at maximum output, but still wasn't quite keeping up with the increased heat being conducted through the skin of the ship from the air molecules slamming into it outside. It occurred to me that the missiles normally carried in the defensive weapons bay of a one-man reconnaissance ship could probably take heat a lot better than a human body could, and I suddenly found myself facing the really nasty prospect that all of Peterson's and Stryker's careful planning had overlooked one tiny, minute little detail like the simple fact that the weapons bay was not nearly as well insulated as the cockpit of the little recon ship, and I just might become a roast Fetterman before the doors popped open and announced I was done.

It wasn't a very confidence inspiring thought, and there wasn't a damned thing I could do about it either, except lie there and watch the slowly narrowing gradient between the suit's internal temperature and the weapons bay's ambient temperature, both of which were well past thirty-seven degrees centigrade and climbing like a startled mountain goat. My mouth felt like someone had stuffed it full of steel wool, and I was awash in enough sweat that it seemed probable I'd soon be able to float inside the environment suit, if I didn't drown in it, which would, if nothing else, take care of all my worries about roasting.

Dimly, through the noise of the buffeting ship and the rhythmically alternating thunking of my helmet against the missile pylon and the bay doors, I became aware of a faintly metallic ringing that I belatedly recognized as the computer's annunciator chime.

"This is no time for another goddamned topography lesson," I thought, but the computer had other things in mind.

"Attention, please. Your attention please. We are approaching the insertion area, altitude ten thousand five hundred meters. The weapons bay doors will open in thirty-five seconds. Please stand by for jettisoning sequence countdown. Thank-you."

I checked the suit readouts on the HUD. Everything was in

the green except the temperature readouts. I didn't like the look of their color at all.

"Attention, please. Your attention please. We are approaching the insertion area, altitude ten thousand three hundred meters. The weapons bay doors will open in twenty-five seconds. Please stand by for jettisoning sequence countdown. Thank-you."

I closed one eye to protect it from the glare, and used the chin switch to turn on the tiny adjustable beam spot-floodlight mounted on the helmet. After a day and a half in blackness, the illumination was dazzling, the beam bouncing back from the forward bulkhead and overhead deck, and reflecting crazily off the weapons pylons, some of which were still hung with missiles, flares, or ECM pods. Quickly I checked my own parachute harness, as much as I could feel, or move my head enough to see, and eyeballed the equipment container and its chute assembly. As far as I could tell, which wasn't very far, we were both ready to go.

"Attention, please. Your attention please. We are approaching the insertion area, altitude ten thousand one hundred and fifty meters. The weapons bay doors will open in fifteen seconds. Please stand by for jettisoning sequence countdown. Thank-you.

"Ten, nine, eight . . ."

I felt the ship lurch sickeningly as the computer deployed the air spoilers and began the programmed braking maneuver. Peterson and Stryker had both said I'd have five seconds to extricate myself from anything I happened to get tangled up in, once the doors opened and before the ship started its series of violent maneuvers designed to resemble a fatal malfunction. I tried to think of anything I might get or be caught up on, but couldn't. The only possibility was the empty pylon above me, and all the harness straps were clear of it. I chinned off the floodlight and waited in the darkness.

" . . . three, two, one. Altitude ten thousand meters. Insertion point. Weapons bay doors open. Have a nice trip."

The fast action doors snapped open and I tumbled out into space. Above me, I could see the little recon ship seem to jump upward and away. I knew that was an illusion, caused by my falling away from the ship, but there was no feeling of falling. A few seconds later, the equipment container dropped clear, then the chemothrusters fired again and the recon ship streaked off across the sky at a crazy angle, pouring out intermittent trails of dense orange smoke before breaking into a snap roll and diving toward the ground.

I tucked in one arm and leg and extended those on the other side of my body so that the wind resistance would turn me over face down, then stretched everything back out in a stable, spread position. In the near distance, maybe a kilometer away, I could see the tiny, slowly tumbling speck of the equipment container, and far off to the left the schizophrenic fluttering of the rapidly dwindling recon ship with its dead pilot presumably still at the controls.

Maneuvering in the environment suit was a bit tricky, since there was nothing about it that was the least bit streamlined, but I finally managed to glide my way over to where I was fairly close to the equipment container. I didn't want to get too close to it, since I didn't want our chutes getting tangled up or it landing on me, or vice-versa, but I wanted to stay in reasonable proximity so I could recover my gear as quickly as possible and bury the evidence of the enduraplast container and chutes. Staying close would save me time and a long walk and keep me from running around weaponless in the Aldebaran jungle, a prospect I considered to be most definitely unattractive in the extreme.

There was no formal landing zone as such, just a general area for me to come down in, not too near the landing site of the rescue ship and the drop zone for Masterson's Pathfinders but not so far away that I shouldn't be able to walk my way to the site within twenty-four to forty-eight hours. I'd let the equipment container's haphazard drop select the approximate terminus of the fall and hope for a clearing of some kind in the general area of its descent. I knew the odds were against finding much of a clearing in the jungle and I'd probably wind up coming down in the trees, every jumper's worst nightmare, but the only decent sized clearing in the neighborhood was the one at the rescue ship. The Pathfinders had used that one, and were presumably now all dead. I didn't plan on repeating their mistake.

We'd discussed the mission in general terms a few days

before Stryker had yanked me out of my hospital bed. If a decision was made to send me in, I'd have ten days to make a careful, thorough reconnaissance of the landing site and as much of the surrounding terrain as I deemed advisable. It was a lot of time, but Fleet Ops desperately wanted to know what in hell was going on down there, and given the losses already sustained, they were more willing to spend time than lives. At the end of that time, a high speed shuttle with aerospace fighter support would make a touchdown at the rescue ship site. It would sit on the ground for one hundred and twenty seconds exactly and then re-orbit. If I wasn't there when it took back off, I could figure on spending my retirement on Alpha Tauri Five.

The idea of the relief brigade had been put temporarily on hold while the Imperial General Staff considered other options, like nuking the shit out of the whole planet until it glowed in the dark. The IGS wanted desperately to know what was happening on Alpha Tauri Five, but not badly enough to risk several thousand combat troops, perhaps several hundred thousand, in a sideshow war to find out. Nor did they have any intention of leaving behind unimpeded a planet which sat astride the supply and communications lines of a SCAF Regional Combat Team and had already amply demonstrated on four separate occasions, an affinity for killing SCAF soldiers. If I didn't come up with some answers for them, IGS's most likely course of action would be neutralizing the potential threat from the planet by sterilizing its surface via thermonuclear bombardment, and that was likely to make any retirement I might spend on Alpha Tauri Five a damned short one.

Since there'd been no discussion about any changes in the mission profile, I operated on the premise that the timetable hadn't been altered. For the next ten days, I was on my own. The fleet would be ready, standing a few light hours off from the system, the advance elements maybe even standing by in planetary orbit, marshaling its assault troops should the IGS change its collective mind, flexing its billions of megaton muscles should the safe option be preferred. But it wouldn't interfere. And it wouldn't help. In fact, there was no way for me to call for help.

The matchbox sized communications transceiver I'd been

given wasn't even a voice communications transceiver. In order to minimize the metal and electronic circuitry in it, and thus presumably decrease the likelihood of enemy defensive sensors picking me up as I now hurtled toward the planet's surface, the transceiver had been streamlined. The only messages it could transmit were either of two brief bursts of energy on two different radio wavelengths. Somewhere in the fleet was another transceiver which would receive the bursts and correctly interpret their meaning, then trigger a pulse of energy on a third frequency which would activate a tiny light emitting diode on my transceiver to tell me that my message to the fleet had been received and noted. Depending on the frequency the brief energy discharge was noted on by the transceiver in orbit, the people upstairs would know one of two things. Either I had found Brigadier General Andersohn and needed an immediate pickup at the coordinates of my transmission, or that I had encountered an enemy so powerful and dangerous that it could only be dealt with by the immediate reduction of the planet to an insignificant, burned out, radioactive cinder. No other interpretations were possible. With that kind of gizmo for a communications link, who needed a cyanide capsule?

I freefell to opening altitude, watching the camouflaged chute of the equipment container deploy and open when the barometric altimeter on the automatic opener activated it at around four hundred meters. A radar altimeter would have done the job at precisely four hundred meters, but a radar altimeter would have been easier for enemy monitoring to detect. My own chute had no automatic opener, on the assumption that I was capable of doing the job myself, and that there was no need to increase detection risk by adding a mechanical device which would have had to contain a few extra bits of metal, just to do a job that a flesh and blood human was perfectly capable of doing. I did have a barometric altimeter to tell me my approximate height above ground level. It was almost identical to the one on the equipment container except that it didn't have the automatic opener attached. It contained a single, tiny, bimetal strip about a fifth the size of a toothpick.

The problem was, I had no way of knowing how accurate

the damned thing was since it hadn't been calibrated for a current barometric setting at the planet's surface. I wasn't real sure how spending a day and a half inside the weapons bay of a recon ship in the vacuum of space might have affected it either. I saw the deploy on the container though, so I knew that it had popped at a safe altitude. I held off for another hundred meters, then chickened out and pulled the main rip-cord handle.

The pilot chute and sleeve ran out, the square canopy cracked open and braked hard, checking my descent with a violent, opening shock. It was almost too late. The altimeter had been off by a good two hundred meters.

There was no time to maneuver and no clearing to maneuver to anyway. Five seconds later I was in the trees. All I had time to do was get my legs together, bring my crossed arms up in front of my face and tuck in my head, and pray. So much for picking your spot and running the canopy on.

The branches clawed at my legs and beat at my chest. One tried to break my back and another to take the helmet off the top of my shoulders and my head along with it. For the first time since I'd suited up in the damned thing, I was grateful for the insulating layers of alternating foam and air space and the plastic armored covering of the bulky environment suit. It transmuted rib cracking blows into merely rib bruising ones, and very probably saved my life.

When the crashing and cracking finally subsided I found myself faced with another problem. The canopy had fouled in the branches, and I was hanging a good ten meters above the ground.

I gave a yank on the reserve ripcord handle and let the reserve chute spill out of the butt pack. The canopy flapped limply below me, but didn't make the full distance. Short or not, it was the only choice I had. I wrapped a leg around the reserve's suspension lines, finally managed, after about a hundred tries to get a grip on some of them with my gloved fingers, then reached down with the other hand and undid the fastex buckles on the chest, waist, and leg straps so I could slip out of the harness. Climbing down the suspension lines was a nightmare, even with the little acrylic and nylon hand controlled descender. When I got to the tip of the canopy, I hung by my arms and dropped.

The fall was about three meters and I rolled when I hit, a PLF like we used to do with the old style round chutes. It didn't work very well wearing an environment suit, but the suit did offer a lot of padding, and I only got the wind knocked out of me. A few seconds later I got up, unsealed the helmet, and peeled it off.

The humidity hit me like a slap in the face from a wet towel, and I felt the sweat pop out on my forehead. Still, it was an improvement over smelling recycled Fetterman like I had for the last day and a half. I looked the chute assembly over, decided there was no way I could get it down out of the tree without some equipment, and set out to find the container.

I had a general idea of where the enduraplast cylinder had come down, having seen its chute deploy and figured it was about two hundred meters away. It turned out to be closer to half a klick and took me until the next morning to locate it. I spent the night in the environment suit, buried beneath the vine and thorn choked branches of a bramble thicket, cursing the whole operation in general and the people who had thought it up in particular, and wishing to hell I had a weapon of some kind, even if it were only Peterson's glass resin and ceramic knife.

Around ten the next morning I spotted the container, hanging from the trees overhead. There was a severance mechanism that was supposed to separate the container from the chute in case it got hung up in the trees, but it had failed to fire. Apparently, with the barometric altimeter being inaccurately calibrated, the device had failed to realize it was caught in the trees and still thought it was fifty or a hundred meters up in the air. I spent a fruitless hour tossing branches at the damned thing trying to get it to slip loose, then finally resigned myself to the notion that if I wanted it, I'd have to shinny up the tree and try to shake it down.

That proved to be impossible to do in the environment suit, so after falling on my duff a couple of times, I squirmed my way out of the suit and crawled up the tree buck naked, barking my shins, elbows, and other assorted anatomical appendages in the process. At least with my fingers and toes I could hold on to the moss covered surface of the trunk.

I finally made it up to the necessary height and crawled out onto the limb where the canopy was fouled, having no idea at all how I was going to be able to work that polyfilm fabric off those branches. If I'd had a knife, it would have been a simple enough task to cut the container free, but the only knife I'd been provided was the monstrosity inside the container, and to get to that, I had to get the container down out of the tree.

It turned out to be far simpler than I'd imagined and much more dangerous. As I crawled out on the limb, it bent under my weight and the canopy slipped free, dropping the container to the ground where it buried itself nose first in the soil and remained upright. The branch, suddenly unburdened of over sixty kilograms of weight, popped back upward and I was swept over the side, nearly losing my grip entirely. While I hung there by my hands beneath the limb with the breeze blowing through my short hairs, the damned release mechanism on the chute finally decided it was low enough and the explosive filled krylon bolts popped off, one of them whizzing right between my legs, as the canopy and lines disconnected.

I hung there for a second or two until I realized that I wasn't going to fall off the limb, be emasculated by flying debris, or piss in my non-existent pants, then hauled myself carefully back up on the limb and hugging it like a long lost lover slowly worked my way by centimeters back to the main trunk and carefully picked my way down that.

I walked over to the equipment container and pushed against it gently to see if it would fall. It didn't, so I pushed in the little access plate and pulled out on the opening toggle to pop the hatch. The container split open and dumped all my gear out onto the jungle floor. Then the cannister decided to fall, and toppled over on top of everything.

I rolled the container aside and found the camouflaged coverall that looked like an ad for a botanical garden, slipped into it, and hunted through the pile until I found my gun, knife, and boots. The knife had its own velcro belt and tie down strap so I fastened it around my waist and thigh, pulled on my socks, and laced up my boots. Funny how after all these decades, laces are still the best way to fasten a pair of good hiking boots to your feet. I found the IFF transponder, made sure it was switched off so I wouldn't be beeping out my position to any enemy snooping devices, and strapped it and the chronometer to my wrist. Then I checked, loaded, and rechecked the flechette carbine and snapped it into its overgrown shoulder holster. After that, I piled everything else up in a heap, stuffed the chute inside the container, and dug out the little folding-handled entrenching tool made out of lexan. It took me forty-five minutes to dig a hole big enough to bury the damned container.

After that I found my camouflaged boonie hat, buckled on the combat harness and shouldered the pack, both of them camouflaged with little plastiform leaves to match the coverall and hat, and headed back toward where my own chute still hung in the treetops. The jungle growth was pretty thick, but I had a pretty fair idea where I was heading, and it only took me about half an hour to find the thing. Cutting it down was another matter entirely. I finally had to cut a couple of the lower branches off another tree and lash them together to form a sort of rudimentary ladder long enough that I could reach the lower branches of the tree my chute was caught in. I climbed up, worked my way out to the chute, and cut it free with the big knife, which, as Peterson had promised, worked quite well. Then I climbed back down and buried it, too.

Having finally finished cleaning up after myself, I shot a bearing with the excellent Silva compass and headed off in the general direction of the rescue ship landing site. According to the magnetometer studies that had been conducted by long range sensor scan from the fleet and telemetry from the rescue ship and Masterson's Pathfinders, the compass should have been fairly accurate. A directional radio bearing relayed from the fleet or homing directly on the telemetry transmissions of the rescue ship or the still open mike from the Pathfinders would have been completely accurate, but it would also have been detectable. At least it would have been detectable with current SCAF technology, and when you're dealing with an unknown enemy, you have to assume that his technology is at least on a level with yours; therefore, Peterson and Stryker had decided I'd have to make do with a plain old magnetic compass. Well, at least it beat hell out of using dead reckoning or a sextant.

At mid-morning on the third day I came across three separate sets of tracks, two of them with the characteristic lug sole tread of my own SCAF issued boots. The size of the footprints told me they belonged to either two women or two small men, and the narrowness of the prints made the female hypothesis more probable. The position of the tracks, where one had apparently squatted down to examine the other, suggested that the slightly smaller of the two was following the other. It made me wonder why. The tracks were at least a couple of days old, judging from the way the corners had been rounded down by the nightly rain's efforts to wash them away. I couldn't tell more precisely than that. I'm a soldier with some combat tracker sense, not a Kalahari bushman or an American Plains Indian. Everything I know about tracking is learned, not innate.

All the tracks meant to me was that a couple of SCAF troopers, probably women, had been through the area, possibly as recently as two days ago, which would mean someone had survived the attack on the Pathfinder camp, and possibly as long ago as a week earlier, in which case whoever made them could now be dead, along with everyone else at the rescue ship site.

The disturbing thing was the other set of tracks. They had a vague similarity to a naked human footprint, but were far too long and narrower than any woman's foot I'd ever seen. The toes were exceedingly long, and ended in claws, judging from the narrow indentations in the soil in front of the toes. I finally determined that there were in fact two separate sets of the strange tracks. I'd missed it at first because both sets were so nearly the same size, but I finally caught on because one of the left footprints had a sort of splayed little toe. The damned things reminded me of nothing else quite so much as a cross between a human print and a cat's paw, considerably enlarged and elongated. On an alien world like this, by themselves the prints would have been only a strange curiosity. The unsettling thing was, their position made it obvious that *they* were tracking the two SCAF soldiers. I didn't like the looks of that at all.

I would have liked to follow both sets of tracks, the strange looking ones and the SCAF bootprints. I had a nasty suspicion those two troopers were going to need help. But the mission comes first, and I had my orders. All I could do was wish them luck and hope they had enough sense to watch their backtrails.

I found the landing site about noon on the fourth day. I didn't just walk right in and have myself a look around. I spent the rest of the day and the night observing the clearing around the ship and scouting the surrounding terrain. I found a lot of bootprints, a lot of the strange catlike footprints, and a handful of very dead SCAF soldiers, at least two of which had apparently killed each other. The next morning I watched the clearing until about ten hundred hours, and then switched on the IFF transponder and went in.

I knew what I'd find. I'd been smelling it for almost twenty-four hours. Decay sets in quickly in the jungle, and the jungle of Alpha Tauri Five was no exception. On Earth there would have been clouds of flies busily raising maggots on the fetid, bloating remains by now, but if Aldebaran Five had an equivalent winged pest, they'd been kept out by the Light Point Defense System which was still quietly humming in the center of the clearing. The laser had let the various bacteria through, though, and they had done their job, just as they would have on Earth.

Painstakingly, I searched through the bodies with a growing sense of despair and fear tinged with hope. These people had slaughtered each other. The incredible array of carnage affected even my hardened combat sensibilities. There were bodies mangled by hypervelocity frangible bullets. Bodies mutilated by high explosive grenades. Bodies burned, scorched, decapitated, dismembered, and hacked to pieces. In all my years in a hundred combats on Tau Ceti Four and half a dozen brushfire wars back on Earth, I'd never seen anything like it.

And not one single, solitary, enemy body among them.

Well, that wasn't quite true. There was one. I found it when I checked out the rescue ship. A storage compartment had been modified into a sort of walk-in meat freezer, and neatly stacked up inside it were the bodies of half a dozen SCAF personnel and an alien. It was part human and part cat and part something else. I don't know what exactly, I couldn't put my finger on it. Part alien I guess. I checked the feet, and they were consistent with the tracks I had found.

Finding the makeshift meat locker stacked full of bodies and the alien was the final macabre twist on the whole nightmare scene. I went back outside and knelt down next to the ship, looking very much the part of a stray bush that had wandered into the clearing and set down for a rest. My duty at this point was pretty clear. I should go back in the ship and break comm silence, use its communications gear to contact the fleet and advise them of the situation at the landing site, and that their much desired specimen of indigenous Alpha Tauran life form was still intact in the freezer. That would undoubtedly alter my mission profile and I'd be ordered to safeguard the Tauran until the fleet could land the PAI Brigade it had standing by to secure an airhead.

But there were other considerations. From the looks of the self-inflicted massacre surrounding me, I wasn't all that sure that landing a brigade wouldn't simply result in a few thousand more dead SCAF soldiers, and right now, the LPDS seemed to be doing a satisfactory job of keeping the specimen in the cooler secure. The corpse in the locker had a transponder strapped to its wrist. Evidently the Pathfinders had had to put a transponder on the thing before the LPDS would let them bring it into the perimeter, even dead, therefore, the Taurans couldn't enter the safe zone of the intruder detector system without getting lazed, and they didn't know what a transponder was, because all the corpses outside the perimeter had been wearing theirs when I found them. Further, the Taurans wouldn't be figuring out what a transponder was either, because I'd followed SOP and collected the weapons, transponders, and one set of dog tags from each of the corpses I'd found, all of which were now piled up next to the LPDS itself.

Besides that, my original orders had been to make a reconnaissance of the landing site and as much of the surrounding area as I deemed advisable, in an effort to determine what had happened at the rescue ship, *and* to attempt to locate Brigadier General Andersohn if possible and determine what had happened to her. I'd been given ten days to do the task. Thus far, I'd used four of them. I now knew what had happened to the

Pathfinders, although I didn't know why. That left the second part of the mission still unfinished.

I knew from what Stryker had told me that the rescue ship crew had only been able to determine the general area in which Andersohn's ship had gone down. That without the emergency beacon which should have been activated if the general's ship had crashed, finding it would be a time consuming process requiring an airborne search with the scout helicopter carried aboard the rescue ship, and extensive magnetic aberration detection studies. Something had killed the S&R crew before they got the chance to carry out those studies, and the follow-up missions had been concerned with finding out what happened to the search and rescue team, not the brigadier. I couldn't fly a scoutcopter, and I didn't know how to conduct a magnetic aberration detection study.

And there was one other consideration. I'd checked all the bodies inside and outside the perimeter carefully, every last one of them. Lara Masterson's body was not among them.

When Stryker and Peterson had told me the officer in charge of the Pathfinder Hard Landing Force was Captain Lara Masterson, I hadn't known whether to laugh or cry. After finding out I'd been frozen like that Tauran specimen in the ship for sixty-one years, I'd given Lara up as lost. I'd figured she'd either be dead by now, or on some ship headed for the other side of the galaxy. Then they'd told me she was on Aldebaran Five, alive and well, for the moment at least, and that there was a chance I'd get to see her again. Then things had gone sour down here and they'd lost all contact. Lara was presumed dead, along with everybody else. I'd spent a lot of time during that day and a half I was locked in the weapons bay of the recon ship thinking what it would feel like when I found her body, to have come so far, across so many light years and so many decades, only to have her snatched away at the final moment by some capricious twist of fate, my final act of our relationship being to bury her in the soil of an alien planet so far from home.

I'd agreed to the mission to begin with only because of the possibility of seeing Lara again, and when circumstances indicated she'd be dead when I found her, I'd continued with the mission so that I might see her again even if it was only in death. It wasn't exactly the sort of motivation I'd have expected of a soldier with my background, but then I'd never been in love before. If this was love. I'd never been in love, so I wasn't sure that this was love, but I was sure I wanted to find out, and there was only one way to do that. Sixty-one years was a long time. I wasn't sure Lara would still feel the same way about me. But I was sure I wanted to find that out as well, and there was only one way to do that too.

Peterson had said I was a natural born survivor. Lara Masterson was too. Her body wasn't among the dead, and I had seen two sets of SCAF bootprints being followed by a couple of Taurans moving away from the clearing toward a high rocky escarpment I'd spotted on my way down in the chute. I made my decision. It might wind up costing me a summary court-martial, but I didn't give a shit.

I checked the magazine in the SETAC meatgrinder, shouldered my pack, and walked out of the clearing and back into the jungle of Aldebaran Five.

9

Masterson, Lara
Hard Landing Force Charlie, SCAF

I'll always blame myself for the fact that the cat-people found us. Even if it really wasn't my fault. I'll always feel like it was. Sometime around 0330 I woke up and had to go. Since I didn't want to risk climbing down out of the tree in the dark and didn't feel like wetting myself, I just worked my way out of the harness and thermal blanket, pulled down my BDU's, and hung my rear out over the limb and let go. Sometime later one of them must have passed beneath the tree and noticed the unusual odor. At any rate, I'll always believe that's how they found us.

The jungle was just coming alive with the early morning cacophony as the night creatures gave way to those of daylight. It was still the gray, pre-dawn twilight, but I was cold, and my muscles were stiff, and I wanted to get down out of the damned tree and get on with it.

I hadn't slept well, not that you can ever sleep really well tied to a tree some dozen meters above the ground on a strange planet. I'd dreamed. For the first time in years I'd dreamed of home, of Daddy and Mom, and my little sister Tara. I'd dreamed, after we moved to Illinois, of our little house in Bloomington, out near the airport, and how we used to sit out on the step in the evening and watch the Metroliners come in to land from New Chicago and North St. Louis, and later watch the stars come out, and how Daddy would point to each one, and tell me its name, if it had one, and then point to Aldebaran and say, "See that one, Lara? That's Aldebaran, the eye of the Bull. Someday people from Earth will go there. Someday they'll go to all the stars."

He was quite a dreamer I guess, my father. Maybe all fathers are, at least when it comes to hoping for their little girls' futures.

It's funny how dreams have a way of coming true, but not the way we expect them to. I'd left Earth eighty-seven years ago. All my family was dead now, except possibly my little sister who might be in a retirement home somewhere, if they still had those kind of places on Earth. Yet the dream had come to pass. People from Earth had gone to the eye of the Bull and had met the Aldebarans who lived there. And the Aldebarans had killed them.

I'd dreamed also of Steve McAllif, a young soldier who'd been drafted under the Universal Juvenile Conscription Act, like I had. He'd been my first boyfriend and my first lover. I'd given up my virginity to him on the top bunk in our squad bay aboard the Assault Training Transport *Erwin Rommel* before I was fourteen. I hadn't really loved him, but I'd liked him a lot, and he'd been my lover for about five years. He died in the tunnel fighting on Tau Ceti Four. I killed the Tau who killed him, then held Steve while he died.

And finally I'd dreamed about Tony Fetterman, a man not all that much older than myself that I'd feared when I met him, later hated him, later still come to respect him, and finally to love. I'd slept with him only once. I hadn't slept with anyone since. There had been offers; I just hadn't been interested. He was both lover and love and father figure to me. I guess that sounds a little incestuous. I don't really care if it does.

The weird thing was, in my dreams. I'd seen my parents and sister grow old and die. I'd seen Steve McAllif die too. It was almost like a reaffirmation of their deaths. But Tony, who I'd actually held in my arms while he bled to death after he'd tripped a geophone triggered land mine on Tau Ceti Four, didn't die. The mine went off and he went down and I held him and cried, and then he got up and walked away. I couldn't figure out what it meant, except maybe that I hadn't really accepted his death yet. It was something I'd have to come to grips with someday. He'd died just after the final battle of the campaign, in a Tau Cetian polar rain forest, over sixty years ago.

Anyway, I hadn't slept well and my joints were stiff, and there was enough light to see well enough to climb down, so I just said to hell with it, and figured we'd get an early start. I worked my way down the tree, avoiding several snakes and what looked like an owl covered with porcupine quills roosting in the lower branches, and made my way over to Chang's tree. She answered my whistle and climbed down, and I was just telling her how I sure could go for a good cup of nice hot coffee, when the cat-people jumped us.

There must have been about a dozen of them in the pack, and they came at us all together in a rush, from half a dozen different directions. They came in low and surprisingly fast, snarling like lions. Their line of attack wasn't exactly direct. They came in at sort of an angle, then pivoted at the last instant and leaped directly at us. I saw or heard or sensed them first, and shouted a warning to Chang, but she was quicker to react than I was, and I heard the bolt of her suppressed submachine gun chatter like a playing card in a bicycle wheel and watched two of the beasts come apart in midair.

I swung around and dropped to one knee with my back to the trunk of Chang's tree, and brought my battle carbine up, snapping off the safety. I put a three-round burst into the face of another of the cat-people and watched its nose and whiskers disappear in a fine spray of red and gray mist as the back of its head exploded, but the thing had too much forward momentum and kept on coming until it hit me, knocking me to the ground. I shoved the cat-man off of me, rolled to the side, and came up drawing a bead on another one. My finger tightened on the trigger and the gun *burruped*, But I don't know if the rounds connected or not because at that exact moment, another one coming in from the side connected his forepaw-hand with the side of my head, and snapped the back of my skull up against the tree trunk. The last thing I saw before everything went black was about a billion exploding supernovas.

●　　●　　●

When I came to, my wrists, elbows, knees, and ankles had been tied together with some kind of rough cord or vine and I was hanging painfully from a tree branch that bounced along on the shoulders of two of the cat-men, while vines and saw-toothed grasses tore at my face.

Chang, similarly bound, was bouncing along behind me, and behind her I could occasionally catch a glimpse of one of the Aldebarans being carried in a like fashion. I presumed he had the advantage of being dead, and therefore not suffering the way Chang and I were every time the cat-men took a step and the pole bounced on their shoulders, causing the vines to cut into our wrists and ankles.

The Aldebarans, as I now thought of them, seemed to be having considerable difficulty carrying us in such a fashion and frequently stopped to readjust the load or take a breather, dropping us unceremoniously to the ground whenever the mood moved them. The only thing good I could say about it was that at least when they dropped us, they weren't dragging us head first through the saw grass.

I gathered from the way I'd seen them move when they attacked us that they could run quite well on all fours, or hop about on their hindlegs in a fashion that would make a kangaroo green as a eucalyptus leaf with envy, but they seemed to have trouble walking upright. It was kind of a half shuffling, half hopping gait, and every step bounced the pole I was hung on and in turn bounced me until I thought my back was going to break and my arms and legs be pulled out of their sockets. Every minute of time spent slung on that pole was an eternity of agony, but my mouth was so dry and I ached so much that I didn't have the energy to scream. Besides, I wouldn't give the bastards that satisfaction. Behind me I could hear Chang gasp sharply whenever she took a particularly brutal bounce, but for the most part, she maintained an inscrutably oriental silence, which was pretty impressive for a third generation transplanted valley girl from Visalia, California. We were both busy acting brave for the other's benefit, but the truth of the matter, I knew, was that we were both too chicken to let the other see how damned scared we really were.

Every soldier who goes to combat for the first time is afraid of death. Don't let anybody tell you otherwise. If they do, they're lying. After you've been in a lot of combats, however, a funny thing happens. You stop being afraid of death, and start being afraid of dying. Death is just the absence of life, and that's going to happen to us all eventually, so finally you come to realize that there's no big deal there. What you worry about after that is dying, the manner of your death. Usually the biggest fear is related to the kind of work you do.

More snipers, I'm told, fear being shot in the face above anything else. Soldiers who've worked near napalm or with flamethrowers fear being burned to death. Tankers worry about being crushed beneath the treads of an armored fighting vehicle, and you'd be surprised how many submariners worry about drowning. Kind of makes you wonder why they'd want to get into a ship that was designed to sink.

But at least those are tangibles, concrete ways of dying that can be seen as well as imagined, and perhaps in being observed, their horror is lessened just a tiny bit. There are other deaths though, that are horrifying in the extreme because they can never be observed by the soldier in the field, only imagined.

I can't speak for Recon Marines or LRRPS, but I imagine it's the same for them as it is for Pathfinders. We spend most of our time working in small units deep in enemy territory, and the thing we come to fear most is the terrible, lingering death that comes only after weeks or months or years in enemy captivity. You can amuse yourself all night long by imagining all the ways to maim and mutilate a human body or break a human spirit, before finally destroying the man or woman that inhabits them.

So I was scared, and I knew it, and was determined not to let it show. And Chang was scared, and knew it, and was determined not to let it show. And we both knew that the other was scared and knew it, and was determined not to let it show, and we were both determined not to let it show that we knew the other knew and was determined not to let it show that she knew. So we both stayed very brave, lying to ourselves that we were lying to each other about not being scared.

When I got done making myself crazy with that kind of thinking, I tried to puzzle out our enemy. Occasionally one would growl or snarl or shake its head or body in a certain way, which I supposed was the Aldebaran equivalent of verbal communications, but they didn't bother trying to talk to us. Further, they didn't seem to have much of a developed technology. True, they did wear a kind of loincloth, which seemed to indicate a modestly developed textile capability, and a societal structure that demanded a certain amount of personal modesty, but I'd seen no weapons of any kind, not even a knife. I suppose the argument could be made that with teeth and claws like they had, they really didn't need much in the way of weapons, but it wasn't exactly the sort of development you'd expect from a race that could wipe out an entire company of SCAF Pathfinders in a matter of a few minutes.

I had to remind myself that things were not always as they appeared. The inhabitants of Tau Ceti Four had been a race of Amazonian women, who in a reversal of typical insect hive structure had served as workers in a highly regimented and controlled culture to a bare handful of Tau princes and kings, an agrarian society that relied primarily on hand tools and a vast pool of cheap human labor, and whose military capability at the outset of the war had been limited to edged weapons and a few crude firearms. Yet they were a race of vast collective intellect and enormous mimicry and duplicative capacity, and by the end of the fighting, had been on the verge of producing an operational guided missile equipped with a fission bomb warhead that had very nearly cost us the entire campaign.

Still, I couldn't shake the feeling that we were dealing with a bunch of aboriginal savages here. Their dress and stoic manner conjured up history book images of the Plains Indians, and I half expected to see one of them produce a bow and arrow at some point, or to suddenly find myself surrounded by teepees or wickiups.

Even that level of technology would have surprised me somewhat. Since they didn't have an opposable thumb, it was kind of difficult to see how they could have made a bow or a bowstring. They didn't seem to have had any trouble weaving loincloths or producing the cord I was tied to a pole with, however, and I've seen surgeons tie sutures using only a forceps, so I suppose it's a bit egotistical of us humans to think only those species with thumbs can be smart. After all, dolphins only have flippers, and they don't make war on their own kind, and back nearly three hundred years ago, a bunch of technological primitives defeated the most powerful technological nation Earth had ever known in an insignificant little country named Vietnam. Maybe all a thumb is, is just a finger that got put on backward by mistake.

Late in the day they suddenly dropped us and ran off, leaving us tied to the poles, but apparently unattended. After fifteen or twenty minutes, when it became apparent they weren't going to come back right away, Chang and I started discussing how we might escape. After another half hour of frustrated effort, we discovered that no matter what we tried, there was no way we could untie ourselves from the poles. The situation wasn't helped much by the fact that our fingers were numb, but it wouldn't have mattered anyway. The way our arms had been rotated inward and the backs of our wrists tied together, there was just simply no way we could use our hands in concert with each other. Try untying a bunch of knots using only one hand sometime, and you'll get the idea.

After that, we just lay there in the heat, wishing we had something to drink and too tired to talk. The irony of the situation was that while they had taken our weapons, evidently understanding what could be dangerous, they'd left us our gear and Chang and I both had full canteens hanging on our belts. It was a punishment reminiscent of Tantalus.

About dark, they came back. One of them looked over our relative positions, and evidently correctly deduced that we'd been trying to untie each other. It summoned two others, and they stood there in a little triangle staring down at Chang and me. For a long time they just stood there, staring hard, and I started feeling really uneasy.

Then suddenly Chang broke loose, but instead of attacking the Aldebarans or running away, she attacked me. There was a look of such intense animal hatred in her face as I've never seen. She was practically foaming at the mouth, and her hands closed about my throat and started choking the life out of me. I tried to fight back, but I was helpless, tied as I was. I tried to reason with her, but couldn't speak, only gasp out a strangled, guttural cry. She kept squeezing and squeezing, and my lungs felt like they were going to burst or collapse, I don't know which, and everything started turning dark around the edges, and then, just as suddenly as it had started, Chang was back tied to her pole and we were both gasping for air, our chests heaving as the wind wheezed in and out of our lungs in great gulps.

I knew for a certainty then that they hadn't hit us with some kind of drug gas back at the rescue ship, and I understood why they didn't need any weapons beyond their own fangs and claws. You don't need an ultrasonic grenade or a laser beam when you can reach into your enemy's mind and make him believe that his buddies are trying to kill him. All you have to do is convince him that they *will* kill him if he doesn't kill them first, and let nature take its course. Why waste time and effort killing your enemy and exposing yourself to danger, when you can stand back safe outside the range of an automated defense system like the LPDS, and project mental images into your enemy's mind, so that he'll do the killing for you?

The little practical demonstration of the mental telepathy capability of the Aldebaran natives we'd just been given was their way of telling us not to try to escape again, if we knew what was good for us.

I didn't know if you could actually be willed to death, that is, if they could really kill you by simply making you believe you were dead, but I had heard of surgeons who had refused to operate on patients who were convinced they were going to die, and I'd seen soldiers die in combat from wounds that shouldn't have been fatal when they gave up the will to live. I had no doubt though, that if they set Chang and me on each other, we probably would kill each other. At least one of us would wind up a murderer and the other a victim. It wasn't a happy thought.

There was one comforting thought to the experience, however. The enemy had tipped his hand in a way I'm sure he'd never intended to. The bastards might be able to *put* images into my mind, but at least I knew they couldn't *read* minds. If they could have, they would have killed me on the spot.

I now knew how they'd killed my troops, and why they didn't need a lot of fancy gadgets for weapons, that they could make us see things that weren't there, create illusions like a magician, if you will, and that they couldn't read minds, even though they could fuck with them. I presumed that they were taking us back to their base, if they were soldiers, or at least their village if they weren't. The only really unanswered question that remained was why. Why bother to capture us at all? Why not simply make us kill each other like they had all the rest of my troops, and Chang's, and the SCAF Rangers, and the MP's and S&R crew?

Maybe there was a conventional military answer to it and they just needed some prisoners to interrogate. Or maybe they were just curious as to why we hadn't become casualties like everybody else. Or maybe like the ancient Romans they just fancied taking a few slaves as booty. Or maybe they were just trophy hunters and thought our heads would look nice mounted on the wall of some Aldebaran equivalent of a den.

I didn't have any really good answers to that one. The only thing I knew for sure was, whenever I found out the answer to that question, I had a pretty strong hunch that I wasn't going to like it much.

10

She that runs swifter than the shadows of the night, but chooses the path of aloneness to preserve the land and the waters, the grasslands and the forest, the fish and the animals, in the ancient ways of our forebearers.

All life is a circle. All death is a circle. The rains that come in the middle of the darkness bring life to the waters and to the soil, and the sun that comes in the time of light brings life to the waters and the soil. The fish are born and live and die in the waters, and return their life force to the waters. The waters give up their life force to the heavens during the heat of the day, and the heavens rain down their life force upon the soil in the time of darkness. Plants are born and live and die in the soil and give up their life force to the creatures of the land. And the creatures of the land are born and live, taking their life force from the plants of the soil or the fish of the waters, and then they too die, and decay, and return their life force to the soil. In time, the soil is washed into the waters by the rains, and returns its life to the waters, and so the circle of life and of death is complete, while the Great Spirit of the Chat, which brings the Moons and the Sun, watches over all.

Thus it was, in the time of our Ancient Forebearers, whom we revere, thus it is now, and thus it shall be forever more, so long as there lives a single descendant of the Great Spirit Chat.

In the Dark Time of History, there came invaders to the

Land of the Chat, where all life and death is a circle. And
these invaders came from the great frozen North, from the
mountains and the valleys of the Everlasting Cold, in the Land
at the Top of the World. And in that vast, frozen land, these
invaders called themselves the Yillii, which meant masters of
the land and all that walk upon it, and of the sky and all that
fly in it, and of the water and all that swim in it. But in truth,
they were masters of nothing, for theirs was a barren, frozen
land.

It is said that the Greatest Spirit of Them All, the Great
Zum Prim Chat Hoiu Tichloucotyl Yil Rhi Kitchimanitou created the Land of the Everlasting Cold when the Sacred World
was young, in the Time of the Great Beginning, when She
scattered the stars in the heavens and made the World, and
divided the soil from the waters and the heavens, and made all
the other Great Spirits so that She might have company and
need not live alone.

And the Great Spirits, seeing that this land was so vast and
so barren, said to the Great Zum Prim Chat Hoiu Tichloucotyl
Yil Rhi Kitchimanitou, "Tell us, O Great Mother of us all,
why have you made such a place? You who have created the
beautiful lands of the jungle and the forest and the grassland,
why have You made a place that is cold and barren, and where
nothing grows but discontent?"

And the Great Zum Prim Chat Hoiu Tichloucotyl Yil Rhi
Kitchimanitou said to them, "I have done this thing My Children, because our Golden Age shall not last forever. There
will come a time when there will be those among you who
will turn greedy and envious of the others, and you shall make
war upon your sisters and your brothers, and slay them all
save one, and you yourselves shall in turn all be slain save
one. And when that time comes, the greed and envy that some
of you harbor even now in your heart of hearts, will banish
you all forever from our Paradise in the Heavens. And the
fallen in battle I shall gather up with me, and those who have
kept the Faith shall travel far with me, and build a new world,
while those who have not kept the Faith shall be no more
forever. But the two of you who shall survive will live upon
the face of the World I have created, but only as creatures of
that World, and not as Spirits. And of the two of you who will

survive, to the one who has kept Faith with me is given the land of the jungle and forest and grasslands and the stewardship thereof, and to the one who has broken Faith with me by his greed and envy and craving for power is given the mastery he seeks, but only over the Land of Everlasting Cold and its great barrenness. For he who is empty inside is deserving only of such emptiness. And the two of you who do survive, you and all the generations of your litters and your litters's litters will live like animals upon the face of the World, until I come again from the Heavens to take you back with me to our Paradise among the stars. And in that time, while you live upon the World, there will be war between you."

And hearing this, the other Great Spirits were very much afraid, but the Great Zum Prim Chat Hoiu Tichloucotyl Yil Rhi Kitchimanitou said, "Fear not, My Children. For all life and death is a circle, even as My own is, and there will come a time when I will return, and when I return I will send down a messenger to the World I have created and my messenger will walk upon it as a strange new creature, and none shall know him by his presence, save one of the Faithful, who will see him and recognize his true form. For he shall come as a friend of the Children of the Faithful, and an enemy of their enemies, and his friends shall be friends of the Children of the Faithful and his enemies their enemies. And when that time comes, I will lift the Children of the Faithful out of the Darkness and deliver them from their enemies, and the Land of Everlasting Cold shall be no more, forever."

Thus it was foretold to the Great Spirits by the Greatest Spirit of them all, that there would come the Great Battle, and with it, upon the World would fall the Time of Darkness, but that in the fullness of the Everlasting Circle, there would come again a time of Deliverance.

In time, there came the prophesied Great Battle, and with it, the Twilight of the Great Spirits, but as had been foretold, two survived, one who would be Master, and one who had kept the Faith. And the one who kept the Faith was the Great Spirit Chat, whose name means World, and the Great Spirit Chat retold the prophesy to her litters, and they to theirs and so on, down through all the generations, until today.

And the offspring of the Great Spirit Chat were themselves

called the Chat, which is their word for World, for the life and
the death of the Chat were as one with the life and the death of
the World in the Everlasting Chat. And throughout all the
generations, the Chat kept the Faith, even though they were
decimated ten times over by their enemies, and ten times
again. And they kept their stewardship over the World despite
the efforts of their enemies to master it. So it was in the time
of our Ancient Forebearers, and so it remains today.

It was foretold that the enemy of my enemy shall be my
friend, and that the enemy of my friend shall also be my
enemy. Thus it was foretold to our Ancient Forebearers, and
thus it remains today.

There is a strange new creature that walks upon the soil of
the World. It is unlike any that any Chat has ever seen in
living memory, nor are there descriptions of it in any of our
folklore. It walks upright, like the enemies of my people, yet
it resembles neither them nor us. It does not speak our language, nor follow our ways, nor does it speak or follow theirs.
Its body is pale, like the light of day or the color of the stars.
It wears strange skins upon its body, after the fashion of our
enemies, but the skins are the colors of the jungle and the
night, like our own, and yet not alike, but not like those of our
enemies either. We do not take the skins of the creatures that
we hunt, but perhaps they must take them to keep warm, since
they have so little hair upon their bodies. I do not think they
wear them as ornaments like the Yillii, for the Yillii wear
skins of different colors, but the strangers wear skins that are
nearly all the same.

The strange creatures are the enemies of the Yillii. When
first I saw them, I thought them merely some new animal the
Yillii had hunted for pleasure, for the Yillii apparently do not
hunt them for food. They were so easily mastered, as the
Yillii master all lesser creatures. Yet I have seen since that the
strangers are capable of fighting the Yillii and killing them.
They kill with great speed, and at a distance, and with a terrible finality, through the magical power of strange objects that
they carry about in their forepaws. In the entire history of the
Chat, there is no memory of any creature that kills in such a
fashion. It is as though they invoke the power of the Greatest
of the Great Spirits, and send lightning bolts to do their killing

for them. Perhaps this is as it should be, for their fangs and claws are poor excuses for those of a hunter, short, and worn down smooth. Yet there is no creature known to exist in the World which kills in this manner, and even the Chat have never been able to befriend the lightning and hunt with them.

I do not know where these strangers come from, but I have seen one of them fall from the sky on a great and strange wing, made not of feathers, but of an unknown skin. It is said in the lore of the Chat that the Great Spirits themselves fell from the heavens, and it is foretold in the prophesy that one day a strange creature will come down from the heavens and walk upon the World, and that his enemies will be my enemies, and my enemies his.

I know that birds too, come from the sky, and many insects, and the sunlight and the rain and the lightning, and that none of these things are messengers from the Greatest of the Great Spirits, the Zum Prim Chat Hoiu Tichloucotyl Yil Rhi Kitchimanitou. But these strange new creatures that fall from the sky and walk upon the World are not birds or insects or sunlight or rain, and they kill with the flash of lightning and the roar of thunder. And the Yillii are their enemies.

But the prophesy foretold of only one messenger, not an entire tribe of them.

I have decided that I shall go to the stranger I saw fall from the sky, and I shall speak with him, even though he may slay me with thunder and lightning, and I shall ask of him three questions.

I shall ask, "Are you a messenger from the Greatest of the Great Spirits, the Zum Prim Chat Hoiu Tichloucotyl Yil Rhi Kitchimanitou?"

And I shall ask, "Are you an enemy of the Yillii?"

And finally I shall ask him, "Will you hunt with me?"

For whether he is a messenger from the Spirit World or not, if the Yillii are indeed his enemies, I will hunt with him, for the enemy of my enemy is my friend. Thus it was foretold in the time of our Ancient Forebearers, and thus it remains today.

11

Fetterman, Anthony B.
Major General (Simulated)
Seventh Rangers (Detached),
Fleet/STC JOITF, SCAF

It took awhile to pick the trail back up again. I tried to find it at first in the region of the dead SCAF basecamp, and worked the east side of the perimeter for several hours without picking up a trace. Finally I worked my way along the slope of the hill to the south of the rescue ship landing site, and after about an hour, cut across a faint set of lone SCAF bootprints.

They weren't the ones I was looking for, however. The soldier who had made these had a much longer foot than either of the prints I'd spotted on my way into the camp, and a much longer stride, too. I judged from the distance between them, and the fact that most of them were prints only of the ball of the foot, that the owner must have stood a shade over two meters tall and been moving with the speed of an Olympic class sprinter when he or she had made the prints. It suggested to me that at least one other person had escaped the madness back at the ship, at least temporarily.

It also got me started on a different tract of thought.

The soldiers back at the rescue ship had clearly killed each other. You didn't have to be a forensic pathologist to see that. I didn't know what had made them do it, but something had made them crazy and they'd killed each other.

All except for a few who had managed to run away. Why they hadn't turned on their fellow troopers and joined the killing was a bit of a mystery. There only seemed to be one factor in common. Those who had run away had done so by themselves. The pair of prints I'd found a few days ago hadn't started out together. One of them had picked up on the other's trail and followed along it later, that had been clear enough from the tracks, and had suggested to me that the people who made the prints had not been part of any organized patrol. My sprinter hadn't had any company with her, either. It made sense. If your buddies suddenly started trying to kill you for no good reason, you'd do one of two things. You'd either try to kill them before they killed you, or you'd run like hell and try to get away from everybody, and I mean *everybody,* as fast as you could. There was one other choice, of course. You could just stand there and die, but SCAF Pathfinders aren't trained to throw their lives away like that.

So given that a few people had survived, and that they'd want to get as far away from everybody as they could, I played the hunch that they'd run in opposite directions. I cut back through the death camp and worked the north side of it until I finally picked up a set of prints that looked to be about the right size and shape and mostly up on the balls of the feet, suggesting that the owner was making tracks like a scared rabbit.

I followed the meandering path through the bush until I came to a spot where the fleeing soldier had apparently run headlong into a tree. Glancing around for the trail, I almost overlooked the camouflaged object with the slightly familiar outline, but it was lying with the open end up, and my eye caught the out of place color of the off-white plastifoam padding inside. It was a newer model than the last one I'd used, but there was no mistaking it for something other than what it was. A SCAF battle helmet. I walked over and picked it up, and checked the sweatband on the inside. There, neatly stenciled in block letters according to regulations, was all the encouragement I needed: MASTERSON, L. SCAF 482373164.

I knelt there on my knees, and held that helmet in my hands, and for the first time in thirty and a half years, or a hundred and eleven, depending on how you wanted to do your counting, I cried.

Don't think I'm some kind of softie who goes all maudlin at the drop of a hat. It's just that Lara Masterson and I had

been through a lot together. We were just about the last of the
dinosaurs from the Old Corps. There aren't that many of us
left from the First SCAF Retribution Army. Besides, we'd
meant something special to each other once, at least, I hoped
we had. I knew she'd meant something very special to me.
She understood better than most what it means to be a soldier,
being a damned good one herself, and could love one anyway.
She'd never actually said it, and neither had I, but that didn't
matter. There are a lot of things in life that don't get said that
should, but sometimes they don't have to be. Sometimes you
just know.

Anyway, the stress of the situation, of thinking she was
dead, finding out she was alive, thinking she was dead again,
and then finally finding some tangible proof that she was still
alive, that she had at least survived the attack on the camp,
was just too much, added into the not inconsiderable stress I
was already under from all the other sources. So I cried a
little, so what's the big deal? Finding the helmet was the best
news I, or SCAF for that matter, had had in a long while. The
assumption had been that if Lara were alive, she'd have contacted the fleet somehow, since she'd been the officer in command at the scene. The footprints and the helmet suggested
that she was still alive, but couldn't contact the fleet because
she'd lost her comm link when she'd lost the helmet. If she
were alive, she could provide an eyewitness account of what,
precisely, had happened. SCAF might not applaud her common sense in running away the way I did, but they'd damned
sure want to know all the details of how an entire company of
trained Pathfinders could be induced to murder each other.

Without a neutrino power pack, the helmet was useless to
me except as a memento, and my basic orders called for me to
maintain comm silence anyway, so I buried the helmet beneath
some ferns at the base of the tree and took out the big knife to
notch the tree so it would be easier for me to identify it again.
The gigantic glass and ceramic resin blade once again worked
better than I'd imagined it would, but the tree wouldn't stay
marked very well. As soon as I cut through the bark, some
kind of milky white sap oozed out into the cuts and gummed
over them, then immediately started turning grayish brown to
match the trunk. It was evidently some form of natural self-

repairing mechanism, but it did leave little ridges where the gashes had been, so at least there was the possibility that there might be some identifiable trace later on.

I followed Masterson's trail until it got too dark to see it anymore, then spent the night in a tree, brushing a big, ming-blue spider about the size of my double fist off my leg with my boonie hat in the morning before he could take an undue interest in me. The spindly legged little fellow had been busily constructing a web between some of my plastiform leaves, evidently figuring I looked like I'd make a good home for him.

I picked up the trail again easily enough, and in late morning came to the spot where the second set of bootprints joined hers, and followed both along. I probably moved quicker than common sense dictated, until late afternoon when I ran into a stretch where the trees weren't quite so close together and the extra light from above had allowed the undergrowth to come up in a tangled profusion. It was harder to follow the tracks there, and just plain harder to walk. There were places I could see where the two people I was following had had to cut their way through the brush. I followed suit, and to my pleasant surprise, found that the big, light bladed knife made a fairly effective machette. After that, I made reasonably good progress until nightfall when I had to stop again.

Early the next morning, I came upon a scene that once again dashed my hopes. The Tauran cat-people had evidently caught up with Masterson and whomever was now traveling with her, and some kind of battle had ensued. I found a large, scuffed out and trampled down area at the base of a big tree with a couple of empty submachine gun magazines and an assortment of equipment scattered about. There was a canteen and cup, some field ration concentrates still in their wrappers, a thermal foil blanket, several grenades, most of the contents of a standard issue SCAF survival kit, one of the new battle carbines I'd read about that fires the 3mm hypervelocity frangible bullets, a Pathfinder's Personal Defense Weapon, and a tiger-striped boonie hat like they issue to Marine Force Recon personnel. A little ways away I found the SMG the empty magazines belonged to. It was an old Kalan M-K, the kind we used to use that fired the 9x25mm caseless expanding boat-tail hollowpoints, with a 25 centimeter sound suppressor screwed onto the barrel. It had SCAF RF/A markings overstamped with *Imperial Marines*. Evidently Masterson's traveling companion had been a survivor of the Recon team that had been sent in to find out what happened to the Ranger platoon.

It was a tough decision to make, choosing what to do with all the weaponry. The grenades and the Kalan especially were tempting. The Kalan I was familiar with, had used before, and it at least looked like a weapon, but I finally decided against any of it. The grenades were unfamiliar models to me, not that I really was well acquainted with the ones I'd been issued, but Peterson had assured me that they all had three to five second delay fuses. I had no idea if the ones I'd found were contact or delay detonated, or what the time delay might be. Some of them might even be zero delay fused, designed for boobytraping. If I pulled the pin on one of those, it would be the last grenade I'd ever throw. Further, every bit of my equipment had been predicated on a minimally detectable hypothesis, very little metal or electronic circuitry. The Kalan wasn't very big, but it *was* stainless steel, and I still had no clear picture of what kind of electronic warfare capability the enemy had. Suppose they *did* have magnetic aberration detection equipment available to them and I decided to carry the Kalan. I figured I didn't need that kind of trouble. Seismic intruder detection equipment and infrared heat-seeking scans were plenty enough for me to worry about without inviting more problems. I finally wrapped all the stuff up in the thermal foil blanket and buried it.

I was a bit surprised that the enemy hadn't bothered to collect it. You'd have thought they'd have wanted it for the intelligence value or as souvenirs if nothing else. I had no doubt that the enemy could have collected it if they'd wanted to. The signs of the struggle, the presence of all the empty magazines and all the discarded weapons, and the complete absence of any bodies, either SCAF or Tauran, pointed to the conclusion that Lara and her companion had been surprised, overwhelmed, and captured. It wasn't exactly the best news I'd had all day.

But it got worse.

There's an old Ranger saying that it's always darkest just

before the storm. I think it goes along with the one that you can lead a horse to water, but he'll probably piss in it. It's kind of like the corollary to Technical Sergeant Murphy's Law. You know who Murphy was, the guy who said that if anything can go wrong, it will. Well the corollary goes something like this: Murphy was an optimist, and an optimist is somebody who doesn't understand the situation.

Anyway, I'd just finished burying the equipment and was struggling back into my pack when something hit me in the back and knocked me clear off my feet. The next thing I knew, it was dragging me backward through the saw grass. I couldn't get turned to where I could see it, it apparently had ahold of my pack, so I did the only thing I could think of to do. I popped the fastex buckles on the backstraps, threw my arms straight up over my head, and let whatever it was pull the pack off me. Then I rolled to the side, drawing the AFC from its shoulder holster, squeezed both grips, and came up firing.

The SETAC meatgrinder growled like a garbage disposal and loosed a cone shaped cloud of krylon flechettes in front of me as my mind reeled at the grade B moviegram monster standing not more than three meters away, and my brain screamed at my finger to get off the trigger before I used up all of my magazine.

The flechettes chewed into green leafy plant tissue and fibrous floral matter and chopped up the nightmare horror like an electric powered vegematic, but not before it had partially digested the contents of my pack. Well, to be fair, the plant, or whatever it was, had a fair amount of help in the digestive process from the AFC. The flechettes pretty well shredded everything the plant didn't get to eat.

It was strange. I'd never come up against a killer plant before. And killing it was like cutting the grass. There was no disagreeable odor like a human emptying his bowels in his death throes, or urinating on himself, no faint, sickly sweet odor of warm blood. There was just a kind of wet, fertile smell. It reminded me a little of new-mown hay.

The thing had been a little over three meters tall, and vaguely resembled a Venus flytrap in appearance. I was so fascinated with it that I almost didn't notice the other one oozing in from the side of my field of vision on what looked like a big snail's foot, leaving a slime trail. I spun to the side and blasted that one too, then crammed a fresh magazine into the AFC. I don't think I killed the second one, but it sure lost a lot of chlorophyll and plant sap in the process.

I was getting ready to blast it again when I spotted the third one oozing up from the other side, and decided that discretion was the better part of valor and I'd better forget about what was left of my pack and get the hell out of there. If Masterson and her friend had run up against those things, there was nothing I could do for them now.

I split and dashed off through the jungle for about two hundred meters, feeling the vines and thorns tearing at my coverall, snagging the plastiform leaves and ripping some of them free. When I'd put a little distance between me and the ambulatory carnivorous weeds, I held up to catch my breath and take stock of the situation.

Most of my gear had been in the pack. My rations, extra water, sleeping bag, climbing rope, pitons, and carabiners, and most of my grenades and explosives, as well as my binoculars, were all gone. I still had five full mags for the meatgrinder, four grenades, my two canteens, the compass, my issue survival kit, the communications burst transceiver, and the knife. Life had suddenly become a lot more complicated.

I didn't realize just how complicated until I turned around and found myself face to face with what looked like a giant Canadian lynx, jet black in color with lazing yellow eyes, and standing a good meter high at the shoulder. I didn't know whether to yank the AFC up and try a snap shot, or work it up slowly, so as not to alarm the critter into jumping.

"You may kill me now, strange creature that has fallen to our World from the sky," said the cat, "but I mean you no harm. I will not attack you. I desire, before you decide my fate, to know the answer to three questions, if you would do me the honor of answering them."

"Well, I'll be go to hell," I said. "A talking wildcat. What do I call you? Loup Garou?"

12

Loup Garou

The stranger's thought patterns were indeed alien, yet somehow vaguely familiar. He had made no effort to raise the thunder and lightning box he carried, and I sensed that he did not mean to kill me unless I threatened him, but he had shown me his teeth, and the warning of that universal sign was clear enough. I understood the implied threat as all creatures do. I thought perhaps that he was as afraid of me as I was of him, but the thought patterns I was receiving from him indicated caution, not fear. Carefully, I formed my next communication and projected it to his mind, which remained open to my efforts.

"I repeat, stranger, that I mean you no harm. I merely wish to ask you a few questions. I will lie down now to show you that my intentions are in no way hostile toward you."

Slowly, I folded my legs beneath me and lowered myself to the ground, fully expecting that at any moment I would be struck dead by a bolt of lightning from the thing he carried in his hand. I hoped that he would understand that I was most vulnerable in such a position and meant him no harm. When I had sunk to the ground, I turned my head to one side and offered him my neck. Among my people, it is an act of complete surrender.

Several moments passed, but the stranger did not take advantage of the opportunity to tear out my throat. When I turned back, I was somewhat alarmed to see him sitting on his haunches, as though poised to pounce. He was still showing his teeth, but I looked at them more closely now, and saw that they were small and rounded, poorly designed for defense or hunting, nor were there claws upon the toes of his forepaws, unlike the Yillii. In truth, even though he crouched and showed his teeth, he did not seem a very dangerous sort of creature, yet I remained mindful of his kind's ability to kill at a distance, without personal contact, and with an almost magical speed and finality.

The stranger sat staring at me for many long moments, and his thoughts were a confusing jumble of images, many of which were incomprehensible to me. There were impressions of concern, I could not really call them fear, and of another creature of his own kind, indeed it was of one of the two I had seen captured by the Yillii, and also of other creatures which ran on four legs and resembled the Chat, but were smaller. Finally, to my amazement, the stranger turned his own head to the side and offered me his throat. I would have been convinced the gesture was intended to allay my fears had he not continued to show his teeth.

"You called me Loup Garou," I queried. "What is the meaning of this name?"

As the stranger sent his thoughts to me, his mouth moved in an exaggerated fashion. I thought this was a very strange way to communicate, but his message seemed clear enough. He projected an image of a creature very like the Chat in appearance, although much smaller, and with fur that was a mottled grey and black.

"In Canada there is an animal that is a member of what we call the lynx family. The people who live there call it a loup garou, I think. I saw one once, and it was the closest thing I could think of," he said.

"I am called *She that runs swifter than the shadows of the night, but chooses the path of aloneness to preserve the land and the waters, the grasslands and the forest, the fish and the animals, in the ancient ways of our forebearers,*" I told him. "I am a Chat, and my people are called the Chat, which is also our word for the World, although we have learned the words of many others, and each has a different name for the World, yet the concept is the same for all."

"Well, I can hardly go around calling you 'She That Runs Swifter Than the Shadows of the Night' and whatever else you said. Would it be all right if I call you Loup Garou?"

"I have no objection, if that is the name in your language by which I would be named."

"I think most people would just call you a cat, but there are many different kinds of cat," he said.

"I am a Chat," I told him. "It is Chat, not cat."

"Chat, not cat?"

"Yes. Chat. My people are called the Chat. There is only one kind of Chat, except that there are male and female, young and old," I told him.

"Yes, but there are many different Chat, are there not?"

"No. There are only a few now. Once there were many, but the Yillii have hunted us until now there are only a few left. We hunt only for food, or to defend our litters and our dens. The Yillii hunt for pleasure as well as food, and to force us from our forests and our grasslands. The Yillii are perhaps not as adept as the Chat at hunting alone, but when they hunt in packs, which is nearly always, they can be very formidible, and they have no sense of honor."

"Still, there are enough Chat that it would be confusing unless each was called by a different name, wouldn't it?"

"Yes."

"And since your name is very long in my language, and difficult for me to say it all, I would like to call you something shorter. Will Loup Garou be okay?"

"If you wish and it is easier for you, I have no objection," I told him. "How are you called?"

"I am called Fetterman."

"That is all? It is such a short name. Do all your people have such short names?"

"Actually, my full name is First Lieutenant, uh, I mean, Major General Anthony B. Fetterman, but most people just call me Fetterman."

"Even your full name is short. First Lieutenant, uh, I mean, Major General Anthony B. Fetterman. Such a short name is easy to remember. Why do you shorten it even more?"

He showed his teeth again, and for a moment I was afraid I had somehow offended him. Perhaps by calling him by his full name I had in some fashion violated a taboo of his tribe, or perhaps it was a matter of honor among his people, having such a short name, but he showed no hostility. Indeed, he seemed amused, but he did show his teeth.

"My people have a very poor memory for names," he said. "The shorter the name the better."

"Ah, then you must be highly exalted among your people to be known only as Fetterman."

For some reason, he seemed to find that quite amusing.

"No," he said at last. "I am not highly exalted. I am a soldier. Just a lowly infantryman."

"Your words mean nothing to me." I was beginning to get a better feel for his thought processes and our communication was occurring faster now, but there was still much in his language that was confusing to me. "Is that what your people are called? Soldier? Infantryman?" He showed his teeth again. It was a most disconcerting habit, but I began to suspect that among his people it was not a threat or warning as it was among all the other creatures.

"My people are called human beings," he said. "A soldier is a special kind of human being, and an infantryman a special kind of soldier. Soldiers fight wars for human beings. Do you know what a war is?"

"Yes," I told him solemnly. "I know what war is. All Chat know war. It was the gift of the Yillii to our Ancient Fore-bearers. It is the suffering and death of people you know, amid the suffering and death of people you do not know, for reasons that are often unclear. It is when two peoples hunt each other until one of them is no more forever."

The stranger growled deep in his throat. "I reckon that's a close enough description of it, although humans usually manage to stop themselves before one group or the other gets hunted into extinction. I suppose we're too profit oriented to waste a resource or a potential market like that."

"But your kind do not all fight their own wars? Some of you fight them for all?"

"More or less. I suppose that doesn't make much sense."

"On the contrary. We who are young and healthy must fight to protect the old and infirm, and the very young. It is the same with your people?"

"Not exactly. What you say is also true of my people, but there are others who are physically capable of doing the fighting, but don't have the guts, the courage to do it. They get others to do the job for them, either by paying them or forcing them through laws."

"This I do not understand," I told him. "It seems to me that such a person is without honor."

"It kind of seems that way to me, too."

"Then why do you fight for them?"

The stranger was quiet for a long time, and his thoughts were once again a great jumble of confused images. At last he spoke.

"I do it because it is what I know how to do best. I'm a soldier. Like the fish swims or the bird flies, a soldier fights. And also because the more enemy I kill, the fewer of them there will be to kill my fellow soldiers. I no longer fight for those who will not fight. Perhaps I did once, but no longer. My fellow soldiers are like my family to me. I fight for them. I know that's not a good answer, but it's the best I can do."

"It is acceptable. Have you a family?" I wanted to know.

"No. All my family is dead," he answered. But there was a strong image of the female I had seen captured by the Yillii. I sensed he was concerned for her, but did not want to express his concern. I did not understand why.

"This place you mentioned where there are people like me, this Canada, I think you called it, is that your homeland?"

"I was raised there, in a place called Quebec. It's the North Regional Administrative Center of the United Americas."

"I do not understand your words. Tell me, what is it like in your homeland?"

"The summers are cool and pleasant, but short. The winters are long and very cold. I lived in an orphanage there, that's a place where they raise very young people who have no families. When I was old enough, I went away to college in a place called Iowa on a government scholarship. A college is where they teach you things about what kind of work you will do as an adult."

"Is that where you learned to be a soldier and fight other people's battles?"

"No. I studied physics and astronomy there, but after a year I was expelled for fighting with a group of students. They were protesting a war the United Americas were fighting against the Pan African Alliance, and they desecrated a memorial upon which was written the names of soldiers who had fought in a much earlier war. One of the soldiers whose name they desecrated was an ancestor of mine."

"I do not understand much of what you say, but in some way they insulted the memory of your forebearer, and when you rose to defend his honored memory, you were punished for it?"

"Basically. After that I joined the Army. I can't really tell you why. It just seemed like the thing to do at the time."

"What is this Army?"

"It's a place where they train soldiers. My ancestor had been an infantryman, and I followed in his footsteps."

"So you are not a messenger from the Greatest of the Great Spirits, the Zum Prim Chat Hoiu Tichloucotyl Yil Rhi Kitchimanitou?"

"I'm afraid not. I just came down here to try and find out what happened to the soldiers who came here before me."

I organized my next question carefully before I projected it. "Why did the other soldiers come here? Was it to make war on my people?"

"No. My people are fighting a war with someone else. One of our important soldiers came here without telling anyone why she was coming, and other soldiers were sent to bring her back. Something happened to them, and I was sent to find out what."

I projected an image of the female human being I had seen fight and be captured by the Yillii. "Is this the important soldier you seek?"

The stranger was so startled that he jerked upright on his hindquarters, startling me as well, then he squatted down again.

"No, but I am looking for her also. Have you seen her? Do you know where I can find her?"

"I have seen her. She has fought the Yillii, but they have taken her away."

"Lara? Captured by those . . . Oh God, no."

"The Yillii are your enemies, then? I thought this must be so when I saw the one you call Lara and the dark-haired one fight them. It was the Yillii who hunted your soldiers in the clearing with the objects that give off the stranges noises. The Yillii are your enemies?"

"If they're the ones who did that mess back at the clearing and they've gotten their paws on Lara, you're damned right they are."

I remembered the words of the prophesy, that the messenger from the Greatest of the Great Spirits would come from the sky and walk upon the land, and that none would know him by his presence, save one of the Faithful, who would see him and recognize his true form. And that he would be a friend of the Children of the Faithful and an enemy of their enemies, and that his enemies would be our enemies and his friends our friends.

This strange creature who called himself a human being and said his name was Fetterman professed not to be a messenger from the Greatest of the Great Spirits. But he had come from the sky, had he not? And he had walked upon the World. And he had done the Chat no harm, but had professed the Yillii his enemies. And his friends that he called soldiers had fought the Yillii, and the Yillii had hunted his friends.

And the prophesy had said that none would know him by his presence save one of the Faithful, who would see him and recognize his true form.

For a Priestess of the Chat, truth is often a matter of Faith.

"Fetterman, the Yillii are your enemies. They are also mine. I ask you now, will you hunt the Yillii with me?"

"Loup Garou, if there is any chance at all, I must try to find Lara Masterson and free her. Do you know where they've taken her? Can you lead me there?"

"I have seen the denning place of the Yillii who hunt in this part of the rain forest, and the tracks of the Yillii who captured her lead in that direction. It is possible that they have taken her there, if they have not tired of the hunt already."

"What's that supposed to mean?"

"Fetterman," I told him, "you must try to understand. The Yillii hunt for food or pleasure, and they breed prodigiously. Even their own dead are not exempt. They have never been known to keep captives for very long. When your friend no longer amuses them, well, they have many mouths to feed."

"She's my friend, Loup Garou. She would try to get me out if I were there and she were here. I've got to do what I can. Will you help me?"

"Your enemies are my enemies," I told him. "Your friends are likewise my friends. I will do what I can to help you, although it will be very dangerous, and perhaps we will be too late anyway."

"In that case," said Fetterman, "I will hunt the Yillii with you, until they are no more, forever."

13

Masterson, Lara
Captain, Hard Landing Force Charlie, SCAF

They carried us all through the night and part of the next day, and by the time we reached the Aldebaran village, the ache in my wrists, ankles, arms, legs, elbows, knees, biceps, thighs, shoulders, and hips had gone beyond the merely excruciating and passed into the realm of the exquisite. My extremities hurt so bad that I'd long since forgotten about the splitting headache I had that still produced occasional blinding flashes of light before my eyes.

Chang was semiconscious. That's the term the medtechs use, I think. Semiconscious. How in the name of hell can you be semiconscious? You're either conscious or unconscious. Or drifting in and out of one or the other. Maybe she was better off that way. The unconscious don't feel pain. I was concerned about her, though. She'd been living in the jungle for a couple of weeks, subsisting on what she could find to kill and eat, mostly small Aldebaran reptiles, and drinking the local water. She'd looked a little thin when I'd found her, or rather, when she'd found me. She'd seemed competent enough, and I've too much respect for Imperial Marines, especially Imperial Recon Marines, to let any sense of false interservice rivalry make me think they aren't as tough as Army Pathfinders. They're probably tougher. But I knew I'd been eating better and sleeping better than she had for a couple of weeks, and I wasn't sure how much her condition had been weakened by all the stress, both physical and mental. Everybody's got a breaking point, I don't care how tough they are. Everybody.

The Aldebaran village was kind of a shock after the massive city-domes of Tau Ceti Four. I don't think there could have been more than a couple of hundred Aldebarans of all shapes and sizes, if that. There were no buildings or houses as such, just a series of cave-like hollows in a rocky cliff face, perhaps thirty-five or forty in all, it was kind of difficult to tell while I was swinging back and forth beneath a pole. Some of the caves were accessible along a narrow trail that ran along the cliff face at an angle. Most of the others had a long pole or branch sticking up into the doorway which the Aldebarans seemed to use as handily as I would have a ladder or a flight of stairs.

I'd seen pictures of vaguely similar dwellings once. One of my grade school teachers had gone on vacation to New Mexico and brought back some holoslides of an ancient Amerindian settlement in a place called Frijole Canyon. I couldn't remember much about those early Americans, but the similarity was enough to reinforce the notion that despite their terrifying ability to project thoughts into a person's mind, these Aldebarans weren't all that advanced. It wasn't a comforting thought, considering the damage they'd done. Sort of like the Zulus wiping out the British 24th Regiment of Foot at the Battle of Isandhlwana, only doing it with twenty warriors instead of twenty thousand. Technological superiority helps in a war, but it isn't everything. There's also tenacity and just plain blind luck.

I'd like to be able to report that despite my personal predicament, I exhibited the detached professionalism expected of a Pathfinder, and made a thorough and accurate visual assessment of the village against the time of my future planned escape so that I'd be able to accurately brief Fleet Intelligence following my return to a friendly area, but that would all be pure bullshit. The truth of the matter is that I was able to see damned little, had no concrete plan of escape, and expected to die in that place without ever seeing another SCAF face, except for Chang's. I did note three items, however, that weren't very encouraging.

First was a large metal object of unfamiliar design, but with the unmistakable feature of a parabolic antenna pointed skyward, which set in a more or less central location in a clearing at the base of the cliff. It was in a circle of bare rock, on a sort of low, rocky pedestal, and nothing grew near it, and the Aldebarans avoided going near it. I had no idea what it was, though an educated guess would have been some sort of surveillance or communications relay device. Whatever it was, it blew my technological primitives theory all to hell.

The second thing was the simple realization that the only cliffs in the area had to be in the region of the rocky escarpment I'd picked as a rendezvous spot with St. Croix. If I'd proceeded as planned, sooner or later I'd have walked right into these creeps. I could only hope that St. Croix hadn't, and that she'd managed to get a message out to the fleet.

The third thing was the ornament the village mayor or chief or whatever he was, was wearing. At least I suppose he was the village chief, because they carried us up to the guy and dumped us in the dirt at his feet, and sort of bent forward and nodded their heads a lot, as though paying homage to the guy.

The Aldebaran chief had a pistol dangling on a lanyard about his neck. The lanyard had a familiar red, gold, and blue color to it, and a closer look at the weapon confirmed what I already surmised. It was the compact little PDW with the engraved slide and the scalloped grips that SCAF issues to General Officers. I had an unpleasant feeling that I'd found the missing brigadier that Fleet had been so interested in locating. I noticed that the slide had locked back on the weapon, indicating that the magazine and chamber were empty. I didn't think Brigadier Andersohn would mind that the Aldebaran chief was using her Personal Defense Weapon for a necklace, though. While he stood there scrutinizing us, the village leader was also absently chewing on a little midday snack, cracking open the bones with his jaws, one at a time, to get at the tasty little morsel of marrow inside. I recognized it, too. It was a human hand.

When the village big shot got tired of looking us over, another group of Aldebarans came and gathered around. There were about a dozen of them in all, and I guess they must have been the local equivalent of a town council. The Aldebarans

that had brought us in showed them a certain amount of defer-
ence, and they all wore a necklace of some sort, usually vine,
from which hung some item or other of SCAF issue equipment: a chronograph, a compass, a canteen, an ammo pouch,
one of them even had a grenade hung about his neck by a vine
passed through the ring of the safety pin. I recognized it as a
fragmentation model with an effect radius of ten meters, and
sincerely wished the fellow would go someplace else. The ends
of the pin had been straightened somewhat, and it didn't look
all that secure to me.

When all the bigwigs got tired of looking at, snarling at,
and kicking their prisoners a few times, the chief gave a nod
of his head and a couple of our captors stepped in and jerked
and yanked off the rest of our equipment, taking most of our
BDU's and a fair amount of flesh with it. They left us lying
there in the dirt, naked for all practical purposes, and bleeding, while they sorted through the booty and divvied up our
gear. I don't think they had any idea what most of it was for.

Finally the chief took one of Chang's boots, which had
been pulled from her foot more or less intact, and with considerable difficulty, succeeded in adding it to the pistol hung
about his neck. I wasn't sure if he just liked the looks of the
thing, or it was his way of telling the rest of them that he had
first dibs on Chang's foot when they got around to dividing up
the body parts. I was glad she wasn't conscious to witness it.

Afterward, the chief snarled and indicated something in the
direction of the cliff with a jerk of his head and a gesture of
his forepaw. We were dutifully picked up on our poles again,
and carried off toward the caves. When they ran out of trail
running up the cliff face, two of the Aldebarans worked their
way up a couple of parallel poles maybe twenty meters long,
with me swinging on my pole between them. When they ran
out of climbing poles, they worked their way along a little
rock shelf for a dozen meters, and then climbed a second set
of poles. They repeated the procedure twice more until finally
we were deposited on a large, flat, rock shelf some two
hundred meters or so above the base of the cliff. St. Croix was
there waiting for us.

It hardly seemed fair to call the pitiful wretch before me
human any longer, but there was still enough skin on her

hands and feet for me to tell it had once belonged to a tall, athletic, black woman that had been my Company Warrant Officer. The rest of it resembled a skinned game animal. Incredibly, it was still able to speak.

"Captain, Masterson. Glad you're alive. Sorry they got you too, sir." The voice was barely above a whisper.

"Take it easy, St. Croix," I told her, "save your strength," and got kicked in the mouth by one of the Aldebarans for having the audacity to speak to her.

St. Croix chuckled, but it came out sounding more like the rattle of dry bones.

"Save my strength? For what? So these butchers can entertain themselves a while longer? No thank you, Captain. I'm dead and I know it. The body just hasn't realized what the mind already knows."

I looked at her and hated myself for asking it, but I had to know. "The Fleet, were you able to . . ."

The pulpy mass with the protruding eyeballs that had once been a head with a fairly handsome female face, shook slowly from side to side. "Sorry. They jumped me almost as soon as I was out of the perimeter. I didn't even have time to kill one of the smelly bastards."

"It's all right," I lied. "It doesn't matter. Just hang on. The Fleet was getting a brigade ready before the attack. There's bound to be a rescue mission mounted. They were monitoring all our transmissions, they know we were attacked." The only reason I didn't get kicked again was because the Aldebarans were busy tying Chang and me spread-eagled between two upright poles, as St. Croix was.

St. Croix laughed again. If you could call it a laugh.

"The rescue missions SCAF has mounted so far haven't done so shit hot, Captain. You'd better hope they don't send another one, or these bastards will start having a weight problem. I only hope to hell I give the fuckers a case of indigestion."

St. Croix was silent after that. I didn't know if she had died, passed out, or was just thinking. I hope I can be forgiven for saying that I prayed she was dead. The Aldebarans had skinned her alive, and she was oozing a mixture of blood and plasma from her exposed muscle and fatty tissues. They can do some amazing things with regenerative surgical implants these days, but I didn't think even the Fleet experimental medical physicians had any tricks in their little doctor bags to fix up something like this and make it look human again.

They left us there, tied upright between the poles, with the heat of the red giant sun beating down on us, the fluids oozing out of St. Croix, then crusting over in the heat, only to break loose in some new spot and come seeping out again.

Chang regained consciousness after awhile and we talked a bit, but there was really nothing to say of any importance, and we were both too exhausted and too thirsty to carry on any unneeded conversation for any length of time.

Some time in the night, four of the Aldebarans paid us a visit. For awhile they amused themselves by making me think my skin was on fire, and then by making me think they were skinning me like they had done to St. Croix, but it turned out to be just an illusion. I had the impression that they'd learned a lot about torturing Earth people from Brigadier Andersohn and St. Croix, and wanted to see how another human being would react to the illusion of torture. By the time they were done with me, my mind was too deranged to know whether I'd been any help to them or not, but they seemed reasonably pleased with their experiment.

Afterward, a couple of them took turns with Chang. I can't clearly relate what they did to her; the whole proceeding had the quality of a nightmare about it, and at the time I thought maybe it was another of their illusions, but I know now that it wasn't. I wish to god it had been. Imagine the picture of a young, smallish woman being raped and sodomized by a couple of creatures that look like something out of an H. G. Wells horror novel and smell like last week's cat food left in the sun too long, while you can't do anything but stand by and listen to her scream, and you'll have a pretty fair idea of why I feel that way.

Maybe what they'd put me through was just too much, or maybe it was the image of what they had done to St. Croix and were doing to Chang. Or maybe it was just that I hadn't had any food or water for something over twenty-four hours and had been bounced around all over the Aldebaran jungle with my hands and feet tied to a pole. The human body is an amazingly resilient organism, but it has its limits. Fortunately, when it reaches those limits, it has a wonderful mechanism for saving itself. When the brain has been subjected to painful stimuli for too long, it finally tells itself to shut down the afferent nerve pathways and stop taking input. All kinds of input. And when that happens, you go to sleep. Not like taking a nap, but sleep all the same. You go to sleep, and while you're asleep, the body gets a chance to repair some of the damage and ease some of the hurt, so that when you wake up again, the agony isn't quite so severe and the body can more or less cope with it until the system gets overloaded once again.

It was sometime late the next morning when I woke up, and it was somebody's screams that woke me. In my foggy brain, I thought at first that it was my own screaming that had done it, then realized that it wasn't me after all. When that realization finally dawned on me, I thought they were still abusing Chang, but that turned out not to be the case either. She was hanging limply between her upright poles, thin trickles of blood oozing down her thighs and from her mauled breasts. The screaming was coming from St. Croix.

I thought she'd died during the night, but she'd only passed out like me. Now the Aldebarans were continuing with their educational experiments. They were being very methodical about it too, using their razor-sharp claws to slowly dissect her still living body, one muscle, or tendon, or ligament at a time, carefully eliciting a verbal response as each one was torn to shreds, noting the volume and quality of their subject's screams.

Insanely, I wondered whether these repulsive creatures were indeed mindless, immoral savages, or the Aldebaran equivalent of a skilled surgical biologist, conducting a vivisection on an alien species that they did not, of course, view as human from their standpoint. Which alternative made them the less monstrous, and would our own scientists be any less monstrous if presented with a living, breathing Aldebaran native? I thought of the Aldebaran specimen in the makeshift walk-in cooler back at the rescue ship, and wondered if at root, our level of savagery was indeed all that much different from the Aldebarans. Scientists experimented on live animals all the time, didn't they?

I couldn't even defend the human race's actions by claiming that our scientists performed their grisly experiments in furthering the cause of scientific knowledge of medical science. How did I know that wasn't what the Aldebarans were doing as they slowly took apart my friend and sister-in-arms. War is full of cruelties, but did it make any sense to torture your enemies to death just for the pleasure of seeing them die excruciatingly? Only a completely alien mind could contemplate such a thing, yet weren't the Aldebarans aliens? And weren't we aliens to them? After all, it was their planet, what right did we have to think that they should behave in ways we were accustomed to, just because we'd seen fit to land a couple of hundred armed troops on their world, hardly a peaceful gesture of universal friendship?

But damn it, they were killing my friend.

And what of the laboratory rat or guinea pig or dog? What do they feel when they can only stand by and watch some human scientist inject their friend full of carcinogens in order to try out the latest cancer fighting drug on them? Or cut them open with a laser knife and play around in their insides trying to perfect a new surgical technique to save humans? How do dogs feel about being sacrificed for the sake of human knowledge?

It occurred to me that that was a dangerous line of thought for a soldier to be pursuing. Keep it up and pretty soon I wouldn't even want to be a vegetarian because of all the little heads of lettuce that would have to be sacrificed to feed me. In some fashion or other, every living thing lives by the death of others, and nature attaches neither guilt nor blame. Some of us are just more efficient at it than others. Should we give up eating meat because we have to kill an animal to get it? Should we give up vegetables because we might cause a green bean to suffer when we snap it, or a pea to cry out when we open its pod? Should we give up breathing because we might injure an oxygen molecule when our cells use it in metabolism? Nature doesn't draw those kinds of distinctions, but it does set limits.

"Yes, damn it," I thought. "There have to be some limits.

Otherwise we aren't any different from the animals or the Aldebarans. If we're humans, we have to set limits."

St. Croix screamed again as one of the Aldebarans excised her uterus and let it drop out on the ground in front of her.

I railed at my captors, throwing a stream of incoherent obscenities at them as I struggled against my bonds, trying futilely to pull the uprights loose from the ground and beat them to death with the poles, trying to tear free and strangle them with my bare hands. I didn't care if they killed me, so long as I could take a few of them with me. Revenge is the best way to get even. That was all I wanted. Revenge for what they were doing to St. Croix, for what they had done to Chang, and to me, and to some general I didn't even know. Revenge for what they had done to the men and women of my company, my troops who had looked to me for leadership and hope, and found only death. I fought against the vines that held me fast until my wrists and ankles were raw and bleeding. If I couldn't get free to kill them, I could at least perform the last act of defiance.

Only I couldn't even do that. There wasn't enough saliva in my mouth to spit in their faces.

Frustrated and angry, I hung there slackly between the poles, feeling the only moisture I could muster, my tears, running down my cheeks, as I helplessly watched them take St. Croix apart.

She lived until nearly sunset.

I gave a small prayer of thanks when they finally tore out her heart.

14

Fetterman, Anthony B.
Major General (Simulated)
Seventh Rangers (Detached)
Fleet/STC JOITF, SCAF

I gave a silent prayer of thanks when the woman died.

There had been nothing we could do for her. Not if we entertained any hope of getting the other two out, and getting any word back to the Fleet about the big dish antenna sitting down there in the middle of the Tauran village. Even the Fleet doctors with all the incomprehensible procedures they'd spent the last sixty-one years perfecting on me couldn't have helped her. All I could have done for her was put a couple of bullets in her and end the suffering, and that would have blown our chances on getting the other two out.

I suppose the smart thing, the professional thing, to do would have been to pull out and trigger the pickup beacon, meet the retrieval ship, get back to the Fleet, and tell them about the antenna setup, whatever it was. In fact, I was almost sure to get myself court-martialed for not doing exactly that. That damned antenna was blowing the hell out of my theory that the Alpha Taurans, at least the Yillii Alpha Taurans, weren't as sophisticated as everybody up at Fleet seemed to think they might be.

But there were still two women up on that big rocky shelf that were alive. I didn't know the others, but I'd got a good look at all three through my binoculars, and one of the two still alive definitely was Masterson. I'd already committed what was probably one court-martial offense in order to find her, and now that I had found her, committing another one seemed somehow fairly trivial. Especially when I considered the treatment she was likely to receive at the hands of the Yillii if I didn't get her out of that place.

My binoculars and a couple of pitons and carabiners were all I'd been able to salvage from my pack after my little encounter with the Alpha Tauri Venus mantrap. I hadn't expected to find that much. In fact, I hadn't even been real crazy about going back to look for anything, but Loup Garou had assured me the area would be relatively safe after half an hour or so, when the giant killer weeds lost interest in the area and oozed off in search of someone else to eat.

I'd gone back and sorted through the wreckage, finding half a dozen ceramo-acrylic pitons and D-rings, and one figure eight descender, the rest having either been chipped or broken by the flechettes from the SETAC meatgrinder, or digested by the plant, which evidently exuded some type of strong acid as part of its feeding process. My Kevlar II climbing rope was gone, shredded by the darts and melted by acid. My ration packs had all been punctured by flechettes or eaten away, contaminating them, and my spare ammunition, grenades, and demolitions equipment were for the most part either completely gone or barely recognizable. The binoculars alone had come through virtually unscathed. The rubber armored covering was gouged and torn, and there was one krylon dart still impaled in the protective coating, but the case itself was still intact and the optics undamaged. It was a real tribute to the engineering and quality control efforts of the people at Steiner. They make one tough binoculars.

Losing so much of my equipment had put my tactical situation in a different light, and after conferring with Loup Garou who had seemed completely lost when I'd tried to explain the concepts of magnetic aberration detection and seismic intruder surveillance, I'd gambled that the enemy's defenses weren't as sophisticated as we'd thought, and gone back and dug up the weapons I'd found earlier.

It had taken me about an hour to clean the things up and put them back in operating condition, mostly because I wasn't all that familiar with the battle carbine, and because I *very* slowly and carefully disassembled each of the grenades and checked the fuses in an effort to figure out if they were time or contact delay. Thank God none of them were booby-trapped.

I was able to figure out most of the grenades from the markings on their fuse assemblies, although I'll admit part of it was educated guesswork, but a few of them eluded me. There were a couple I couldn't figure, and I re-buried them. I was willing to take a chance on the ones I could make reasonable guesses about, but not on something totally unfamiliar. It was just too good a way to get myself blown up.

When I finally took stock of it all, I felt a little bit silly at all the weaponry. I had the SETAC AFC with its five magazines, the suppressed Kalan with eight and a partial one in the grip, a fully loaded PDW, eleven assorted grenades of various types plus my own four frags, a couple of ration packs that hadn't been contaminated, and a SCAF battle carbine with an even five hundred rounds of 3mm hypervelocity frangible bullets in ten fifty-round magazines. I figured it was about twice as much weaponry as I could ever live long enough to get to use.

I improvised a rucksack from what was left of my poor, half-digested pack, the thermal foil blanket, and a few short pieces of my climbing rope that had survived, and we set out on the trail again. I let the big cat lead, since I figured that her senses were sharper than mine, and she was familiar with the terrain. Besides, she knew where we were going, I didn't.

It occurred to me that I might very well be walking into a trap, but I just didn't buy that. I believed the cat's story, and it checked with what I'd found at the rescue ship site. Once I'd accepted that I could carry on a telepathic conversation with a giant wildcat, accepting that it wanted to help me hadn't been so difficult to do.

Along the way, I'd picked up a rudimentary lesson in natural history from Loup Garou, who had related to me a highly selective, partial retelling of her people's story, if you could call a race of sentient cats a people. The Tale of the Chat was mostly a pretty fanciful legend, full of Great Spirits and not so great ones, with a lot of ancestor worship mixed in, but a couple of important points emerged from the long, purring discourse. Just as on Earth primates had risen to a stature of ascendency over the other animals by virtue of their stereoscopic vision, opposable thumb, and advanced mental capacity, so too had the Chat and Yillii risen from among the other creatures of Alpha Tauri Five by virtue of being blessed, or cursed, depending upon how you viewed things, with special traits that were either the natural process of Darwinian selection occurring over millennia, or gifts from the Greatest of the Great Spirits. You pay your dollar, and you pick your religion.

By the gross similarity in their appearance, it seemed possible that the Chat and the Yillii had once shared a common ancestor in the distant, murky past. Whether or not that was in fact correct is a matter I'll leave to the exo-anthropologists to fight out one of these days, but if they did share a common root, it might help to explain the amazing mental powers that both species developed. It just could be that at some point, the physical development of each line diverged from that common ancestor, and the mental capacity that we humans think of as extra-sensory diverged with it. Such a theory fits, at least, with the fact that the religious history of both the Chat and the Yillii acknowledge that once they had a common ancestor. The Zum Chat Hoiu Tichloucotyl Yil Rhi Kitchimanitou.

At any rate, each species developed a discrete, suprahuman mental skill that set them apart from all the other inhabitants of their world.

The Chat, who were highly intuitive, developed a limited capability for direct mental communication among their own and certain other species. They could, in effect, read minds over short distances. As Loup Garou explained it, it was really more like a process of getting certain mental impressions from one Chat, and then correctly interpreting their meaning. The other Chat would then form a series of impressions, and make them available to the first Chat. It allowed a nonverbal communication that permitted the Chat to exchange information and ideas, and to warn others of impending danger.

It was a conscious process, requiring a purposive mental effort on the part of the mind reader much like speaking, but because any Chat could look into the mind of any other Chat, it had resulted in a society that, although it had a term for alone or apart, had no real concept of privacy. It was perhaps because of this that most of the Chat chose to live their lives in small family groups, coming together with other families of

Chat only occasionally, since the mind-reading ability was limited somewhat by distance. I suppose everyone thinks it would be nifty if they could read the thoughts of everyone around them, but how would you like having everyone else know exactly what you're thinking from moment to moment?

At any rate, the mind-reading capacity was the Chat's form of language, and just like human linguists, some of the Chat were more adept at it than others, could reach out farther with their minds to contact others, and could "speak" with a greater variety of other animals, much like some people can speak several languages. The greatest of the adepts were accorded a revered status among the Chat, somewhat like the shaman or medicine man of the American Prairie and Plains Indians. An understandable honor, since, after all, they exhibited a greater skill than others at what the Chat regarded as a gift from their Holiest of Great Spirits. Not surprisingly, most of the Chat class of holy cats chose a solitary existence, shunning even to take a mate and living in relative isolation, much as the fabled wise men of Tibet.

The mind of the Chat was not open to all other species, however. The Alpha Tauri Five equivalent of a squirrel, a big olive-gray mammal about the size of small kangaroo, for instance, could not look into the mind of a Chat unless the Chat permitted it, yet the Chat would communicate with them, after a fashion, when they desired it. It was this ability, combined with the ability to mind-link across reasonably short distances, a few kilometers or so if I understood correctly, that had given the Chat an excellent Intelligence network and enabled them to keep from being completely eradicated by the Yillii who were more numerous, more vicious, and who possessed a frighting ability of their own.

The Yillii could not read minds, as the Chat did. They relied on keen eyesight and hearing to hunt their prey, but they did possess a sort of one-sided telepathic ability. The capability to project mental images, terrifying illusions, into the minds of others. They could not read another's thoughts, but they could create literally, waking nightmares in the minds of their prey, and then capitalize on the panic thus caused. Their prey, fleeing blindly, would stampede, and in their unreasoned flight, were easy victims for the Yillii. Until the Yillii had encountered humans.

The Yillii had hunted the humans as they hunted all other creatures on Alpha Tauri Five, but unlike all the other creatures save the Chat, humans when confronted with danger, at least human soldiers, reacted not by fleeing, but by fighting. And unlike all other creatures, including the Chat and the Yillii, humans exhibited the ability to kill at a distance. Because of this ability, the Yillii learned that humans could be a dangerous foe, but perhaps a manageable one. For the Yillii learned that humans would use their ability to kill at a distance against any threat, including other humans.

As I sat on a tree limb, studying the Yillii village through my binoculars, I wondered about Loup Garou's motivations for helping me. She had said the Yillii were the natural enemies of the Chat, yet they came from a common ancestor. I wondered if humans would have accepted help against a human enemy as readily from an alien. True, I had accepted Loup Garou's help, but it was against an alien enemy, not a human one.

There was also the fact that I really knew nothing at all about Loup Garou's people. I had met only one representative example of the Chat, and had only one Chat's word for the character and history of the entire Chat people. For that matter, as far as I could actually prove, there might not be any Chat people, just the one single Chat currently inhabiting the tree limb next to mine.

I wondered if Loup Garou were reading my thoughts about her. If so, she gave no sign of concern. Perhaps she'd switched off for the moment and was sifting through her own thoughts about me, or perhaps she was simply being a clever Chat and picking my mind without giving any access to her own.

I decided it didn't matter. I'd seen the massacre back at the rescue ship, and I'd watched the Yillii take apart a human being, a soldier like myself, a piece at a time, apparently just for their own amusement. From the looks of things, they had every intention of doing exactly the same thing to their other two prisoners, one of whom was somebody very special to me. That alone was justification enough.

And if it hadn't been, there was still that damned big parabolic antenna on top of its little metal cylinder sitting at the base of the escarpment to think about. Loup Garou claimed to have no knowledge of its significance, and theorized that it was some form of Yillii religious shrine. She said she'd never seen anything like it before, except for the machinery back at the rescue ship, and wanted to know if it could be something we had brought with us from the sky. I was pretty sure it had come from the sky all right, but not from us. The design was too unfamiliar, and while I'd be the first to admit that SCAF had come up with a lot of unfamiliar stuff since I'd been killed sixty-one years ago, I'd observed that one thing about SCAF hadn't changed. Everything in SCAF was camouflaged for the terrain of intended use. We used to call it painting things "Army ugly." The antenna and cylinder down below were polished to a mirror finish.

"How would you get them out?" I said at last.

"I would not," said Loup Garou. "While you have been studying the village through the strange device you hold to your face, I have made my own assessment. It is a difficult procedure, to be able to look into the mind of a Yillii without stimulating their awareness that they are being probed. Further, you must also understand that it is . . ." she searched for the right terminology, "repugnant.

"They mean to kill your friends of course. Slowly, one at a time. The dark-haired one will be next because she is the weakest, but I do not think they will begin with her until the return of the light. Tonight they will feast, and the council of their leaders will dine on the flesh of the one they have killed in order to take the power of her spirit. She was strong and endured their torture for a long time. The leaders will take her strength and add it to their own by consuming her flesh."

It seemed like a lot of mystical mumbo-jumbo to me, but I remembered that there were cultures on Earth where eating the liver or the heart of an enemy slain in battle had been considered a necessary part of taking the strength from your enemy's spirit. For the first time, it dawned on me that the Chat and the Yillii weren't merely fighting a war with each other, they were fighting a holy war. By establishing their dominance over the

Chat, the Yillii hoped to establish the dominance of their Great Spirit over that of the Chat.

"I say I would not get them out," continued Loup Garou, "because I do not believe it can be done without our being killed. There are nearly fifty adult male Yillii in the village, and almost as many adult females. There are perhaps three times that number of small ones. The cubs are not of as great concern as the adults, for the Gift of Causing Panic is not as well developed in the young as in the adults, but even discounting the cubs, which we cannot, that still makes the odds a hundred to two against us. Even in the hunt for food, it is not a sound tactic to attack something stronger than you are."

"The weapons I have brought with me can kill a great number," I said, trying to sound confident, and sounding rather foolish even to myself.

"Yes. I have seen them used by others. They kill from a distance, without touching, and with great speed and certainty. Someday you must explain to me how such magic can be possible, if it is permitted for a messenger from the Greatest of the Great Spirits to tell such things to a Chat."

"For the last time," I said, "I'm not a messenger from any Great Spirit."

"Perhaps not. And perhaps you are merely testing my Faith. It matters little. I would not attempt to rescue them, if it were my choice, for I know that such a thing would not be possible without the intervention of the Great Spirit Chat. Only someone who had the protection of a Great Spirit would even consider such a task. Yet, I have said that your enemies are my enemies and your friends my friends. If it is your decision, I will go with you."

It wasn't a very confidence inspiring pep-talk.

"Have you a plan?" asked Loup Garou.

"Not much of one," I admitted. "This ability of the Yillii to project illusions into someone's mind, is there anyway to guard against it?"

"No, but it can, like all fears, be overcome."

"I don't follow you," I said.

"Fetterman, there are many things in life that we fear, yet as we mature, we learn to overcome our fears, do we not?"

"Yes," I agreed, "but I don't see how we're going to do

that while they're putting images into our heads."

"You must learn to ignore the images."

"Ignore the images? That's it? That's your big idea? Just ignore the illusions? You seemed to be forgetting that the whole key to an illusion is that you can't tell it from reality. How the hell are you supposed to ignore that?"

"And you seem to be forgetting that an illusion itself cannot harm you. Only your reaction to it. If you look for the truth, you will see the illusion for the falsity that it is."

"Pardon me, but I'm a little weak in the existential Buddhism department. Suppose you tell me just what in the hell you're talking about."

"What is existential Buddhism?"

"Never mind that now. Just tell me how I'm supposed to know the truth and ignore the illusions."

"This is truth, is it not? Your friends are bound between those distant poles. They cannot move when tied thus, so whatever else may happen, whatever else you may think you see, they will remain there."

"So?"

"And you are the only other human, so any other humans you see will be an illusion."

"So what?" I said. I still wasn't getting the picture.

"And I am the only Chat, so any other Chat you see will be an illusion."

"And just what in the name of Sam Hill am I supposed to do when I see one of these illusions, ignore it?"

"Certainly not. You must kill it with your magic weapons. If it is only an illusion, your magic will not harm it, and you will then know that it is an illusion and cannot harm you. If it is a Yillii disguised as an illusion, you will kill it and it will die. In either event, there is no danger that you will kill your friends by mistake, for they will be on the flat shelf of rock, and unable to attack you. Further, you will not be able to see them from below, so there is no danger of you mistaking them for something else."

"And just how am I supposed to get my friends down off that rock shelf without going up there where I can see them and possibly mistake them for Yillii?"

"That should be an easy enough task afterward."

"After what?"

"After you have killed all the Yillii," said Loup Garou.

I stared hard at the big cat. "You can't seriously expect me to just walk in there and wipe out a whole entire village."

"It is up to you. If you wish to rescue your friends, it is the only way. Personally, I think the odds are very much against your survival, but I have seen the power of your magic weapons, and perhaps it is possible, given that you will be at least partially able to tell the truth from illusion."

"And just where are you going to be while I'm supposed to be pulling this John Wayne stunt?"

"Who is John Wayne? It is a very short name. He must truly be highly exalted among your soldiers."

"Just answer the question," I said sourly.

"I will be where you cannot mistake me for an illusion, and I cannot mistake you."

"I thought you said you were going with me?"

"I will be with you, in a manner of speaking. Is that the right phrase? Yes, I see that it is."

"Where?"

"It is better, I think, if you do not know. That way, there is less chance of a mistake occurring. What you must do, I can have no part in. What I must do, you would not be able to help with. You should gain some advantage from the fact that they will be largely assembled at the base of the cliff for the feast. It should make it easier to find all of them. Afterward, we will meet, if you survive. If not, perhaps we will meet anyway, before the Greatest of the Great Spirits."

I felt like reaching out and punching the big cat right in the nose, but it didn't seem advisable.

"That's the whole plan, then? I'm just supposed to walk in there and shoot everybody?"

"Unless you have a better idea, that is the plan."

"Well the plan vacuums."

"You have a better idea?"

"No," I said. "I don't have a better idea, but this one still vacuums."

"I can see no alternative, except to sit here and watch your friends be tortured to death."

I said nothing for a moment. Picking up the binoculars I

studied the outcropping. I could see Masterson's face clearly, pained, a little bit scared, but still proud and a touch defiant. She hadn't changed much over sixty-one years.

"You know," I said, lowering the Steiners, "I really like this plan of yours. I'm real enthusiastic about it. Let's do it."

"Certainly," said Loup Garou. "It should be easy for a messenger from a god."

"And an overgrown alley cat," I thought before I could catch myself.

There's an old Ranger saying, "Take the hard way in, the easy way out." I wasn't real sure it had ever been intended to apply to situations like this one, but I couldn't think of anything much harder than killing a hundred plus of the enemy by yourself, even if they didn't have firearms, or anything easier than walking out after everyone else was dead.

I could have triggered the pickup beacon, but I had no way of knowing whether the response from the Fleet would take minutes or hours, and all it would do was confuse the issue anyway. The damned cat was right. The only chance of the crazy idea working at all was if I could be sure anything I saw wasn't a friendly troop. Well, I could be reasonably sure of that. The cat had gone off shortly after dusk to do its thing, whatever it was, and I was on my own. I didn't really think she had deserted me completely, but there was damned little comfort in knowing Loup Garou was out there somewhere while I was metaphorically walking into the lion's den.

I didn't exactly walk in. To be perfectly accurate, I crawled the last hundred and fifty meters on my belly, coming face to face with, and finally staring down the Tauran equivalent of a porcupine in the process. It was shaped about like a hedge apple covered with fifteen-centimeter quills and had one red eye more or less in the middle. It studied me for awhile, evidently decided I was bigger than it was, and rolled away on the tips of its spikes.

It took me nearly two hours to rig up the three grenade booby traps at the main avenue of approach to the village, then work my way around to the other side, setting up two booby traps there and stringing another four along the way. It left me with only six grenades, but the basic plan was to kill all the Yillii, and I figured that meant not letting any of them get out alive if they panicked and ran. Running didn't really seem to be in their nature, but I thought they might feel differently when things started popping. That only left them one avenue of escape, up the cliff face and across the top of the escarpment and down the other side. There wasn't anything I could do about that. I only had so many resources.

It occurred to me as I crawled around out there in the darkness like some mobile bush that I was contemplating causing the death of what a Board of Inquiry might later decide was a bunch of noncombatant civilians, including women and children, thereby earning myself a place in the history fiche alongside Lieutenant William Calley. These Taurans weren't really warriors. But I reminded myself that they or their friends had been responsible for the deaths of a couple hundred SCAF troopers, and I had a hunch that Fleet Ops would see it as a justifiable retribution.

Which presumed of course that I pulled it off. Otherwise I'd probably be joining Masterson and her Imperial Marine Recon buddy up on the shelf and these bastards would be enjoying a noonday Fetterman snack in a day or two. That's what happens in war. People you know suffer and die, against the backdrop of people you don't know suffering and dying. There's nothing glorious or heroic about it. It's a killing business, pure and simple. It's survival, or not surviving, nothing more or less.

I finished rigging the last of the booby traps and checked the set. The grenades were all three to five second fused, as near as I could tell, which would ordinarily have been a bit too long for booby-traping, but I was banking on Tauran inexperience with grenades to make up for that. I hoped that when they hit one of the vines I'd used as tripwires, they wouldn't be smart enough to dive for cover, and if they did figure it out, by that time it would be too late.

The traps were all rigged, and the Yillii party was in full swing, the stench of burning human flesh filling the night air. I was a bit surprised that the Taurans had a knowledge of fire for some reason. It made my task harder and easier at the same time. For one thing, the Yillii tended to cluster around the one big central fire, which grouped them all nicely to-

gether, held their attention as I approached, and reduced their
night vision. On the other hand, the fire was big enough to
light up a pretty good sized area, which would make it easier
for them to see me, but which also lighted them up as pretty
good targets.

I found a filth and water filled ditch with excrement float-
ing in it which ran along the base of the cliff, and which the
Yillii apparently used as a kind of open sewer. It stunk to high
heaven, but offered the best cover available and would put my
back to the cliff wall, which meant I wouldn't have to worry
about anybody sneaking up behind me, although they could
still drop a boulder down on my head if there were any
Taurans left up on the cliff in their cavelike houses.

I slipped into the muck, and trying to hold my weapons up
out of the putrefying mass, crawled along the ditch and into
the middle of the Yillii encampment. When I was where I
wanted to be, I laid out the SETAC AFC and its four extra
magazines in front of me on the edge of the ditch, and put the
Kalan and its magazines next to the meatgrinder. I slipped the
makeshift pack around to where I could get at the battle carbine and its magazines, and laid four grenades out in front of
the AFC.

I checked my position one last time. I was about twenty-
five meters from the campfire. The nearest of the Yillii was
about ten meters away. I picked up two of the grenades, one in
each hand, and pulled the safety pins. Then I raised up in the
ditch and threw one of the grenades as far as I could, threw
the other one just this side of the campfire, and ducked down
in the ditch. When the grenades went off. I picked up the
meatgrinder and started firing.

I shredded the nearest Tauran with a short, controlled
burst, since he was near enough to be an immediate threat.
After he went down, I just held back on the trigger and hosed
down the whole area, trying to remember to fire low. At that
point I was less concerned with causing fatalities than I was
with causing casualties and provoking the optimum amount of
panic and confusion. I was outnumbered a hundred to one. If
the Yillii figured out they were up against only one human,
and where he was, they could wave-assault me and I wouldn't
stand a chance of holding them. When the AFC went empty, I

picked up the Kalan and emptied that, then tossed another grenade and hunkered down in the ditch to change magazines on both weapons while I waited for the grenade to go off.

There was instant pandemonium. Taurans were falling, getting up, falling again. The air was filled with a cacophony of shrill panther-like screams and snarls. Dimly, I was aware of the sound of my own voice, screaming incoherently back at them.

I burned through three more magazines in the meatgrinder, the enormous clouds of krylon darts cutting down Taurans like a scythe, then pulled out the SCAF battle carbine and started picking individual targets, firing in three round bursts. Directly in front of me a Tauran's head exploded as I shot it in the face. I shifted aim, fired again, and watched a huge, gaping hole appear in another's chest. My aim was a bit off on the third one, and I only cut off his arm at the shoulder. I spotted a fourth running away and shot it in the back.

Some of the Taurans were beginning to spot my position now, and a group of three tried to rush me. I flicked the selector to full auto and blasted away. They crumpled together in a pile of broken limbs.

I couldn't tell if I was shooting males or females or cubs. Everybody was running in different directions. The only sound of a weapon firing was my own, but a thousand different roars, snarls, and screams split the night, almost drowning out the sound of the carbine and completely masking the muffled Kalan when I brought it back into play.

I just kept shooting and changing magazines and shooting and changing magazines and shooting some more. Across the clearing a Tauran hit one of the tripwires and a grenade booby trap went up. It turned out to be an incendiary, white phosphorus mixed with thermite. I could see three Taurans, their fur in flames, run several meters off into the darkness before collapsing.

I had a bad moment when I saw Masterson and the marine running straight for my ditch, but there was something funny about their gait, and I remembered what Loup Garou had said about knowing the difference between truth and illusion. It was probably the longest five seconds and the hardest decision I've ever had to make, but I brought the carbine in line, sighted carefully and put a three round burst through each of their abdomens. Both of them went down, revealing a few agonizing moments later the badly eviscerated corpses of two Yillii males.

Their second attempt was much more subtle, and almost worked. Masterson loomed up again from out of nowhere and locked her hands around my throat, trying to choke the life out of me. It *felt* real, and I was coughing and gasping for air, but the effect was somewhat spoiled by the fact that they'd already used Masterson's image for one feint, and it hadn't washed the first time. I pulled out the PDW and pumped five rounds into her chest. When nothing happened, I knew it had to be an illusion. It was contact range, the muzzle of the pistol pressing right up against the lower curve of her non-existent left breast. The image wavered then, and I felt her grip loosen about my throat. I picked the carbine back up and continued dinging away at any Taurans I could still see. As I did so, the image flickered, then faded away entirely.

On either side of me, more grenade traps went off, one of them momentarily lighting up the entire night like a half-kilo-ton nuke. I had no idea what kind of a grenade it had been, but was damned glad I hadn't tried to throw it. The overpressure from the shock wave physically knocked me down into the ditch. When I pulled myself back up, a curious silence had descended over the entire scene, and I thought for a moment that I'd been rendered deaf by the blast.

A few seconds later though, there started up a pitiful mew-ing and wailing from the wounded. I knew that any Taurans caught in the open must have been stunned by the explosion and used the next couple of seconds to check my weapons, making sure each had a full magazine in it, in preparation for the anticipated counter-attack, but the counter-attack never came.

After awhile, I stuck the meatgrinder back in its shoulder rig, slung the carbine, and picked up the Kalan. I don't re-member throwing my fourth grenade, but I must have, be-cause it was nowhere to be found. Maybe the blast from the baby nuke grenade had knocked it into the ditch or someplace. I don't know. I never found it again.

I took the PDW in hand, and walked out into the flickering

light of the campfire to administer the *coup d' grâce* to the maimed and dying, without regard to sex or age. It wasn't exactly a shining moment in the history of the mercy of humanity.

I've gotten pretty hardened to the realities of combat over the years, I guess, but some of what I saw and did sickened me just a little. No soldier likes making war on women and children, not even if they're not particularly human-looking and have been trying to kill him or his buddies.

When I'd finished doing what had to be done, I walked back over to the base of the cliff and started climbing up the narrow trail. Eventually I ran out of trail and had to shinny up one of the rolly poles. The others had been knocked down by the blast from the supergrenade, and after that, I had to resort to hand and toe holds and the pitons I'd scavenged from the wreckage of my gear, using the PDW as a hammer to drive them into crevices in the rock. I cringed inwardly each time I had to use the pistol for a purpose other than what it was intended for, but I had no choice. I had nothing else to drive them in with.

It was damned tricky making that climb in the dark. I was physically and emotionally exhausted after the slaughter down below, and more than a little apprehensive about what I might find when I got up top. As I pulled myself up onto the rocky shelf, I came face-to-face with a familiar, giant black form with gleaming yellow eyes. There were three dead Yillii lying near Loup Garou's feet, their throats ripped open by those long teeth in those powerful jaws.

"Glad to see you made it, Fetterman," said Loup Garou.

"Just how in the hell did you get here, and what are you doing here anyway?" I wheezed, gasping for breath after the long, excruciating climb.

"I came over the back side of the escarpment," said the Chat. "A difficult climb to be sure, but not impossible. As to your second question, I came to make sure no harm befell your friends when you started shooting... Is that the right word, shooting? When you started killing the Yillii down below?"

I gave the big cat a hard look that I'm sure must have been

visible in the light of the triple moons. "You knew there would be someone up here with them, that's why you came. You said the Yillii wouldn't start on them until tomorrow, you knew."

"Yes," agreed the Chat. "I fabricated a falsity."

"You lied."

"Yes, that is the word. I lied."

"Why?"

"There was no point in alarming you unduly, or giving you cause for more concern than you would already be faced with down below. Further, I did not wish you to know where I would be, as an added precaution against the Yillii using us against each other. I knew that as their celebration wore on, the Yillii would seek new entertainment and begin to play with your friends. It is their way, whenever possible, to play with their food before eating it."

"Sort of like a cat toying with a mouse," I said, and was instantly sorry for having done so.

Loup Garou was most distressed that I would even consider such an analogy.

"The Chat are hunters, Fetterman. They kill only for food or in self-defense. We are a people of principles and honor. Not like these savages." She indicated the dead Yillii with a shake of her head. "We kill what we must for survival, but we do not make our prey suffer needlessly. Even these three enemies of my people were given a quick death. I did not torture them."

"I am truly sorry for my words, Loup Garou, and for the careless thought behind them," I said immediately, sensing that I had greatly offended the big Chat's honor. "I intended no slur or aspersion. The small animal I mentioned is like the Chat in appearance only, and as you have taught me this night, appearances can be deceiving. The important thing is to look beyond the falsity and see the truth. You have said that my enemies are your enemies and my friends your friends. Are we not, then, friends ourselves, and will you not accept the apology of a friend for thinking without thinking?"

The Chat considered this, and inclined its great head. "Your apology is accepted, as is your friendship. Now let us see to your other friends."

Loup Garou walked over to the marine, reared up and put a paw on either side of her, the upright poles creaking beneath the pressure of two hundred plus kilos of Chat, and lapped at the marine's face. The little dark-haired girl woke up, looked at the Chat, and fainted dead away again. Loup Garou gave me a puzzled glance.

"Think nothing of it," I told her. "She's just not used to seeing Chat, that's all."

I took out the big knife Peterson had given me and cut through the vines holding the marine to the poles, helped her to the ground, and made sure she had an open airway. The kid was in bad shape. She'd been mauled pretty bad, but I didn't see any wounds that looked life threatening.

A dazed Masterson watched me as I approached her, rustling the plastiform leaves attached to my camouflaged coverall. I hadn't really considered the psychological aspects of approaching an injured soldier looking like an ambulatory plant with a knife in its branches, especially an injured soldier who had already had some experience with the lethal flora and fauna of Alpha Tauri Five. She strained at her bonds and definitely didn't seem glad to see me.

"Take it easy, Lara," I told her. "Everything's going to be all right. It's me, Tony."

"Tony?"

"Tony Fetterman."

"Fetterman, you're alive. I saw you . . . die."

"Things aren't always what they seem," I said, cutting her loose. She stumbled, and I caught her in my arms and held her upright.

"Indeed," said the Chat. "All life is a circle. All death is a circle. Life and death, they are one in the same."

"Jesus!" said Masterson. "I must be hallucinating. What is that thing?"

"Lara," I said, "meet Loup Garou, one Chat who's real Ranger material if ever there was one, my friend. Loup Garou, meet Captain Lara Masterson, my very special friend."

"Loup Garou?" queried Masterson. "His name is Loup Garou?"

"He is a she," I said, "and her name is about five klicks

long and impossible to remember. I call her Loup Garou."

"Why Loup Garou?'

"What else are you going to call someone who looks like a giant Canadian lynx?"

"Fetterman, you idiot, a Canadian lynx is a *loup cervier*. A *loup garou* is a lycanthrope."

"Oh well," I said, shrugging my branches, "zoology never was my forte. Anyway, she's a Chat, not a cat, and she doesn't mind being called Loup Garou, and she can read minds, so be careful what you're thinking."

"If I am reading your friend Masterson's mind correctly," said the Chat ingraciously, "you had both better be careful what you are thinking. This is no place to be making cubs."

I pulled the thermal foil blanket out of my survival kit and wrapped it around Lara, helping her sit down on a rock, and gave her one of my ration packs and a canteen.

"How's Lance Corporal Chang?" asked Masterson, nodding toward the marine.

"Kind of rocky, but I think she'll make it. I need to check on her again, if you're all right. Here, I think this is yours." I handed her the SCAF battle carbine.

"Thanks," she nodded. "See to Chang."

I went back over and rechecked Chang's airway, then did a quick exam with the aid of my flashlight. Her body was covered with deep scratches and a few teeth marks, and she'd apparently suffered both a vaginal and a rectal bleed, although both had dried. I bandaged things until I ran out of dressings and bandaids, then poured some water in my hand from the other canteen and wiped her face with it. At first nothing happened, then she suddenly came up off the ground and went straight for my throat.

"At ease, Marine!" I barked, trying to hold her down and keep her from strangling me at the same time. "At ease! You're among friends. I'm Major General Fetterman, Seventh Rangers. You're all right. You're safe now."

I wasn't sure that last bit was strictly true, but so far at least, there'd been no indications that any of the Yillii had survived and were mounting a counter-attack. I finally got Chang calmed back down, covered her up with the tube tent from the survival kit, and went through the process of explaining Loup Garou again. I left Chang and the Chat discussing the finer points of the Yillii in very unsavory thought patterns, and went back over to Masterson.

She eyed me with a distinct curiosity. It wasn't exactly the glad-to-see-you reaction I'd expected, especially after what Loup Garou had said about her thoughts. It only took a moment for the aloofness to become clear.

"So you're a General Officer now," she said. There was something in the voice that told me that made all the difference in the world.

"Before you go jumping to any conclusions," I said, "I'm not. It's a simulated rank."

"Simulated Major General? What in hell is that?"

"It's what Peterson called it. They made me a temporary Major General in case I had any trouble dealing with Brigadier General Andersohn. Part of my mission was to find her."

"You're a bit late for that," Masterson told me. "Those cat-people found her first."

I glanced at the third set of poles where I'd seen the woman tortured to death. "Was she . . . ?"

"No. That was Rhiannon St. Croix, CW-2, my company warrant. I think you can safely assume the same thing happened to Andersohn, though. When they brought us in here, the village head man or whatever he is had a General Officer's Model PDW hung around his neck like an ornament, and was sucking on the bones of a human hand."

"I'm sorry," I said. "There was nothing we could do." I meant about St. Croix. Andersohn had been gone before we got there.

Masterson nodded. "I understand. Nothing anybody could have done I suppose. Where are the rest of your troops?"

"There are no other troops," I told her. "It's just me and Loup Garou. I was sent to make a reconnaisance of the situation after the Fleet lost contact with your people. I met Loup Garou in the jungle, and she threw in with me. She says her people have been at war with the Yillii—that's what she calls those felinoids that gave you such a rough time—for thousands of years. The Yillii have hunted her people virtually to extinction."

"There's one thing about all this I don't understand," said

Masterson. "Sixty-one years ago I saw you trigger an antiper-sonnel mine. I'm not a doctor, but I would have sworn you were dead."

"I was, technically speaking. My heart and lungs had stopped. That's clinically dead. They got me onto some advanced life support systems before the brain cells started to die, however. Eventually they managed to correct all the problems and brought me back."

"So what have you been doing for the last sixty-one years? How come you never tried to let me know you were alive?" There was accusation in her voice.

"I couldn't, Lara. I was lying frozen in an experimental medical cryonics lab while they used me for a guinea pig. I was the perfect subject. After all, I was already dead."

A look of utter contempt crossed her face. "Bloody sadists!"

"It doesn't matter," I told her. "What's past is past. I'm alive now. Peterson got them to thaw me out for this job."

I heard the thermal foil blanket rustle slightly, and felt her hand touch the back of mine.

"I needed you, Tony," she said. "I needed you and you came. You came back from the dead for me."

"An easy enough feat for a messenger from the Greatest of the Great Spirits," said Loup Garou smugly.

"Mind your own damned mind," I told the Chat sourly.

"Loup Garou seems convinced I'm some kind of paragod," I explained to Masterson.

Lara snuggled up close to me. "You may not be a paragod, but you look pretty damned good to me, leaves and all. Tell me, Mr. Major General Bush, simulated, how the fuck do we get out of this place?"

"Elementary, my dear Captain Masterson," I said. "We employ the old Ranger adage, Take the hard way in, and the easy way out." I dug the burst transceiver out of a thigh pocket on my coveralls, flipped up the safety cover, and punched one of the two buttons.

Belatedly, I hoped I'd pushed the right one.

15

Masterson, Lara
Captain, Hard Landing Force Charlie, SCAF

What do you say when you suddenly come face to face with an old lover? Especially one you haven't seen in sixty-one years. Most especially one you saw die sixty-one years ago.

"Fetterman, you're alive. I saw you . . . die."

Somehow it seemed kind of inadequate. I mean, what *do* you say when an old lover comes back from the dead?

I don't know exactly what I should have felt. Surprise, shock, joy, curiosity, relief, even anger would have been normal enough sensations under the circumstances, but I don't think I experienced any of those. Perhaps it was just that I was still in something of a numbed state from all that had happened in the last few days. Or perhaps the truth of the matter was that having already given him up as dead, having accepted his death for so long, I just couldn't accept finding him alive, or more precisely, his finding me.

I already knew the Aldebarans were capable of projecting nightmarishly real illusions into my mind. I considered for a moment the possibility that it was some Aldebaran's grisly idea of a joke, that perhaps one of them had somehow looked into my mind and dredged up the image of Tony Fetterman as I remembered him, and then was reprojecting that image as part of some ghastly prank. It seemed consistent with their apparent policy of torturing prisoners.

But there were other inconsistencies that seemed to dispel

that notion. For one thing, I'd never seen Fetterman wearing such a ridiculous costume as he had on now, a camouflaged uniform that made him seem like an ambulatory bush. For another, I'd never seen anything like the giant cat that was with him. Period. Never. Not anywhere. Not even in nightmares. So that at least, wasn't something they'd pulled from my mind, and if the image didn't come from me, why bother with it at all, since although unusual it was hardly terrifying. Indeed, it seemed quite friendly, if a bit nosey. Did it all mesh together to form some sort of bizarre trick? Was it all part of some weird Aldebaran interrogation process? It was kind of a crazy notion, but it made at least as much sense as the rest of the whole damned planet seemed to make.

I finally opted for none of the above and decided to just accept Fetterman's improbable tale of where he'd spent the last six decades. The story was as good as any of the others, and it made my head hurt less, not having to try and figure out what was reality and what wasn't. Besides, even if it were just some illusion the Aldebarans had conjured up to soften me up before they started tearing me apart, the feel of his arm around me, holding me once again after all those years, made it worth it. I gave in, and let the fantasy, if it were one, run its course.

Irrationally, I'd been a little bit pissed-off when Fetterman told me he was a general now. I mean, the guy had been dead for sixty-one years, while I'd been working my buns off, well, for eighteen months or so anyway, so now he's suddenly a major general and I'm still a lousy captain. Come on, give me a break, will you? But I'd gotten over that fairly quickly, even before he explained to me that it was only a simulated rank.

For awhile it felt good just sitting there with Fetterman's leafy branches, uh, I mean, arms, wrapped around me. I remember wondering insanely once if I might get poison ivy from him, and breaking out in long gales of laughter that finally degenerated into hysterical giggling and then sobbing as I pawed at his leaves. It must have looked pretty funny, a battered, half-naked female crying into a bush. I finally got control of myself, dammed up the flood, wiped some of the excess fluid away on the back of my dirty hand, and looked up at him.

He was still there.

"I'm okay," I said. "It's just the stress. So much has happened. St. Croix dead. My command wiped out, all those good troopers gone off to Post Everlasting. Finding you." I glanced over at the Chat who appeared to be intensely involved in deep conversation with Chang, although neither of them were speaking. "Not to mention being introduced to your friend there. I guess there was a lot of pent-up adrenalin looking for someplace else to go."

Fetterman didn't make a big thing out of it like a lot of other macho types would have. He just squeezed my shoulder and nodded, telling me he understood. It was more than a gesture of a friend. It was the gesture of a true comrade-in-arms. I could have kissed him for not making a fuss about it, like some typically overprotective military males, then thought, "Why not?" and did. Just lightly on the cheek. My lips came away smeared with camouflage makeup and tingling slightly from insect repellent.

When I finally got my act together enough to try a little movement, I had Fetterman help me up. It felt like there were a thousand pins and needles sticking me in the ankles, and my knees were too rubbery at first to get the job done. I'd been tied spread-eagled between the poles for so long, my toes barely touching the ground, not enough to take any real pressure off my wrists, which were already numb after being carried about the jungle on a branch, that my thigh muscles knotted up in a spasm that proved to me I *could* still hurt in places that I didn't think would ever even feel again.

I fell, but caught myself. Fetterman made no move to help. He had sense enough to realize that what few shreds of my pride I had left couldn't have stood that. He was just there to give me something to catch myself on and pull myself up on. He kept himself available to help, but only if asked. I didn't, so he didn't either.

When I had myself stabilized, I just stood there swaying for a minute while I tried to decide whether to be sick or just pass out. When I finally realized I wasn't going to do either, I tried a step. I just had time to realize my mistake before the big rock came up and hit me under the chin. Fetterman had a hard time not grabbing me on that one. As I ran my hand along the underside of my chin and felt the thin trickle of blood there, I almost wished he had.

I eventually made it over to Chang under my own power. She was conscious and alert, but looked like death warmed over. Her skin was diaphoretic, the color of a midwest snow-fall, and not much warmer. Except, of course, for the areas covered by dirt and crusted blood, or showing ecchymosis. She smiled bravely and said she was doing just great, but I believed that about as far as I could have thrown her, which right then wasn't far.

The Chat confirmed my suspicions when she ratted on Chang, telling me what areas she sensed were hurting her worse than others. That, coupled with rapid, shallow breath-ing, a rapid, thready pulse, and guarding of the abdomen, told me Chang's major problem, for the moment, was most likely some kind of low grade internal bleed resulting from blunt trauma, if I remembered my combat first aid classes correctly.

That was *medicalese* for saying Chang was slowly dying, and from the indications, unless we got her some real help soon, the process would accelerate rapidly as hypovolemic shock set in. That thready pulse indicated that her heart was already working a lot harder than it ought to be to keep brain and kidneys perfused while she was lying supine.

The situation was complicated by the fact that we had to get down off the rocky shelf. True, a Search and Rescue me-devac sprint chopper could have picked us off the outcropping easily enough, despite the partial overhang, but we had no reason to expect a dustoff. The pickup Fetterman had signaled for would most likely be a high speed assault shuttle with aerospace gunship support. Neither category of vessel was equipped to effect a stationary cliff rescue. If we wanted to leave Aldebaran Five when the pickup vessel showed, and I sure as hell did, we had to get ourselves and Chang down off of that escarpment. Hanging around waiting until an S&R me-devac could be arranged for, and giving the Aldebarans time to figure out what had happened and send in some reinforce-ments, didn't seem like the hottest idea in the universe. When the pickup ship lifted, I wanted to be off planet.

Fetterman managed to find a quantity of twisted and inter-woven vines that the locals had evidently used as ropes, and mistrusting them implicitly and with the aid of a beat-up look-ing carabiner, I managed to rappel down to the narrow trail that wound part way up the face of the cliff. After that, with me functioning as ground man and Fetterman as climber, we succeeded in lowering Chang, using the tube tent cocoon-fashion as a sort of makeshift soft-sided stokes basket. The Chat simply scurried down the climbing poles.

Well, maybe not exactly simply. She lost her footing to-ward the end and fell about a dozen meters, but landed on her feet, natch.

Once we were down and had Chang as comfortable as we could make her, Fetterman wanted to check out the antenna assembly.

Loup Garou was against the idea, insisting that since the object was in the Yillii camp, as she called the Aldebaran felinoids, and hadn't been put there by the Sky People, as she persisted in referring to Fetterman, Chang, and me, that it was obviously some sort of Yillii monument or shrine, and there-fore no good could come of it. To approach the shrine of a Great Spirit without knowing which one it represented was, she insisted, to invite disaster.

We knew of course that we weren't dealing with any sort of religious shrine, but the concept of approaching an unknown device with caution made a great deal of sense to us, as it should to any soldier, and we opted to toss a rock at the thing first while crouching down behind a big boulder ourselves.

Fetterman made the pitch, and the rock sailed beautifully toward the antenna assembly until it got within about ten meters, and then it simply vanished.

Fetterman repeated the experiment a second time, with identical results, then, after considerable gnashing of teeth over how pissed-off the Fleet Intell people would be if we damaged it, he pulled the last grenade from his equipment belt and chucked it at the thing.

There was no blast or flash, no rain of shrapnel. The gre-nade just disappeared as completely as if it had been sucked into a black hole. For all I know, maybe it had. At any rate, bullets proved just as ineffective when we tried them, and after that, there wasn't much else for us to do but sit around waiting for the pickup ship and staring at the enormous metal monster with newfound respect. I remembered seeing the Aldebarans avoid going near it, and now I understood why. How do you fight something that absorbs all your weaponry, not to mention you personally? I decided that whatever the thing was, it would make one hell of a garbage disposal.

We moved into a little irregular circle of rocks that might have been a Yillii store room, or a shrine, or a barbecue pit for unwary space visitors like ourselves for that matter. If it had been used for anything recently, there was no longer any telling what that, or the original purpose, had been. It was just a little enclosure of rock in the midst of a dead Yillii village now. The assumption was that it must have served some purpose, or they wouldn't have left it cluttering up the village square that way. At any rate, it offered the most defensible position at ground level, and provided some concealment and protection, although not, of course, from an illusion-evoking, thought-wave attack.

Since Fetterman's burst transmitter contained no homing beacon, the pickup ship would have to land at the last known fix, that is, the one the original burst had come from, so we had to hang around and wait for the ship. Making your troops stand around and wait at the scene after a big battle was lousy tactics, since it gave the enemy time to marshall a counter-attack, but typical of the tactical blunders the higher-ups in the chain of command were famous for. To be fair though, Fetterman's transmitter hadn't originally been intended to be used after a major battle. He was just supposed to find the Brigadier, if possible, and get her and himself out, not shoot it out with an entire village of Aldebaran mind-killers. Still, it seemed to me to be typically short-sighted of SCAF not to have considered the possibility that it might have to do *some* shooting to get the job done, and that *any* shooting might bring a whole bunch more of the enemy down on your head.

Which is exactly what happened.

I don't know for sure how long we'd been waiting for the extraction. It must have been at least a couple of hours. The Yillii campfires had pretty well burned themselves out, but visibility was fairly decent out as far as the tree line that marked the beginning of the jungle, because all three of the planet's moons were up and nearly full. Not the kind of light you'd want to read the fine print in a military technical manual microfiche by, but enough to see the clearing fairly decently, say about two and a half times the reflected light of a full moon back on Earth. The problem was, we were in the clearing, and the enemy was out there somewhere in the jungle, hiding in the shadows.

It was Loup Garou who alerted us, silently slipping the message into all our minds simultaneously.

"Be very quiet and do not move," she said. "I sense the presence of more Yillii. They are coming this way, and although they do not seem alarmed, they are exercising considerable caution. I believe they are aware that all is not as it should be, but I do not think they know exactly what has happened here."

"Can you tell how many?" Fetterman immediately thought.

"Not precisely, but I get a great many impressions. I believe the number is quite large."

"Well, shit, that tears it," thought Fetterman. "Can you tell what their intentions are?"

"I am attempting to penetrate one of their minds now. As I told you before, it is not an easy task. To look into a mind that has not willingly opened itself to communication, and do so without disturbing it, without making it aware that it is being probed, if I have the right word, requires a certain amount of . . ." She searched for the proper term. ". . . finesse. Also, it is difficult to . . . expose . . . one's own mind to thought patterns as base and primal-hate filled . . . as that which emanate from the Yillii. It seems obvious, though, that they intend to investigate this place, and while they are not able to mentally search for other conscious minds, when they physically search this place . . ."

"They're sure to find us and attack us both physically and mentally," Fetterman finished for her.

"Yes. And although we all understand the nature of the threat now, we do not have the . . . safeguards that we had earlier."

"Which means they'll be able to make us kill each other," I interrupted.

"Nothing is certain except the Great Circle of life and

death, but it is a strong possibility which we must consider."

"A real strong possibility if there's enough of them. I'm out of grenades, and we're not all that flush on ammunition," said Fetterman.

"I do not understand ammunition," thought the Chat. "Is it important?"

"Only if we want to stay alive. It's what makes the uh, thunderbolts operate."

"Thunderbolts?" I asked, confused.

"Without these ammunitions, you cannot kill at a distance, without touching the enemy?" asked the Chat.

"You got it."

"I have what? Ammunitions? I do not think so."

"I mean yes, you're correct. We need ammunition to make our weapons work, and while we've still got a couple of hundred rounds for the carbine, we're just about out for the Kalan and this thing." Fetterman shifted the strange looking weapon he'd drawn from its shoulder holster slightly.

"I see," said the Chat. "That is, although I do not understand exactly, I comprehend that you will be unable to slay the Yillii at a distance once you have used all your ammunition. I take it that there is a limit to your spells or incantations."

"That's accurate enough," thought Fetterman. "When we run out, even if they aren't able to make us do each other in, they'll be able to overwhelm us. If there are enough of them."

"I'm afraid that there are enough of them for that," replied the Chat. "A larger group is following the first. I sense the active thoughts of nearly as many as you have already slain, and there may well be more. It is perhaps all the Yillii who inhabit this area of the forest. Apparently, knowledge of the capture of Masterson and Chang, and the others you called St. Croix and Andersohn has spread. Several villages of the Yillii were called together by the head man of this one. Evidently, he was what you would call the chief of the surrounding tribes. I am afraid that I read the thoughts of the others, earlier, badly. I knew only that they were preparing for a celebration. I did not realize that the entire clan had been invited. I apologize for this, but as I said, the procedure is a difficult one."

"Any chance we can slip through them and get away?" asked Fetterman.

"Very little. Alone, I could perhaps do it. It might even be possible for you, but the Yillii are fair hunters even without the gift that causes panic, and they are used to hunting this jungle at night. Also, I sense that you would not leave Masterson behind, and in her weakened condition, I do not think she could make it."

"Thanks a lot." I almost grumbled it outloud.

"You are most welcome, Masterson, although I am not exactly sure what for. In any event," the Chat continued, "Chang could not make it. I sense she may not survive long here, but she cannot function on her own, and taking her with us would only increase the likelihood of our being caught."

"Well, I guess that's it, then," replied Fetterman. "You'd better take off, Loup Garou. Thanks for all the help."

The Chat showed no inclination whatsoever toward the sensible course of action.

"I have told you that your enemies are my enemies, Fetterman, and your friends my friends. You have offered me your friendship, and blooded it by hunting the Yillii with me, have you not?"

"Yeah, sure," answered Fetterman, "but that's no reason to . . ."

"Then please do not insult the honor of my people by suggesting that I, a Priestess of the Greatest of the Great Spirits, the Zum Prim Chat Hoiu Tichloucotyl Yil Rhi Kitchimanitou, should abandon any of my friends in the face of the enemy," the Chat thought with finality.

"Loup Garou, try to understand. This isn't some test of your faith. There is no Great Spirit coming to help us. The only people coming are just soldiers like Lara and Chang and myself. If they come at all. For the last time, I'm not some messanger from some Great Spirit. I'm just a man."

"I have known this for some time now," the Chat replied. "But you are more than just a man. You are my friend. The bond of the hunt is a bond not easily broken or to be lightly formed. We have hunted the enemy together, Fetterman. That is the strongest bond of all. You are not only my friend, you are now my Brother of the Hunt. I will not leave. Besides, I am curious to meet more of these people you call humans. You make much better conversationalists than the animals of our World, and since you do not read minds, you permit a degree of . . . privacy . . . that is normally attainable only by living a solitary existence. I believe that meeting more of your kind would prove to be an enriching experience. And should the rescue not come to pass, and we fall in battle as the Greatest of the Great Spirits chooses to will it, I shall still count myself fortunate in the Hereafter World to have been privileged, if only for a short time, to have known and been a friend to the race of Man."

"I wouldn't be too sure about that, if I were you," Fetterman told her, "but if that's what you want, I sure hope you get the opportunity for extended discourse. Otherwise, things are going to get awfully terminal around here real fast."

We readied all our weapons and waited.

"I suppose you figure to let as many of them into the village clearing as possible before we hit them," I asked. It wasn't really a question, more of an observation on the tactical situation.

"Might as well," Fetterman whispered back. "They're going to know they've got trouble as soon as we open up, and it won't take them all that long to figure out where to project their illusions. Our muzzle flashes are going to give us away. I figure we might as well take as many of them with us as we can initially, and the clearing offers a pretty good field of fire."

"Suppose they only send in one or two scouts to begin with," I said. "That's the way we'd do it."

"Lara, we're dealing with an alien life form here. At least it's alien to us, as much as we are to it. There's no reason to suppose they'll act like we would at all."

"But suppose they do," I persisted.

Fetterman pulled his knife out, and stuck it blade first into a crevice in the rock in front of him. "In that case, we'll take them out as quietly as possible. Either Loup Garou and I will do it, or if necessary, you use the Kalan. Maybe we can nail them before they figure out where it's coming from. If we can't draw the main body of them out in the open, we've got no chance at all."

Chang was slipping in and out of consciousness now. I picked up the Kalan and pulled back on the cocking handle, making sure a round was chambered, then tightened down the threads on the suppressor. I laid the carbine between Fetterman and me, where either of us could reach it.

"Tony," I said, violating military protocol by using his first name, and not much caring that I had, "in case things don't exactly work out, there's something I want you to know. I, that is . . ." I knew exactly what I wanted to say to him, but given the circumstances, it seemed like such a corny thing to say that I kind of choked on the words. He leaned over and kissed my hair, which by now had to be one of the more unkissable parts of me.

"I know," he said. "Me too."

I knew precisely what he meant, even if he hadn't actually said it. I guess there are some things in life that should get said that don't, and some things that really don't need saying when the time comes. Strangely, it made me feel angry. Not for what I'd tried to say, or he almost had, but for all the times and opportunities we'd missed, and all the ones we would miss. It made me so damned mad I almost felt like crying. Instead I cleared my throat and said, "I don't suppose there's any chance of the cavalry showing up in the nick of time?"

He shrugged, and said lightly, "Captain Masterson, in the entire history of the Tri-D moviegram, the United States Cavalry has never failed to arrive in the nick of time."

"Yeah, but we're not talking about the United States Cavalry. We're talking about the Sol Combined Arms Force," I reminded him in a whisper.

He shrugged again. This time his reply was serious. "I'm not sure what difference it would make anyway. If we had some way of communicating with them, we might be able to get them to lay suppressive fire along the perimeter while the pickup ship comes in, assuming they've got an escort, but I don't even know if that would help, and anyway, we've got no way of talking to the Fleet."

"Excuse me," said the Chat mildly, "but that should pose no greatly significant problem."

"If you call not having any neutrino or radio communications no significant problem . . ." began Fetterman.

"I beg your pardon for interrupting," said Loup Garou impatiently. "I do not understand this radio or this neutrino, but if I have correctly assessed the difficulty, you have friends coming who could be of help to us if only you could communicate with them."

"Which we can't do, which makes their possible intervention just about a useless theory for discussion," snapped Fetterman irritably.

"But Fetterman, you are wrong," said the Chat. "I can communicate with them, as soon as they are sufficiently close. Indeed, I sense a sentient presence even now which is more like that of your mind than that of the Yillii."

Fetterman and I both stared at the Chat as though dumbstruck. I mean, it was such an obvious ploy, that I couldn't believe neither of us had thought of it. Here we had the perfect military communications channel, instantaneous and secure, right under our noses, and it hadn't occurred to either of us to use it to contact the Fleet. I didn't know if Loup Garou could mindcast clear out to whatever elements of the Fleet were orbiting about the planet, but she could damned sure communicate to the pickup crew and their aerospace gunship support, which evidently, had finally got off their collective butts and were coming to pick us up. If she could persuade the pickup vessel that her thought transmissions were genuine, and let them know our situation and the location of the enemy, there was a good chance the gun team would be able to lay down enough suppressive fire to keep the Yillii at bay while we extracted, provided they got here soon enough.

It's amazing how a drowning man will grasp at straws. It keeps his spirits afloat if nothing else. And anyway, it was the only game in town.

Fetterman formed the command almost instantly and thought it at the Chat. "Tell them what our situation is here. And tell them to hurry. And keep telling them until they reply."

"By the Greatest of the Great Spirits," said the Chat, "it shall be done."

Of course, things didn't work out quite as simply as all that. In fact, to be fair, even though the rescue did arrive in time, about the only way you could describe the mission would be unmitigated disaster.

16

Fetterman, Anthony B.
Major, Seventh Rangers (Detached)
Alpha Tauri Five Military Assistance Advisory Group
(Provisional), SCAF

I had a new rank and a new job. At least, temporarily. Although why anyone in their right mind would have thought I was the least bit qualified for the position, Christ and the Imperial General Staff, only, knew.

I kind of missed the old rank. I'd had a lot of fun being a Major General for about three and a half days after I'd gotten back before anyone remembered it was only a simulated rank and blew the whistle on me. Just long enough to spend a couple of sixteen-hour days being debriefed and analyzed for any toxic microbes I might have accidentally brought back from the planet's surface with me, and to discover the joys of the Tau Cetian Brandy supplies available only to members of the General Officer's Mess, and my guests.

Loup Garou had created quite a stir by her appearance in that most venerable and hallowed bastion of exclusivity, but then, she created quite a stir wherever she went aboard ship.

It was the same every time we went in. Masterson and I hardly got noticed for the first twenty minutes or so, then someone would finally wonder who the officer was who had had the audacity to bring such a beast into those sacrosanct halls, and I, having slammed down half a dozen brandies by that time, would feel the hackles standing out on the back of my neck and be compelled to remind the miscreant fellow that he was referring to the ambassador pro tempore of the Chat of

Aldebaran Five, holder of the SCAF Silver Cresent with "V" device, and the Medal for Military Merit, Valorous Class, and a Combat Meritorius Battlefield Commission, and that it was probably only her standing and long years of study and training as a High Priestess of her race's religion that kept her from tearing his goddamned throat out. Or, wasn't the poor simpleton aware that the Chat was a race of mind-reading telepaths?

This display of verbal affrontery on my part invariably got me noticed, especially if the loggerhead I was addressing happened to be an Admiral, Senior Chief Air Commodore, or STC Field Marshal.

They had of course, all heard rumors about what had happened on Aldebaran Five, although most of them had no idea of the extent of the debacle; *that* was being carefully suppressed by Fleet-STC JOITF. But the rumors were enough. None of them wanted to risk insulting a newfound ally of the Empire of Sol, and the Chat usually helped out by giving them a friendly smile, having learned that humans displayed their teeth to one another as a sign of friendship. Of course, when the smile came from a giant lynx that stood a meter high at the shoulder and had a mouth full of teeth like bayonets, the friendly human gesture tended to lose something in the translation.

In any event, the trouble-causer would rapidly develop a profound interest in refreshing his or her drink from the bar, and being unsure whether or not he could mask his thoughts sufficiently from the Chat, would transfer them to me, which suited me fine just so long as he didn't verbalize them. Having once broken their thoughts away from the Chat, it was then a bit easier for the stuffed brass shirts to notice Masterson, first as a drinking companion of the ambassador and her loud-mouthed Major General friend, then as a reasonably good-looking young female who had recently had her beauty temporarily spoiled by a severe battering that she made no effort to conceal with makeup. Sometime after that, one of the regulars at the bar could invariably be heard whispering that after all, she was *only* a captain, to which his drinking buddy would dryly reply, having noted the scarlet and magenta ribbon with the crossed palms centered above her other decorations, "I see, Old Boy, that for being only a captain, she's managed to earn herself *two* Imperial Medals of Honor. I haven't got one of those, and I don't believe anyone else in this room has either." That invariably moved the discussion on to other matters.

They were wrong, of course, butt then, since I wasn't wearing my decorations, they couldn't have known that.

The second IMH was a touchy subject with Masterson who couldn't see anything deserving of such a high honor in getting her command wiped out. She'd come by the first one honestly during the final hours of conflict on Tau Ceti Four. I don't know what she was complaining about. All I'd done to earn mine was butcher a village full of civilians. At least mostly civilians. At least the Yillii equivalent of civilians. All things considered, a more appropriate honor might have been the SCAF Health and Sanitation Award for eradicating vermin.

But IGS had seen things differently, and by Christ, the Commander of SCAF Second Retribution Fleet/Army, Plenipotentiary to His Imperial Majesty—or was it Her Imperial Majesty by now? No matter—was damned well going to see to it that the survivors of the first contact with the indigenous hostiles of Alpha Tauri Five were accorded an appropriate expression of the Empire's gratitude, even if he couldn't be present to pin the medals on us himself.

On the express command of that august authority, the Commanding Officer of the 504th Stellar Strike Command had been pleased to make the presentation. He hadn't been too pleased about making it in secret in the crowded office of the Director of Combat Intelligence Star, or about repeating it later at Chang's bedside in the ship's infirmary, but he'd done it just the same, while one of the Petersons stood by with watchful eye and a look of great good humor on his face.

Oh well, they could make me take the damned medal, but they couldn't make me wear it. Personally, I'd have been a lot happier with a couple of cases of good scotch and a week's vacation to drink it in.

But I digress. Someone had found out I wasn't really a general and used it as an excuse to bar us from the club. I think they were really just upset with the rate at which we were going through their brandy. Loup Garou had developed a real affinity for the stuff, and her capacity for dissipation was awe-inspiring to behold. The bartender considered, I'm sure, cutting her off more than once, but the master-at-arms was disinclined to tangle with a drunken Chat, let alone an ambassadorial drunken Chat.

Ambassador-Lieutenant Loup Garou had had a bit of difficulty making contact with the rescue ship. As I understand it, the problem was primarily one of being able to focus in on the correct consciousness. The Chat was mind-casting for one particular sentient, that of the rescue ship pilot, and expected at most to have to pick it out of a small group of others, a relatively simple statistical solution with a probable ratio of less than twelve to one. The problem was, *that ratio* was off by about ten orders of magnitude.

It seems the saber-rattlers had finally won out over the cooler heads in the debate that had raged in the inner circles of the Imperial General Staff while I had been bopping about the jungle in my plastic foliage, and, in what was undoubtedly the worst tactical military decision since a distant ancestor of mine had tried to ride through the Sioux Nation with a few good men, the choice had been made to go for broke. SCAF very nearly did.

They jumped a reinforced para-amphibious infantry brigade, right smack-dab on top of my burst transmitter's radio trace, which put half of them into the defensive field of the alien antenna assembly. The field, we later discovered, extended upward and outward like an inverted cone to a height of twenty-one kilometers with a base diameter of seven kilometers, and was a little less than twenty-two meters wide where the apex touched the ground, surrounding the antenna array. Fifty-two hundred men and women, twenty-five heavy assault shuttles, and eighty-seven fighters, gunships, and support craft of various types, flew into that cone of nothingness and vanished without a trace.

In the ensuing bedlam that resulted among those troops that finally reached the ground and closed on their objective, about a third ran into the remaining Yillii, and assuming the Taurans to have been responsible for the deaths of their comrades, immediately joined them in battle. The Yillii were caught off guard by the sudden onslaught and staggered beneath the massive fire power of the SCAF PAI assault troops. It took them some time to organize an effective defense, but when they did, the Yillii accounted for nearly ten SCAF troopers for every one of their number lost. In the end, the Yillii were annihilated, but SCAF casualties amounted to nearly three regiments, give or take a battalion, mostly dead. There were very few wounded.

A couple of days later, a company of combat engineers and a few dozen scientists from Fleet Intell's Foreign Technology Division bought the big one when they tried to penetrate the antenna array's defensive field.

The geniuses in the white lab coats, it seems, were having a hard time explaining why anyone could plainly see the antenna within the field or the terrain behind it while anything that entered the field from outside just disappeared. After the light beam from a high intensity laser failed to emerge from the other side of the field, even though it was aimed at an area of open space well to one side of the antenna assembly's physical structure, the engineers and scientists gave it one final go with a twenty kiloton nuclear device.

They tied a time delay fuse into the detonator, backed off thirty klicks or so, and used a radio-controlled remote manipulating arm to push the modified glide bomb through the perimeter of the alien device's defensive cone. They cracked the field, all right, but not exactly the way they'd intended.

The blast, which occurred prematurely the instant the warhead penetrated the field, was a rather small one by modern standards. However, it had the coincidental side effect of triggering a counter-blast from within the alien device that left a smoking, but very radioactively clean, crater, fifteen kilometers deep and measuring ninty-two kilometers along the semi-major axis of the elliptical depression.

The remaining FORTEC scientists, safe aboard the fleet, could offer no explanation for the lack of radioactivity, or why the blast, which had obviously produced intense heat within the crater, judging from the finely powdered ash residue filling it, had failed to ignite the surrounding jungle as was to be normally expected following a nuclear blast. For the moment, all they could do was theorize that the SCAF device had in some fashion triggered the sudden release of a form of energy hitherto unknown in the Empire of Sol. The best guess was the sympathetic detonation of a self-destruct mechanism within the alien device.

A few of the more esoteric thinkers timidly hazarded the dissenting opinion that the bomb had merely triggered a critical reaction in the antenna array's power pack, since a self-destruct mechanism of such devastating proportion seemed unduly excessive.

The majority rejected the notion, applying the minority's own argument that a power source of such capacity was hardly necessary for the operation of a simple transmitter.

The counter-argument was that you couldn't call the thing a *simple* transmitter since no one had any idea what, or even if, it transmitted. No emissions had been detected from the unit, so perhaps it was a receiver of some sort. But then again, why protect either device with such a powerful defensive field? Surely it must have been some sort of automated battle station.

One of the surviving FORTEC experts, who was apparently something of a maverick, offered the idea that perhaps the thing had only been some kind of super land mine, just waiting for something big enough to come along with the necessary pressure to set it off.

To me it made as much sense as any of the other explanations. Maybe they were all partially right.

I remember reading a story once, decades ago, when I was still young and naive enough to believe that things other than casualty radii and fields of fire and maximum effective ranges could be important to know about. It was by one of the literary giants of a couple of centuries earlier named Clarke. It was called *The Sentinel* and it was about some explorers who found a strange object where it shouldn't have been, that was incased in a material that couldn't be cracked. Somebody finally did crack it, of course, and the artifact was destroyed in the process. But the point of the story was that it wasn't just some artifact left behind by another civilization at all. It was a beacon that for thousands of years had simply set quietly, beaming out a signal that said, "I'm still here," until one day someone came along with enough pressure to turn it off.

For close to a century now, the combined armed forces of the Empire of Sol have been searching the stars for an elusive enemy that no one has yet met face-to-face and lived to tell about it. We still had no idea where the enemy's home base was, or even what he looked like, but I had a gut-level feeling that we were getting uncomfortably close, and that the maverick FORTEC genius was right. There's really not all that much difference between a warning beacon and a mine set out on your perimeter. In either case, when the enemy hits the tripwire and sets it off, you know he's there. After that, you simply do everything you can to kill him before he can kill you.

I think we can expect to meet the enemy face to face now, though whether it will be next week or next century I've no idea. But we've bumped up against the bastards' outer wire, and they know we're out there somewhere on their perimeter. I'm sure of that.

I'm not so sure I look forward to the meeting. Not with a foe whose idea of a warning device is a portable black hole capable of implacably defending itself until a critical threshold is reached, and then blowing up roughly thirteen hundred square miles of planetary surface, just to let you know that the enemy is in the outer wire.

I think Brigadier General Andersohn must have had some inkling of what she'd find on Alpha Tauri Five, although what, exactly, it was that made her steal a scout ship and go running off to look for it, I've no idea. I'll leave the answer to that one to the investigative teams still sifting through her notes and personal effects, and trying to crack the cypher she used to encrypt her private journal. My concern with the general ended when I learned she'd become lunch for a bunch of hungry Yillii Taurans, a fate I don't believe she had any inkling of.

At any rate, I had more important matters to think of now than eating a general, like being appointed military advisor to the Chat of Aldebaran Five, or Alpha Tauri Five if you prefer. For some reason it had become instantly fashionable to refer to the Chat as Aldebarans and the Yillii as Taurans. I'm sure either would have considered such reference a great insult.

There had been no debate about a military assistance program to support the Chat in their struggle against the Yillii. SCAF IGS had been quick to realize the tactical and strategic potential in a cooperative ally that could read minds and communicate on an extrasensory level. I'm sure they'd have been interested in the illusory capacity of the Yillii with equal rapidity, but the Chat were friendly toward humans, while the Yillii were decidedly hostile. In warfare, you take your allies where you can find them. I had a hunch that in this case at least, we'd picked the right side to be on, although I'm relatively sure that the rightness of the issue never entered into SCAF's decision making process.

My immediate task was developing a TO&E for a provisional advisory staff who would assess Chat military assistance needs, propose and select solutions to meeting those needs, and then implement those solutions, in addition to developing field study criteria for joint SCAF/Chat operational procedures.

It was enough to make any holder of the Combat Infantryman's Badge vomit.

While it's true that I've always considered myself to be a professional soldier, the term means something different to me than it does to the keyboard tappers who run today's modern military. I've always felt a commander should lead his troops in battle, not manage them from behind a desk. Call me an Alexandrian dinosaur if you will. I know all about combat actuarial studies and cost-effective analysis, and how SCAF IGS and Cost and Accounting Corps considers field grade officers just too valuable to be allowed to risk themselves in the front lines, which is why they provide them with fortified Tactical Operations Centers and Mobile Armored Combat Command Centers, and why the grunts who do the killing and the dying hate their senior officers' guts. I'd rather shoulder a pack and pick up a rifle any day. Not smart maybe, but it's just the way I'm built. I prefer the field.

But SCAF hadn't given me any choice in the matter. The logic was, I had to admit, inescapable if a bit thin. I was the first human to ever meet a Chat; therefore, I had more experience in dealing with them than anyone else; ergo, I was the logical choice to head up the initial advisory effort.

I was free to select the members of my own advisory team,

within reason, which was stupid. I knew nothing about heading up a planetary advisory team. I'd run a couple of small advisory detachments dealing with direct training and patrolling in South America and Africa back on Earth. That's like giving a Boy Scout Senior Patrol Leader a SCAF PAI combat division and expecting him to be able to take it into battle against three-to-one odds and win. Further, as I've already noted, it goes against my basic philosophy. I'm a leader not a manager. Finally, how could I be expected to pick a team when I had no idea of the capabilities of its members, or even what its composition should be? The only reasonable selections I could make were Masterson and Chang, if she lived, and that only because each had the same qualifications for the job that I did, more experience with the Chat than anyone else. To be precise, with one Chat. And of course, against the Yillii in combat.

I'd have tried to get Lara on my staff anyway, of course, just so I could be near her for awhile, and I don't give a damn how unprofessional that sounds, although I probably wouldn't have been able to swing it if she hadn't gone down on Aldebaran Five. The two of us winding up working together again after all those decades was one of those incredibly improbable things that can only happen when the SCAF Battle Planning Computer gets into the act and starts matching up the best talent with the dirtiest jobs.

So why in the hell couldn't the blasted piece of worthless junk reach down into some molecular corner of its microscopic bubble memory and tell me what the composition of the rest of my advisory team should be? I pushed the console key pad away from me in disgust and rubbed the grit from my eyes. I hoped to hell Loup Garou was having more luck putting together her counterpart team, although it took a bit of imagination to figure out how she might be going about it. Just how do you develop requests for military assistance when you're a member of a race that has no understanding of lasers, gunpowder, or even the bow and arrow? When you don't know what a grenade is, or have a hand to throw it with? How do you develop concepts like fire teams, squads, platoons and companies, when you come from a race that hunts alone and fights alone, and lives alone, primarily, because on your planet, there's danger, not safety, in numbers?

I had a sudden, absurd vision of Loup Garou seated in front of a computer console, tapping away on the key pad, and pausing periodically to scratch her head. It gave me the first good laugh I'd had in sixty-two years, and I stood up and stretched and then went out and wandered down the corridor to see just exactly what the Chat *was* up to.

I found her seated on the floor in her quarters. In front of a computer console. Using one long claw to tap delicately at the key pad and pausing occasionally to scratch at one ear.

I had a sudden, uneasy feeling that the earlier vision wasn't entirely my idea, although the Chat had repeatedly disclaimed any ability to project images to other minds, such as the Yillii possessed. I was beginning to develop the notion that perhaps there was a very fine line between telepathy and psycho-illusory projection.

"Ah, Fetterman. Good of you to drop by," said the Chat.

She didn't turn around. There was no insult intended. A race that communicates directly from one mind to another has no need to face a friend when talking to him.

"This is a most fascinating, uh, thing. One touches these small squares, and lighted pictures appear in the front of the box. Each picture is different, yet each is exactly the same as the picture shown on the square. When the front of the box is full, the top line of pictures disappears, and a new line may be added at the bottom. It is most entertaining, yet I cannot for the life of me understand what its utility is. If it is a form of protective coloration, it should alter its entire surface pattern, not just the front. I suppose it could have some sort of mating function.

"Can you tell me its name?"

"It's called a remote console," I said. "It's a way of communicating with the ship's main computer, which can, in turn, communicate with other computers. Sometime when I've got a few minutes, I'll show you how it works." Then I realized that I'd probably better leave that particular task up to a linguist, since the Chat had no written language.

"It is not a living thing, I think," said the Chat, "for it does not move of its own accord, nor eat, nor breathe as far as I can tell. At least, not living in the usual sense with which I am familiar. Yet I have a vague sensation that it is somehow almost, if not quite, alive. I receive faint impressions of a sort of rudimentary intelligence within, yet capable of great capacity. I have been unable to communicate with it, yet you say that it can communicate with these computers, as you call them. Perhaps if I were to meet one of these computer creatures, I would be able to communicate with it."

I didn't have a good answer for that one, so I ducked the issue by asking Loup Garou if she'd seen Lara.

"Not for some moments," replied the Chat, still poking experimentally at the key pad. "I spoke with her earlier and she mentioned that she was going to visit Chang, and then go to her den and sleep for awhile. Perhaps you will find her there."

The Chat continued to clack away, absorbed by the meaningless letters and symbols filling the screen, and I nodded, then realized she couldn't see the gesture, said "Thanks," and walked out. It wasn't until much later that the full significance of what Loup Garou had said occurred to me.

"Lara," I said. "What's happened? You look sick." She was sitting on the edge of her bunk with her hands clasped between her knees. She looked pale as a snowflake, and was shaking like an old man with Parkinson's disease who had forgotten to take his medication.

"I feel sick," she said. "I am sick. I just haven't decided yet whether or not I'm going to be sick."

"Lara," I said gently, "make sense, please."

"It's Chang."

"Christ! I thought she was supposed to be doing better. Is she . . . ?" I let the question trail off, not wanting to have to finish it.

"Pregnant," said Masterson.

"What?" It didn't make any sense.

"I said she's pregnant!" She practically yelled it at me.

"I'm sorry," I said, "I don't understand what you're telling me."

"Sergeant Chang is pregnant. Her contraceptive implant failed. They're only about ninety-nine point ninety-nine percent effective, you know. It happens once in about every ten thousand intercourses." Her voice was heavy with sarcasm, as though she was parodying someone else's speech.

"I didn't think Chang was in any sort of shape to be doing that kind of thing," I said stupidly.

Masterson gave me a withering look that made me realize just exactly how stupid. "It happened on the planet, idiot."

"With one of her Recon teammates? I wouldn't have thought they'd have had the time." I still hadn't gotten the picture.

"With one of the Yillii, you dummy. Or more precisely, one of several of the smelly bastards. St. Croix wasn't the only one they had a lot of fun with before you and Loup Garou got there."

I just stood there for several seconds, letting it sink in, then slowly sat down in a chair opposite the bunk. "I just can't . . . How could it . . . I mean, they're not even humans. I thought different species couldn't . . ."

"Apparently they can. At any rate, they're enough like us in one department."

"My God! What are they going to do about it?"

"*They,*" she said disgustedly, "are going to take very good care of *it,* and momma, until they see if *it* carries full term or not."

"You can't be serious."

"That's exactly what Chang told them. I wish I weren't."

"I can't believe that Chang would let them . . ."

"Chang isn't letting them do anything. Those bloody sadists down in experimental medicine are doing it to her, with the full approval of FTC Intelligence. They've got her down in the med labs in a set of four-point restraints, surrounded by a dozen SETAC guards, with more fiber optic probes and wires and tubes sticking out of her than a neonatal intensive care ward. Chang has suddenly become medical history in the making, to say nothing of the Intelligence aspects, and those Frankensteins aren't about to let anything happen to her, or let her do anything to herself. Not until they've got themselves a nice little half human–half alien to play with."

I had to admit that it made me want to be sick too.

Masterson looked at me and her expression was almost pleading. "It's disgusting, Tony. They've got fiber optic trideo probes stuck into every orifice in her body. They've got central venous monitors and intra-arterial catheters, ECG and EEG traces, they've even got her hooked up to a fetal heart tone monitor. Christ! It's nothing more than a fertilized egg right now. It'll be weeks before there's any heart for them to listen to. They're treating her like some piece of meat. It's as bad as what the Yillii did to her. Worse."

We both knew she didn't really mean that, but I could understand how she felt and agreed with her. More importantly, I could understand what it must be doing to Chang, perhaps better than Masterson could, given my own previous experience at the hands of the so-called researchers from Experimental Medicine.

I immediately ran through all the options and rejected them one by one. There was no possible legal recourse. An Imperial Military Court, the only court that held jurisdiction over SCAF personnel, would unquestionably rule that Chang, as a soldier, was military property, and any military property could be reassigned or reallocated wherever SCAF pleased under the pretext of precedence of Imperial security. They probably already had a Top Secret, Need to Know, Eyes Only classification slapped on Chang under the Imperial Official Secrets Act. Springing her was out of the question as well. Lara had said Chang was under heavy guard, and I was already well acquainted with the kind of weaponry they'd be armed with. From what Stryker had told me about SETAC guards, I had no doubt they'd shred first and ask questions later. Besides, where would we go? How would we hide? Steal a ship like Andersohn and hide out in the jungles of Alpha Tauri Five? An unattractive proposition at best, with a practically guaranteed limited life span. SCAF would take the planet apart a molecule at a time looking for us. Besides, none of us could fly an antigrav ship or a conventional shuttle. There was no one we could appeal to, and if we raised any kind of ruckus at all, we'd only get ourselves in hot water. The sad truth was, there was nothing we could do for Chang except feel sorry for her.

It was a hell of a way to treat a recipient of the Imperial Medal of Honor, and it left a very bad taste in my mouth. I said as much to Lara.

She leaned back against the bulkhead behind her bunk and stared at me, an expression of grim resignation on her face. I thought it a very beautiful face, despite the black eye and the split lip and the mediplast covering the deep scratches on her cheek. I thought once again how incredibly clear her eyes were. I had never seen eyes so blue.

"So," I said, "what are we going to do about it?"

She sighed, brushed her hands along the legs of her khaki trousers, and got up off the bunk and pushed past me.

"I've got the same damned taste in my mouth," she said, rummaging around in a desk drawer and coming out with a bottle of Tau Cetian brandy, "and I'm going to try washing it out. Care to join me? I pinched this from the General Officers' Mess the other night while you were arguing with that Admiral. The red bearded one with the gray temples and the bald head."

"Oh, yeah," I said, "her."

Lara stuck her tongue out at me, uncapped the bottle, and poured a metal canteen cup half full of the fiery liquid, handed it to me.

"Sorry about the cup," she said. "It's the best I can do."

She put the bottle to her own lips, tilted it, and swallowed deeply. A thin trickle escaped and dribbled down her chin.

"Best be careful with that stuff," I admonished. "I don't think we'll be getting any more of it unless you stole more than one bottle."

"Alcohol abuse," she agreed, wiping it with the back of her hand and licking off the droplets. "Christ that's smooth. I suppose we can always go down to the O-Club and suck down some of that ersatz Scotch they serve when we run out."

"Ugh," I said. "Can't stand the stuff. How can you enjoy a good time on something that only leaves you drunk for an hour and doesn't cause a hangover? If it were, say, Glenlivet or Johnnie Walker Red, now that would be different."

"So how *do* you suggest we spend the rest of the evening?"

I shrugged, then after a moment looked at her and grinned. "Well?"

"I was just thinking," I said, "about something Loup Garou said when we were down there in the village."

"Such as?"

"That this was no time to be making cubs."

Masterson sat the bottle down on the desk and looked at me.

"Well," she said, "at least it'll give us a chance to find out if *my* implant is still working."

"Some days you've just got to say, 'What the fuck?'," I agreed.

We did.

ACE
SCIENCE FICTION
SPECIALS

Under the brilliant editorship of Terry Carr,
the award-winning <u>Ace Science Fiction Specials</u>
were <u>the</u> imprint for literate, quality sf.

Now, once again under the leadership of Terry Carr,
<u>The New Ace SF Specials</u> have been created
to seek out the talents and titles that will lead
science fiction into the 21st Century.

MORE SCIENCE FICTION ADVENTURE!